The 13th Round

Sometimes Relationships go into Overtime

DEVON CALLAHAN

authorHOUSE®

AuthorHouse™
1663 Liberty Drive
Bloomington, IN 47403
www.authorhouse.com
Phone: 1-800-839-8640

First published by AuthorHouse 4/25/2011

ISBN: 978-1-4567-5320-7 (e)
ISBN: 978-1-4567-5319-1 (sc)

Library of Congress Control Number: 2011905141

Printed in the United States of America

Before I get started

Dreams come true. It takes time and hard work. Just think about Mr. Tyler Perry. Do you wonder what was going through his mind about 11 years ago? I wonder all the time. I wonder if Tyler knew that one day he would be providing jobs for people – jobs for *icons*. I wonder if he knew that his plays would turn into motion picture success – films and plays that are loved by millions. I don't know him but if he knows the Lord, then I believe that he knew it would all happen.

Never stop dreaming. Never stop trying to accomplish your goals. You only fail when you stop trying.

If you want something; give something. It is better to give than receive but when you give, you always receive more than you gave.

Hope you enjoy the book. I took a break but now I got my head right and I won't stop this time. I promise.

Peace and God's Love,

Devon

1

She was bad and I should know – I've seen my share of fine ones. She was yellow like a banana and had that silky hair like a baby's. She had a fetish for down-South rappers like the Ying-Yang twins. You best believe she was shaking it just like a salt shaker too. She had a name to fit her actions: Karma. She was taboo, but to most people, taboo is hard to resist. I just stood by in my living room watching. I had never touched Karma sexually, because my best friend Tracey tried to get at that. She didn't want Tracey, but he never stopped trying. At this juncture, I would say that Tracey had run out of time. He was getting married tomorrow so of course, I got to send him off right. So I did the traditional best man thing. I hired a couple of strippers to shake some ass for him – tease him a little bit to remind him of what he was going be giving up.

I had to get Karma here just to make Tracey feel good.

She told me that she would dance for him if I promised to play some Eight Ball and MJG, but I had to turn it all the way up and keep the drinks coming to her. She was a slippery nipple and fuzzy navel kind of girl, and I had what she needed. Karma was putting it on Tracey. She was teasing him, and I enjoyed watching. Tracey was sitting on top of a bar stool and she was straddling him and grinding on him, this dude didn't know what to do. His smile was almost permanent. She grabbed his hands and put them on her stomach while she grinded on him some more. The boys were in my spacious living room throwing dollars and for a minute, it seemed like another regular night, instead of a bachelor party. This one cat named Rob put his brew on the counter and ran to the fridge. By this time, the stripper was whistling to **Don't Flex**, by 8 ball and MJG. She was riding Tracey like she was influenced. As she worked up speed, it was clear to everyone that the bachelor just couldn't handle it; Shorty was riding that thang so hard. I was watching the bar stool wobble. She freaked him so hard until the barstool broke. They landed hard on the floor, but that didn't stop either of them. She kept riding, and as Tracey palmed her supple ass with both hands, she just kept bouncing that ass with a smile. The boys were cheering while holding their drinks in the air. For a minute, I thought that Karma would fuck my man right there in the middle of the floor, even though I knew that just wasn't her style. She liked to dance for strange men. She liked the attention, and more than that, she liked for men to lust over her. Yeah, she was a tease, but she was the most convincing tease, rubbing Tracey and making eyes at him like she wanted to do something.

Rob came back with a can of whip cream that he gave to Tracey. Karma's fine ass twisted her waist and healthy thighs until she was on her back. Tracey shook the can anxiously. The dancer's body was shiny from all the all hard work she'd put into her performance. She looked me dead in the face until the zealous man sprayed her bikini area with chocolate whipped cream. She was giggling as Trace licked the short woman's belly button. If the bride-to-be could see him, there would be no wedding tomorrow. I thought about running to the back room to get the digital camera so I could send her pictures. Yeah, I was hating, but I couldn't stand that hoe. I thought my friend deserved way better than her.

I was looking at my partner who was acting like he had a mission. He was licking and touching her so much until I thought she would come out of her thong right in front of us. I had that no touch policy for the rest of the fellas. I ain't got time for no chick hollering rape in my house. I'm retired, but people still remember who I am. They seem to think that I got the same kind of loot as I did when I was in the boxing ring. While there were some things I could still afford, I definitely couldn't afford to let things get out of hand in my crib.

The dancer finished dancing to her song and walked up on me. I was looking at her titties and I wanted to grab one. She knew what I was thinking. She saw me staring. She toned it down to a smile and asked where I kept my towels.

"I got you," I said.

"I can't believe them niggas poured beer on my pussy." She looked down and said, "Ooh, this shit really burns."

I laughed. She shot me a dark look, but I didn't care. Why would she let them do something like to her? As far as I was concerned, if she let them, then she deserved it.

"It burns?" I asked.

"Oh God yes!" She grabbed herself, like doing so would make her feel better.

"Come on, I'll get you a towel."

"Yeah, whatever just get this shit off me."

She walked up the steps with her legs gaping. "Look at me, whipped cream and shit."

I looked back and asked, "You want to take a shower? I'll get you everything you need so you can handle your biz."

"Please," she said. "Let me go get my fucking clothes."

Shorty definitely had a foul mouth on her. Baby was sexy, but I couldn't get down with her language, and besides, she was a stripper. All I could do with that was hit it and quit it– I couldn't wife somebody like her.

***

The fellas were congregated out front. We had to be careful. I lived in Chevy Chase. There are a lot of white people that live there, and a bunch of noisy black people hanging out in the front yard across from them could look bad. Some white people just *killed* me; they hate on us because they don't know how to have the kind of fun that we have.

"Keep it down," I told the fellas.

Tracey had this smile on his face. He slapped my right hand and threw the other around me to show his gratitude for the party.

"That shit was off the chain, dog."

"Anything for you, bruh. You know that we have been down like pimps without hoes since the second grade."

"That's why I love you man. You always look out for me."

"You look out for me too, Trace."

We released each other and I was smiling this time. "You like that, huh?"

"You are a funny dude," Tracey said.

"What I do?"

"You know what I'm talking about; hiring Shorty to dance for me."

"Man I hired her for me – you're getting married tomorrow."

"Just so you know Zay, I didn't want her."

I chuckled. "Okay, you didn't want her. So is that why you were smacking her on the ass like you owned it?"

Tracey didn't say anything. He just smiled and walked towards his car.

"You're smiling, but I was hoping she would take you upstairs and do some things to you to make you forget about tomorrow."

Tracey stopped and stared me in the face. "That is fucked up, Zay."

I laughed it off, even though I was serious.

The brothers were getting in their cars and thanking me for the party. I didn't want their thanks. They were only there because it was Tracey's night. He is my only true friend. The other cats were for show, just some people to make it look like a real party. They weren't my friends. They were people who I met when I was living the champagne high life. Most of these people I hadn't seen since my boxing career ended – they'd just disappeared.

2

"What's up," she greeted.

"Not a damn." I rolled over and looked at the clock. It took only a few seconds for my eyes to adjust.

"It's only eleven-thirty and you are asleep already?"

"Just fell off to sleep," I told the female on the other end of the line. It was getting cooler in the room. I pulled the covers up closer to my neck.

"Thought you were a night owl?"

"Not tonight, had a long day. I was working the shop solo."

"You didn't have any performances tonight?"

She barely knew me, and she was talking to me like she knew my schedule. "Nope," I responded. I was lying in bed wondering why I was staying on the phone for this long. I didn't have anything to talk about, and it was more than obvious that she was just making small talk, so she didn't have anything to talk about, either. She had been throwing out the one-liners for the sake of conversation, and I wasn't paying her much attention. There was a slight pause before she asked if she could come over.

"Not tonight doll. I need to sleep."

Instantly, she got an attitude. "Need some sleep? You better take a power nap between now and when I get there."

"Nah baby, I'm saying no tonight."

"Why don't you be a man and tell the truth."

"'Scuse me?"

"Just say that you got some bitch over there."

By then, I was fully coherent, and I didn't appreciate this, especially since we met only last week. She was carrying it like I was her man. I took a deep breath and bid her good night. I didn't have time for this.

I hung up the line and rolled over to go back to sleep – but I just couldn't. I got angry at Sheryl for calling me up, and then I got mad for allowing myself to waste time like I'd been doing. I rolled back over and looked up at the ceiling. I was thinking about my life, evaluating it. Messing with these different women was getting old, and so was I. Age was kicking up, but it was still fun. I wasn't sure I was ready to give up the player's card just yet, but what did I have to lose?

And that damned Karma. I didn't know what I was thinking. All I saw was that ass. I got to stop thinking with my dick. That was what kept getting me in trouble. I saw her strictly as an opportunity. She called me up talking 'bout come by the carry out. I'm thirty-seven years old and I am still seeing women that have roommates or stay with their moms. I'm too old to be messing with these types of women. I'm too old to be fucking women like Karma, women who work in mom-and-pop fish joints. I guess that's what I get for messing with some Northwest chick from Upsher Place.

I went to the bathroom and took a look in the mirror. I mean, I took a long look and began to examine myself. I used the mirror to look into the inner me, and I wondered if I was all that. I stood 196 pounds and six feet even. People have always said that I have a baby face, but I didn't see it. I admitted some youthful characteristics; my head was kind of small, I sported a short, neatly-trimmed haircut and goatee, and I kept my hair faded high. I was an even brown. When I had my glasses on, they said I looked like an English professor– a young English professor. Maybe I didn't deserve those classy-ass women that I saw dudes come into the shop with. I couldn't seem to do it right. *Maybe I really did have a problem*, I thought. My last girlfriend told me that I'm a commitment-phobe. Maybe she was right. I would attract quality women, but for some reason I did something to run them away, but I let the bums hang around for handouts when I knew they should go.

I went outside in my boxers, ready to smoke one. I love going outside in my boxers. It is such a liberating feeling. Too bad my next door neighbor didn't seem to think so. Every morning, I smoked a cigarette, and every morning, the lady next door was out doing something to her yard. She was an old white lady, aged really bad, and she flipped me off when she saw me in my boxers, or she'd say, "put some fucking clothes on."

That morning, she was not outside. The traffic on the avenue sped by. It was only nine-thirty. I puffed a little more and tossed the cigarette. My morning cigarette was usually the shortest. I never finished the whole thing. Once I got back inside, I reflected a little more. I looked at the large shadowbox in the living room.

In the beginning, it was a good idea. Me and Tracey bought this joint downtown and had it renovated. We put our heads together to figure out how to compete with all the clubs in DC. We had to come with it if we were going to make some bread. We put in some pod lights, built a stage, and got some live bands in. It was a cool, laid back, over-25 club, and before I knew anything, we'd gained recognition as the hottest jazz spot in the metro. We made good on it for a while. I was happy, and so was my business partner. I was led to believe that the customers we got in the beginning were only there because of my name. The spot was hot, but the truth was, most of the partygoers were under 25 and they don't know anything about jazz, so we changed our face – mixed it up a bit. Mondays through Thursday were jazz nights and Fridays through Sundays were hip hop and go-go nights. We got more business, made more money – but with all that came more problems. The youngins liked to fight. We'd had at least three lawsuits filed against the club in the last year. I was getting tired of it.

Our other spot, on the other hand, was the coolest. We bought some space and turned it into a coffee shop. Coffee has been the style, it seems, every since the Starbucks craze. We decided to eat off that. I love Lotta Latte, our coffee shop. It's painted in the warmest colors and it has that mild coffee smell all the time. I come to the shop even when I'm not working sometimes, just to escape. About six months ago, the old man who ran a printing shop next door went out of business. We bought his space, added a connecting door, and used that space to host poetry slams every first and third Saturday of the month. Besides using the space for a lounge, we also used this room for our business meetings.

Some would like to say that I perpetrate like I'm still balling. Deep down, I believe people wish I was still balling like I was when I was with the boxing association so they could have something to associate themselves with. But I did right by my money. I put up a lot, and I bought some assets.

It was the first Saturday of September. The first Saturdays were usually the busiest. We got this regular poet named Dufonties who came down once a month when he wasn't touring. People paid big money to hear this guy speak. He always brought a big crowd. I hired this one lady to MC, and she could really draw a crowd, but the crowd that gathered tonight was a tough one. You had to be pretty good to impress them.

I was solo. Tracey had gone out of town. When I scanned the crowd like I always do, I saw some familiar faces. I walked up the aisle and slapped a few hands, and then I posted in the back. There was this one lady. She was a dime piece. I had seen her somewhere before. I didn't think she'd been to the club before. I'd seen her somewhere else before, but I couldn't remember where. I tried not to stare at her, but it was killing me. I didn't want to ask her where I knew her from, or if she knew me – that would come off like such a line. I was too old for one-liners. I watched momma for the entire show until it was time for me to go up on stage to close. Once I put the mic down, I was high-stepping for the exit; I couldn't let momma get away.

I made it to the exit. She knew what was up. I could tell by the way she took her time getting up from her seat. I took the opportunity to light up a cigarette. Uh, uh, uh, baby had class and style. She was wearing a light studio fix foundation, Vegas Volt paint on her lips. She definitely had the skin tone for that shade of lipstick. Her French-manicured hands were laid one on top of the other. She had man-made crystals on her wrist and pinky finger. She had some shine in her earlobes, as well.

Finally, she stood up like she just got out the beautician's chair. She was like a painting, and I'm not lying. When I said momma got style, momma got style. She looked back towards the exit and we locked eyes. She had this powerful, intimidating look, but at the same time, she looked so innocent. Can't tell you how that's possible, but that's how it seemed. I looked off and took another pull from my cigarette when she grabbed her purse.

She walked towards me and was fumbling inside her bag, maybe to find her car keys. I put the cigarette to my side and asked, "Enjoyed the show?"

She looked up and said, "I would have enjoyed it more if you weren't back here smoking."

I looked around. "Other people are smoking too. You didn't say nothing about them."

"Well, they aren't standing as close to me as you are."

"That's funny. Do you know I was *just* thinking about quitting today?" I put out the cig in a nearby ash tray.

"Really?" She looked into my eyes and I looked down; what I saw made me feel like I was falling in love. She had some pretty feet. Now, I'm no poet, but seeing those feet inspired me. I wanted to take her home and just rub on her feet. I'd oil them down and everything.

I looked up, and momma was walking off. I reached for her instinctively. I wanted her to stay. Some part of me wanted to get to know her. I felt like I had to, so I said, "Let me buy you a drink."

She smiled. I was starting to warm up to her some, until she barked at me for making the offer. "How do you know that I drink? I drove my car here and plan to drive my car home... sober."

"Okay, cool. Forget that, how about a cup of coffee?" I persuaded. If she hadn't known until now, she wasn't getting off that easy.

"Don't need anything to drink anyway, and besides, I have a press conference tomorrow."

"Not like I would try to take advantage of you."

"Don't worry, playa, I could be incapacitated, and you still couldn't take advantage of me."

She started to walk off in those low-rise skinny jeans.

"Because I respect you."

She stopped. When she turned around, her face was wrinkled. "What did you say?"

"I said, 'I couldn't take advantage of you because I respect you.'" *How could I not respect a lady that carried herself the way she did?*

"Besides, I'm a bitch when I drink."

"Okay, fuck the drink. Let me take you to dinner, and we can order some waters with lemon."

She giggled. "Fuck the drink? Is that how you expect to get a woman?"

"I already have one."

Her expression changed, but I wanted to be straight up with her. I didn't want to run game on her. I knew I'd have to start being honest with women one day, and I guessed this was the day. I had to get to know this woman. It was like something was pulling on me to do that.

When she stopped laughing, she asked, "You have one?"

"Well, kind of, sort of. It's nothing serious."

"Well, you don't need to take me to dinner."

"I mean, why not? All I got to do is talk to my man and have him lock up, and we can cruise."

She laughed at me. "You can't do that."

"Yes I can. It won't take me long. Just give me a minute."

"No, I mean you can't take me to dinner when you have a girlfriend."

"You act like you know her – and besides, I just asked for dinner; I'm not trying to marry you."

****

She didn't say anything, she just looked at me.

"What are you looking at me like that for?"

"You look like somebody I know," she answered.

"Funny. You look familiar to me too. But if I'd met you before I wouldn't have forgotten it."

She had the cutest little-girl smile. She pointed her salad fork at me and said, "You really need to work on your compliments. They are old school."

I didn't feel the need to defend myself. I knew I had her by at least ten years, and it was cool. I thought baby was dazzling. She looked like a Vicki C model. She was a perfect ten to me, and it wasn't all her looks that made her that way. It was her whole vibe. She was so classy – her mouth wasn't too dirty, she wasn't too uptight, and she didn't seem too wild, either.

People looked around, acting the way people often do when a cell phone rings in a nice restaurant. I detached it from my hip and looked at the display as the lady across from me stabbed her salad. I flipped the phone open. My dinner date looked me in the mouth as I told the person on the other end of the line that I was busy.

She said, "Look, I don't want her coming to look for you, or deciding that she wants to blow the place up after she sees me with you."

I held a finger up and leaned over to her. "This is my man," I whispered. I was happy to hear from him. It was about time for him to come back. I didn't stay on the phone long. I gave him a rundown on the evening, and with that, I was gone.

"You get a lot of calls. Surprised you keep a girlfriend, the way your phone rings."

"My phone only rang twice, what are you talking about?"

"I peeped you out at the poetry show. You had you your phone on vibe, but you got a lot of calls. You kept putting that little phone to your ear."

"Well, I'm in the type of business where I need my phone."

She put the fork down and asked what I did.

"That's easy. I promote concerts and run the coffee shop. The dude that was on the line helps me run it."

"That's cool. I heard that the coffee spot is a busy spot. That's why I went there."

"I knew you weren't from around here," I chimed in.

She smiled and picked up her fork again. "So that was your partner, huh?"

"Yeah, I wish you could've met him. He just wrecked his life. He's on his honeymoon," I said dryly.

She frowned and asked, "Do you have any morals? Do you stand for anything?"

I looked at her, my face showing how confused I was. She explained.

"I mean, you are cheating on your girl by having

dinner with me, you are shitting on your friend because he got married. What type of impression do you think you're making?"

"I'm not trying to make an impression. I'm not trying to impress you. I'm not cheating, and I'm not shitting, I'm just being myself. My boy married the wrong person and knew it before he tied the knot with her but chose to do it any way."

"So, what about your girlfriend?"

I pushed my glasses up and looked her in the face once more. "She's not really my girlfriend; she's more like a hobby. I like her right now, so she is what I like to do." I slapped the visa on the table, ready for the check. I wasn't feeling this. Maybe I shouldn't have invited her to dinner. "If you didn't want to come here, you wouldn't have come, so don't be throwing this girlfriend stuff in my face."

She looked down at the credit card I had just placed on the table. She smiled and covered her mouth with her napkin. "I knew it! You're Nyza Stevenson! My father loved you when you used to fight."

I didn't care that she knew who I was. That kind of thing happened to me all the time. I was still ready to go. I wanted to tell her to grab her Louis bag so we could go. I wasn't about to argue with a woman who I didn't even know. I didn't owe her nothing. This started out a good night, and I'd been enjoying myself. There I was, breaking bread with a fine-ass woman who seemed to be as pretty on the inside as she was on the outside. For a change, I'd been myself. I didn't throw any lines at her, and I wasn't trying to get her in the bed with me.

I pulled out my Newport box, ready to light up. As I pulled a single from the box, I complained, "I can't believe I asked your evil ass to dinner."

"Cause you a damn dog and you probably thought you were going to get in my panties."

"You *ain't* wearing any," I said with a firm look.

She cracked up laughing. This was genuine, I could tell.

"Don't try and get on my good side now, Tammerine. That probably ain't your real name. What kind of name is that?" I blazed up and looked back at her. "Looking like a broke-down Nichelle Phillips."

She smiled and said, "That's Nichelle Tammerine Phillips."

My cigarette fell out my mouth and onto the table. "Get the fuck outta here. Nichelle T. Phillips, the female boxer?"

"Just keep calling me Tammerine." She looked at me, looked at the box of smokes and said, "I thought you were quitting today?"

"The day isn't over yet."

Nyza

What would the fellas say if I told them I'm dating a boxer? What would they say if they knew I was messing with a boxer? That's kind of masculine. I couldn't stop the worries from sneaking into my thoughts. But Nichelle Phillips was all feminine.

Over the last week, the shop had been pretty empty. The morning crowd had come and gone. Usually around ten, we would have maybe three or four come through, and they'd usually get a tall coffee that would last them the whole time they read their newspaper or their magazine.

I was polishing the cups, just to have something to do. I felt stupid. How did I not know who she was? Then again, I'd always seen her with a blue mouthpiece and her hair braided. That makes a huge difference. Besides all that, I didn't even follow female boxing.

I hung the cups up by the finger rings and pulled out

the spoons. I chuckled on the inside, thinking about how I got played. She said she would call me, and it'd been a whole week. After thinking real good, I was happy that I met a woman like that. That night put some things in perspective for me. I was tripping a little on the phone call though. I knew she was busy but, if she said that she was going to call, then I expected a call. I chuckled again, because that was how I'd treated plenty of women, and now it was happening to me– it was a turn-on. I thought about her all day, and I didn't know why. That didn't happen to me often. Tammerine was so different from the rest – she wasn't about a bunch of nonsense, she was refined, and she had her own money and career. It was a shame that after thirty-seven years, I finally knew what I wanted in a woman, and Tammerine had it all.

I put the spoons down and thought about all the different kinds of people that run through here on a regular basis. They wore business suits from Neiman Marcus, and they had a purpose. They would come through, discussing the plans for the day on their cells. Some of them would pull up a table to place their notebooks on. Before you knew anything, they would be typing purposefully.

I looked over at Tracey, who was doing the same thing that I was, and on top of that, his wife was into real estate. She sold property all over Maryland. I felt too old to be hustling gigs at a club and making coffee every day. It more than paid the bills, but I didn't necessarily like where

of my sister and always have been. I didn't want her to mess with any of my boys, especially, because it could cause problems. I knew that no one would love her like I thought she should be loved. She'd been with this one cat – even married to him – and I didn't like him. Good thing they got divorced, because I knew I never would have fully accepted him. He wasn't good enough for Arvette. Tracey had always made jokes about getting with my sister to get under my skin. At first, it used to make me mad, but I got used to it and counted it as something that only me and him could joke about. Tracey looked at me again and asked if I was alright.

I was not alright. I sat in my TV room, where I had a flat-screen mounted on all four walls. I watched one of my old fights. I looked at what I used to be. I was good at boxing, and it was all pissed away. What did doctors really know, anyway? Was he paid? Did the promoters see something coming? Were they trying to protect their investments? A brother was so pretty in the ring. My footwork was so dazzling. I watched myself bob and weave. Flurries were delivered every time I got in the zone. They called me the best pound-for-pound boxer in my division. I got mad at the TV, and then for no reason at all I found myself thinking about mom and dad divorcing. Everything went down the drain after my sister graduated. They were waiting for her to leave the house before they got divorced. My life was shit. I felt like a pregnant woman, the way my thoughts were jumping. It was driving me crazy how emotional I had become in one day. This wasn't the kind of thing that was supposed to happen to me.

When the phone rang lately, I wouldn't answer it. I was over all the chicks who used to call me. I hadn't talked on the phone since I met Tammerine.

After the fight went off, I thought about loading another video, but instead I went downstairs to the weight room. I threw up 205 like nothing. After three sets of ten, I grabbed a 50 pound weight to assist with my sit-ups. Felt like I still had it, even though I hadn't worked out in months. I got up from the bench. The sweat was beading up under my shirt.

I wasn't tired. I was just getting started. I looked in the mirror as I got in my stance. Put the weight under the balls of my feet for balance. *Bend your knees,* I said to myself. You have to learn the proper stance before you do anything else. This set up supports you as you swing and it keeps you from getting knocked on your ass. It's the difference between the strong fighter and the weak one. Your stance has everything to do with survival in the ring. I found myself pumping myself up by chanting my own name softly, 'Zay. Zay. Zay.' I was concentrating on my jab. The right jab is the most important punch. Sixty percent of boxers use it most. That's why people study strategies to oppose left-handed fighters, or South Paws, as we are called. Before I knew it, I was shadow boxing. I could feel it, I could see the earlier days when I struck fear in people's hearts. Some didn't want to fight me. I was among the top ranks, so if they wanted a shot at boxing the best they had to come through me. I was swinging and releasing frustration all at the same time. I attacked the heavy bag, and I didn't even have my hands wrapped. I aggressed the bag, picturing my opposition, and thinking about all the hood rat hoochie mommas who I'd wasted my time with.

As long as I was downstairs and occupied myself, I was cool. When I decided to stop, I was feeling down again. I still had that unsettled feeling, so I went to my desk top to search the web. I needed some answers – I was in search of a probable diagnosis. Within fifteen minutes, I sat looking at the results to my search. The results described my symptoms to a T: discontent with life, boredom with people and normal routine, confusion about where my life is going, questioning the meaning of life, wanting to do something different. All of those things described where I was at this point of my life. I wasn't happy with what I found, but it had to be true. There was that feeling of relief. I had to share this with somebody.

The phone rang about three times before it was answered. I checked my watch again, even though I'd glanced at it before I picked up the cordless.

"Hello?" the person answered.

"What the deal, black man?" I said.

"Zay?"

"Hey, I figured it out." I was excited. I'd found the answer to my problems.

"What's up, man?" I could hear his wife behind him asking who was on the phone.

"You won't believe this, but I could be going through a mid-life crisis. I think that's my problem– why I been acting crazy lately."

"Zay, I'm happy for you man. It is 2:30 in the morning. Go to sleep."

We had this nice little jazz cut on by Pieces of a Dream. Me and Trace were slouching in the blue leather lounge chairs. We were positioned like models for Kenneth Cole, you know – not too casual, just relaxed. I had on some paper-washed jeans with a linen-blend button-up with double breast pockets and leather uppers that I bought when I was in Brazil; they kind of felt like tennis shoes when I walked around in them. My boy had on something similar. See, we stayed up on the new styles. Only difference in our fashion sense was in the jewelry department. I had about twenty watches, and the cheapest one I own cost me about nine hundred dollars. I was a Cartier and Bvlgarri man, while my partner rocked Seikos and Citizens. I'd tried to convert him, but it didn't work. It's not like he didn't have the money. He was just really conservative.

Today was a good day. We were checking out the customers. The morning rush had just left. I slouched in the chair some more and allowed the sounds of that CD to massage my ears. That crisp, clean sound was what the customers loved about the spot. I always pushed them to fill out a comments card. Some would talk about the personal experience, while others would talk about the color of the walls. We had this chick named Aiyanna come in to decorate. She is a friend of my sister's. Aiyanna was the bomb, she'd get some color swatches for you and have your spot laced up in no time. Her colors never clashed; they blended, but they were never too defined. We got the pod lamps dropped from the ceilings. Some brothers even brought their dates here some nights. We had a vision before we opened. We saw people coming in to read their morning papers, throwing their laptops on our bar-height tabletops to put the finishing touches on their presentations due that same day; we saw people with their backpacks discussing homework after class; we saw people doing all kinds of things while sipping on a warm latte or some flavored coffee. We had cold coffee drinks for the youngins. We did well with that. The shop made some good money. Like I said, I even went there to chill some days when Tracey was the one supposed to be holding it down. Those days, we didn't even say much to each other. We knew that on those days it's about self, and both of us respected that.

I looked over to Tracey, who was slouched so much in his chair. I thought he would fall asleep any second. I reached out and tapped him on the leg. "How was the honeymoon?"

"It was cool."

"I mean, you have been back for a minute, and you never said much about it."

"Not much to say about it. I got some bomb head."

"Got to be careful, man. It's good right now, but that's how they get you. Just wait till a few years down the line, she go'n be slipping on the head game, sex ain't going to be as often. You going to go from once a day to every other day to twice a week – and that's if y'all ain't had no fights that week!"

Tracey started laughing. "Well, you need to settle down too, Zay."

"Man, I love sex too much. Whoever I get with has got to bring it." I looked at him, and I couldn't believe what I was about to say. "But I want to."

"Right," he said sarcastically.

"I do, man. I want to settle down. I've been thinking about it lately, and I'm serious."

The newlywed started laughing.

"Oh yeah, I forgot, you're going through a mid-life crisis."

"I'm for real. That shit ain't a joke."

"You really believe that?"

I turned to the co-owner. "Man, the information that I found on the internet was on point. It says that you get tired of the same old people and things that restrict you, and I am sick of these old, tired breads. I haven't even talked to them."

"Oh, this is serious. I think you are really going through a mid-life crisis. I thought you were playing, but now I know for real."

He was being facetious, I could tell. It mattered to me what he really thought.

"See, why it got to be about the dross?"

He looked at me crazy.

"Because it's always been about the dross," my friend said.

"Some things get old."

"No, the same types of women get old."

"Nah, the article online said, 'discontent with life'. I'm tired of the club. I feel like a nickel-and-dime hustler. I'm too old for that stuff."

"Right, you said you're tired of promoting."

"It's not my bread and butter. It's not like I need it."

Tracey hiked up his pants legs as he leaned back in the chair. He placed his palms on his knees.

"No bullshit, Zay, you are really serious." He looked at me in amazement.

"That's what I've been trying to tell you."

"Well what – how do you feel? The other days you were lunchin' and today you alright."

He reminded me of Arsenio Hall when he crossed his legs and rested his chin in the palm of his hand. His forehead was wrinkled, and he looked like he was in deep thought. It was starting to feel like an interview.

"I don't know, I mean, I feel good today."

"Why don't you get some help, Zay?"

"You know, I felt different a couple weeks ago, but it got worse when I met that chick."

"You're talking about the boxer?" He asked. He then cut his eyes like he didn't believe me.

I held my hands up as if I were offering them.

"Trace, we been down like a pimp without hos since second grade. When have you known me to lie about a female?"

He looked towards the front door. He was still, and he didn't blink. He wasn't paying any attention to me.

I turned my head. I wanted to know what was up, too. Other cats watched my light brown-eyed champion walk through the door. She had on some of those sexy, silk Palazzo pants that stopped above her ankles. She swung her arms in her three-quarter sleeve shirt. Her hair was done this time. I sat as others did, appreciating.

I let her get to the counter. I played it off. You have to, sometimes and besides that, I didn't want to appear too anxious. After all, she owed me. What happened to my phone call? I knew I wouldn't ask her.

She looked straight behind the counter. The clerk hadn't made it in yet. Me and Tracey were running the shop. I didn't know if she saw me right away, sitting in the cut.

"Who works here?" She asked to anyone who would answer.

She turned her head in my direction, finally. My hands were folded, cool-like. I was in no hurry. Maybe I was waiting for a special invitation.

I smiled and rose from the seat. Looking at my boy, he was speechless.

"What can I do for you?" I asked the soft lady. Frankly, I addressed her like a total stranger.

She played the game. She asked for an espresso.

I raised my thick eyebrows and asked, "Like that?"

"Like that," the lady standing 5' 9" in heels confirmed.

I sneaked peeks at her. I actually missed her face, and I'd only met her once. Her nails were polished, manicured, no acrylic. These were her nails. I knew. My sister had spent years getting those fake tips.

31

"What you doing tonight, Playa?"

I pretended not to hear her.

"I was working this machine. What did you say?"

"I said, 'what are you doing tonight?'"

I flipped it. "What are you doing?"

She smiled and said, "Depends."

"Trying to roll with me?"

I sat the warm cup inside of a protector before placing the contents before her.

"I'll call you."

I started laughing. "Get the hell out of here. Call me like you called me a few nights ago?"

She looked around, grabbed another one of our Lotta Latte napkins, and starting writing.

She was fast.

"Here is my cell number." She held up her fist and said, "Give it out and we fight."

"Yeah, when you leave I am going to write digits all over the bathroom stall."

The boxer laughed as she grabbed the straps of her Gucci bag.

"Leaving?"

"I gotta go. Thanks for the coffee."

Her clipped ends swung as she turned in the opposite direction.

"Let me walk you out."

"Imma big girl, but thanks."

I cuffed her arm like one of those expensive escorts. "I'll walk you any way."

The coffee shop looked at us as we walked out the front door. Soon as we got outside, she took the top off the cup and tossed the hot liquid. She then looked at me and said, "Sorry. I don't drink coffee."

The elegant athlete pressed a button on her remote to open the Cabrio doors. She got in and I held up the napkin. "Tonight," I reminded her.

Tammerine

He was cocky and a bit over-confident. But I was more than certain that I could handle it. I decided to take him on as a student. So far, he wasn't remedial. He had some experience. I could tell. He knew where to put his hands and how to move. I wondered how many miles he had on his track record, because I was mesmerized. If he had this effect on me, then I couldn't help but wonder how many other women had gotten bitten by his bite.

I was moving and he moved with me; never missed a step. Hands were on me, touching a respectful place on my hips – didn't have his hands on my booty, but he wasn't too far from it.

We were at this club on the waterfront called H20. The place felt like it was on fire – it was so hot. The whole place seemed to be grooving. I had my hands up, moving my hips from side to side when that new joint from Dwele came on. In the chorus, the singer was asking to know this girl's name. It was such a smooth groove. The first time I heard the song, I was in L.A. The former boxer was grooving with me. He was looking all cut-up like he just left the gym. I looked at him just as hard as he looked at me through those Cartier frames – his cute four eyed self. I could take small bites of him, never get full, and take small bites to savor his flavor. Part of me hoped the evening would stay like this. Part of me wanted to leave the club with him. Right then, I wanted to run out the side door. I knew that I had to pull myself together. You are not about to "HO" out like that, I told myself. No ma'am. Can't do it. Just keep on dancing. Don't think about it.

I was wet and loving it. I didn't want to stop. Sister was having too much fun. Brother was such a good dancer. He moved in his Calvin Klein's, taking the same steps I did at the same times. He dipped when I dipped. He stood back when I dropped it to the floor. I was teasing him. When I thought about it good, I was teasing myself too. Could I be his lady? I don't know. Maybe I should have been asking if he *could* be my man. Will he do me right? He held me right as we went from fast to slow. He didn't try and cop cheap feels either. So I knew he respected my body – if nothing else.

Nyza looked down and smiled as he held me in is

his strong arm. They were playing "Believe", by Raheem Devaughnn.

"I love this song," I said as he led me from side to side. It was only a dance, but I was getting wet dancing with him. Like I said, a brother wasn't grinding all on me or nothing like that, but curiosity and anticipation were getting to me. I knew that I wanted him a little too bad. My panties were sticking to me. I was so glad when he asked to take a break. We'd danced for about seven songs straight.

"What are you drinking? He asked.

"Tequila with lime," I said, as I walked off in search of the bathroom.

When I got to the stall and undid my pants, I thought about the night I was having and I didn't want to lose my self-control. The women in the room must've thought something was wrong when I started laughing to myself. It felt good. I felt free. I was having fun for a change. Looking at the inside of the stall reminded me of how Nyza said he would write my number on the walls of the men's bathroom. I smiled some more.

When I got back outside, he had his drink turned to his lips. We drove separate cars and met at the club, so neither of us could afford to drink much. Then, I had the mind to pretend to be drunk as an excuse for him to drive me home. Brown skin with glasses raised a short cup to me. I was standing still, trying not to appear too sexy. Even as he sat on the stool, I still couldn't see over his head, and that was good. Don't like men shorter than me. If I had to guess, I'd say he was a good 6'1".

"Is that for me?" I yelled over the music. He nodded. He thought he was so cool, didn't he? I continued to check him out with his cute haircut.

Those damn cigarettes, I thought as he lit up. When I was little, I thought it looked sexy – especially when a man did it. But that smell gets all in your clothes and your hair. I let him take about three more pulls from it before I took it from him. I took one pull from it and put it out.

"You quit today," I yelled.

Surely he would trip, I thought. But he didn't. He reached for my hand and asked, "Are we finished? My song is on."

I took his medium-sized hand and we were doing it again on the floor.

The DJ was playing "And Then What", by Young Jeezy. I don't get down with all that rap stuff, especially all that down-South stuff. All they talk about are rims and gold fronts, but this cut did have a nice beat. They played it on 95.5 some mornings. This song had the floor packed. There were guys on the floor with their boys. Girls were shaking their asses like it was going out of style. I knew if I shook my ass – I mean really shook my ass – he couldn't handle it. I'd hurt him. 'What the hell,

I'll give him a taste,' I thought. I cocked one leg up and pivoted. My back was facing him, and I was shaking it at him. Then I stuck my ass out and backed it up on him. He had his arms out while I did my thing. I wanted him to grind on it, but he wouldn't. It might have been better that he didn't, anyway.

Right then, they put on "Don't Start None, Won't Be None". I was in Atlanta the first time I heard that song, and the whole club lost their minds. They reacted the same way on this night. A sister was sweating and it was falling into my brows. Nyza was sweating too. I could actually see the wet spots in his dress shirt.

Before long, the DJ slowed it down again. The crowd left us on the floor and I found myself wanting him again, but I couldn't break my own rule. He grabbed my hand and said, "Come on. Let's be out."

The tower of muscles sat me at the bar and told me to wait for him while he used the bathroom. He walked off as I thought what I could be to him. He looked for that strong woman. He waited for her maternal instincts to kick in. He wanted that nurturing figure at the right times. If he's right, I'll be his momma. I'll love him like no other woman can. I'll love him more than his own damn momma. His style, his taste, and the way he carried himself was on point.

My thoughts were interrupted. There was a rap video

reject who stood in my face, wearing a chain that hung down to his dick and clothes that were 4 sizes too big.

I turned around but he didn't go away.

"Want to dance?" The man asked.

"I'm cool," I said.

"You look like that boxer."

I didn't respond. I told him I wasn't interested. Then he asked if he could buy me a drink. By that time, my date came back and grabbed my hand in a non-territorial way. He led off and, of course, I followed.

This was the club that all the hip hoppers go to. Mike Tyson even had his after-party here. The club sat on the waterfront. It was twelve thirty and I could still smell Old Bay seasoning and fresh seafood from the wharf. I'm told all the basketball players, ballers, rappers and kids that want to be Big Willie, hung out there. They had security thick in the front because people liked to cruise slow and hang in the front. It was the same way at home, around Magic Johnson's in Ladera Heights. These brothers cracked me up, pulling up in their Benzes and Bentleys. Some of them were rentals – I could tell by the plates. The tall cup mocha and me must have been sharing the same mind.

"Look at them cruising in that rental."

I smiled. "How do you know it's a rental?"

"Look at the plates. Some of the VA rental plates start with the letter R."

Before we crossed, he asked if I was hungry.

"We're right next to Phillips Flagship."

"Nah baby, I'm cool," I said

"Sure? Good seafood. You would like it."

I shook my head as we crossed the street; didn't even realize that he was holding my hand. It felt so natural when he touched me. I didn't mind this evening at all. It was so easygoing, even up to the point where he opened my car door for me. He stood with one hand in his pocket as the other rested on the top of my door. I started the car.

"So, what's up?" The tempting brother asked. I smiled deviously, as I had a thought.

"You like games?"

He was a bit hesitant, trying to figure it out.

"What kind of games?"

"Cat and mouse."

I snatched the door handle and took off. Having picked up on the vibe, he jetted to his Mercedes. He had a V-12, but still, I thought my Porsche could take him. I waited for the brights of his headlamps before I screeched out of the parking lot. All the lights were green. I did a reasonable speed for the residential limit.

The light at the intersection of South Capital caught me. Finally, I could see his funny looking headlights coming up behind me when the traffic light turned green. I must've been about a half a block away from him and already I was in 4th gear. Took off past the D street / Capital, exit and kept up the ramp to 395 South to Richmond/ 95 Baltimore. When I looked in the rearview, Nyza was right behind me. The ramp leveled off and my engine was roaring, until I shifted into 5th gear. The car jolted forward. I put my other hand back on the steering wheel. The engine purred. I looked up and every time I switched lanes, he did too. His car was fast but it wasn't nearly as small as my car. I flipped my blinker as I looked at the tachometer. Got into the far left lane and took off from him. Wow! When I looked back up he was so close, it seemed like he was inches from my bumper. I dropped it for a few seconds, up-shifted into turbo again, and quickly switched lanes.

Nyza

That little motherfucker couldn't beat me. I had a S600 V-12. What was she really thinking? The car was sexy enough for her though. Showed me that she was adventurous. We'd have gotten fined out the ying-yang if we get caught. I'm doing a buck twenty, so she had to be doing more than that. The engine was loud but quiet at the same time. I had to be careful not to run that little Porsche over. But I was on her ass. She couldn't get away from me. But I liked this version of cat and mouse. This let me know that she knew what she wanted out of life and needed confirmation from me, wanted to know if I planned to stick around. I knew what this was all about. She wanted to make me her subject. Thought I was typical and was looking to reshape me. That's how women always get caught up – trying to change us.

See, women concentrate on how to out-think men. So

they put on this façade. Try to fake us out, like we don't know what time it is. We already know, but we can't let them know that we know the time. Then women will have to switch the game up, which further complicates things. Yep, I knew what she wanted.

Traffic was medium, which was good for what we were doing. It was harder to get a ticket this way, with too many cars on the freeway for the cops to pick us out. We were passing signs for Alexandria. If we kept it up, we would be on our way to Woodbridge. I was keeping up with the little black car. My cell was vibrating against my hip. When I looked down, I couldn't see the display, so I reached down and stuck my hand underneath the lap belt to get the cell phone. *What did Tracey want?* I thought. Whatever it was, it would wait until tomorrow.

Madison Square Garden

She was defending her title. She had only been fighting in the professional division for about 2 years and 3 months. She had a gang of fights under her belt and was still undefeated.

Watching her footwork, I got into it. Found myself moving my shoulders with hers. There was so much confidence about her – but a little fear mixed in, too. There was nothing wrong with a little fear. It's what keeps you moving and on the defensive. I was scared every time I got in the ring, even if it was some scrub, a no-name. Fear was the difference between a winner and a champion. This didn't seem like the same woman I had just shared my evening with. This woman here in the ring looked hungry, violent, unforgiving, and otherwise unrelenting. It was the look the dog had in its eyes for the master when it wanted to make him proud. I watched beauty turn into a beast from the opening of the first round.

I yelled for her to keep her guard up, while the cheering fans backed me up. They called her L.A. Loke. People were urging her to wrap it up. We were into seven rounds, and I knew damn well that Tammy could have finished the girl off a few rounds ago. I smiled because I knew the game. When the managers set the fight, they want a show. That was what she was giving all of us: a show. My baby was throwing flurries of combinations, and the crowd was clapping, cheering, and waving. I was still, though my heart pumped fast and I could feel chills in my chest. The opponent was getting her wig rocked. I enjoyed the fight, but I didn't think the lady in the white trunks could take it anymore. He eyes were swollen, lip busted up. The champ in the blue trunks dropped her hands when the bell rang.

I had a front-row seat. Tammerine's face was shiny from sweat. She didn't have on make-up and of course, we could all see her traumatic marks. She was still beautiful to me, bloody cuts and all.

End of the eighth, the defending champ went back to her corner, breathing hard but looking anything but hurt. She spit out her blue mouthpiece. Her corner coached her, while in the other corner they were applying the cold compresses and Vaseline. You know the corner is in trouble when the boxer comes out of the corner wearing too much Vaseline. They know they're in trouble, too.

Both ladies in sports bras squared off, when the ref stopped the round and sent the challenger, Carlotta, back to her corner.

"Too much of this. Take some of that off."

The corner was upset, but they took it off and sent her back.

She was tired. I could tell. The knees, eyes, and shoulders let you know. The eyes show emotion, mental capacity; the shoulders let you know where the next punch is coming from; the knees show stability. You have to keep your knees underneath – well in-line with your shoulders. Right now, Shelita was unstable. The eyes weren't right. One solid punch to the chin, and it would be over. Carefully, the contender watched the champ. Moved like she was trying to avoid her, maybe even buy herself some time. It wasn't long before she was aggressed and landed straight on her back. When you land on your back, you are not getting up for a minute. I hadn't seen a knockout like that in a long time. The contender had her eyes open. The crowd went crazy, chanting "Loke". It took me back to the days when they used to love me, the days they would holla out my name. I, too, stood and yelled out "Loke".

As I stood, I thought about the noisy crowds, the cheers for me, the pictures, and the posters. I missed the love, but I wasn't hating on Nichelle T. Phillips. Baby was too good at what she did. I loved the sport, so how could I hate on a person like her?

After the press and everyone was done with her, I went to get some personal attention. I stood outside her door for a few minutes, replaying the night in my head. She was bruised up a little, and all I wanted to do was just love her face. I would ice her down and kiss her bruises. I wanted to be a friend. When I thought about being her friend, I decided that inside her hotel room wasn't the best place for me to be that night. I smiled as I looked at the numbered placard on her door, turned, and walked away.

****

I flew back to DC, only to hear Tracey bitching about the adjustments to married life. My mind was still in Madison Square, so I didn't pay him too much attention – actually, the last few weeks, I had been occupied mentally. Tracey would get mad because he didn't see me as much. This morning, I'd gone in early, which is rare for me. I'm not a morning person. I put the towels down and observed my friend like a lab rat. His nerves were shot. He had been keeping himself busy. And he slammed everything he touched, so it was pretty obvious. I hoped he wouldn't look up to catch me smiling or else it would have been a misunderstanding.

"Trace, you okay?" I asked.

"Hell no, I'm not okay." He starts patting his chest and then his front pockets. "Fuck. Where are my – they must be in the car."

He looked at me like a fiend when he asked me for a cigarette. I patted my pockets and started laughing. Tracey had a look of disgust on his face.

"What are you laughing at?"

"I left mine at home."

Tracey didn't seem to find anything funny. His face was wrinkled and his eyebrows were arched like a feline's back when he asked, "And that's funny to you?"

"Trace, I haven't been even thinking about cigarettes. I don't think I've had a cigarette in about three weeks."

"Mid-life crisis?"

"No." I was happy for new reasons, and I had a new take on life. "I haven't missed cigarettes. Do you know what that means?"

"Yeah, it means that some broad got your head fucked up."

We kept walking. I was smiling, but I didn't respond

to the hater's comment. He continued to push, to shake my high. It wasn't going to work. He should have been the last man to talk about a person's head being messed up.

"See, that's what I'm talking about. She got your head all jacked up."

My chest was kind of heavy. I had so much I wanted to tell him, to share with my boy, but for some reason I felt I couldn't. My man didn't want to hear about what was going right in my life when things were going wrong in his. I just looked at him and wanted to tell him that he was totally wrong on this one. For the first time in thirty-eight years, my head wasn't jacked up. By now, I would've tapped that ass, but I wanted to be her friend first before we did the sex thing. I was almost convinced that she was the one for me.

Tracey opened his car door. I stood on the side like his body guard. He fumbled for his cigarettes. *Is that what I used to look like?* I thought to myself.

My friend found his box of Newports and backed himself out of the coupe. Tracey, shorter than me, slammed his car door. He didn't get to the point soon enough, so I decided to draw it out of him by provoking the situation.

"I see she let you drive the good car."

He shot me a killer look. "Fuck you."

"I mean really man, you bought yourself a – what's this?" I rubbed the body of the car as I walked around the it. "This is a Saab, right? She had that raggedy Volvo wagon when you met her. So is that how marriage is supposed to work? You got to compromise like that all the time? If it's like that, remind me to never get married."

I thought Trace would set me on fire with his cancer stick with all the trash I was talking to him. He chose to give me those messed-up looks instead. The brother would break soon.

"Well, at least you didn't buy her a new one. You said she makes all that money. She could buy her own Saab."

"The cars are ours, jackass. That's what happens when you get married. You share shit. What's yours is hers and what hers is hers."

"Except the car note," I added with a chuckle.

Tracey walked off. He was already upset. I knew that he wanted to talk but was playing the role. I was trying to bring him out. See, with Tracey I could say what was on my mind and it was no crime. I won't beg another man, even if it's my boy, I guess on this day I would just have to wait on him to tell me what was up on his own. It wasn't going to happen today. I really hated to see my boy hurting like this, but I'd tried to be a friend in the beginning. I knew the type of woman that she was, and I definitely knew that she couldn't and wouldn't appreciate a cat like Tracey. Deep down, he knew not to marry her either, but he decided to anyway. Like my mother would say, "You made your bed, so lay in it." In laying in it, you have to lay with whatever is in that the bed until you have the strength to move it. I wondered all the time how long it would take for my man to gather the strength to move his wife.

I watched Tracey, and he was out there. He was in a place where he couldn't be reached. Lately, he had the tendency to be so one-sided. I knew that this marriage thing had to be wearing on him some. We were both near 40 and had never been married. We were married to our careers and all that came with it. He had started feeling guilty about all the different women we ran through before I did. He would tell me that we were wasting our time, but I didn't think that guilt drove him to get married to her. I know that it wasn't the sex, because he would have to beg for it some nights.

Tested

The lights were off. It was quiet for the most part in the house. WHUR, Howard Radio was playing the slow jams. It was the quiet storm. Sometimes I played the radio or the TV to fall asleep to. It got too quiet for me in this big house. I got a bit paranoid. It was a bit chilly in the house at that. It was about that time. Fall is okay, but it seemed like winter sometimes in D.C. Last year, we got two and a half feet of snow during the first week of November. You never could tell with D.C. weather. The electric bill was outrageous. I got under a lot of blankets until the real cold hit. It was no fun in bed by yourself. But I thought back to all the women I had in my bed. I kept a woman in the bed at night. But I didn't miss them, not at all. Man, they were headaches. I rolled over to the left and turned off the radio. The bright green numbers read 2:03.

The phone rang. I rolled over again, and this time the numbers read 2:37. Felt like I had been sleep for at least a couple of hours. I was hesitant. I almost let it ring, but it could have been important – an emergency, even, so I reached for the cordless. The number wasn't recognizable, but I answered it anyway.

"Yeah."

"Sleep?"

"What do you think?" I asked, irritated until I caught the voice.

"I can't sleep," she said.

"For real?"

"Uh-uh."

Tammerine

He sounded so sexy with his sleepy voice. There was extra bass in his tone. It was a bit rough around the edges. He continued to talk to me.

"You should try some noise. TV or the radio, I've done it for years."

"That's what helps you sleep?"

"Sometimes."

"Other times?"

"Something that smells good."

I couldn't help it, he caught me off guard with that one. Didn't know if he was serious, but everything he breathed to me sounded good. I looked towards the foot of my king-sized bed. I was getting that feeling again, that tingling feeling in my lower stomach. I quickly crossed my legs and squeezed them tight. God, he sounded so good, as I could feel him, like he was here with me ready to climb into my bed. *Don't think about it, Nichelle. Don't think about it*, I told myself. *Don't think about the sound of his voice. Concentrate on the words.*

"Why are you laughing?' He sounded surprised.

"How does something that smells good help you sleep?"

"I meant a woman."

"Oh. Not all women smell good."

"The ones I mess with do. But I don't want you in the bed. You probably would smell good – but you probably got hairy underarms."

I laughed again. He was funny. "Whatever. I do shave under my arms, thank you. I box, but I am still a woman."

He made a noise and agreed that I'm all woman.

"There's no mistaking that."

I didn't know what else to say, so I said thank you. "Listen. It's late, but I did call you for a reason."

"Yeah."

"We have been spending a lot of time together." He was quiet. "I don't know how serious this can get, but if we are going to go farther, then I want us to get tested for HIV."

There was a silence. I could hear the leaves falling from outside the closed window, it was so quiet. The man on the other end of the phone started laughing. He was laughing too hard.

Zay

There I was, hoping she wasn't planning a booty call. This would have messed up my views of her. Like I told myself, this woman is so different, and I wanted to take things slow.

"What's so funny?" Her emotions folded inside out.

"No," I began. "No woman has ever asked me to do that before, I mean, came out and told me, 'let's get tested.'"

I laughed some more. Couldn't believe what she just asked me, I thought.

Tammerine

I was ready to hang up. I didn't see the irony, nor did I see the humor in what I said to him. I began to regret calling him. My feelings were kind of hurt.

"Baby, that has got to be the coolest thing a woman has ever asked me," he said. I held the phone away from my ear so I could get it together. I smiled big. He was actually willing to do it.

I couldn't get a word out before he asked, "So when do you want to do this?"

"Um…" I didn't know what to say but I didn't want to seem real anxious. "I mean, you know, it's whenever you can get around to it. If I am going to be with you, it is going to be only me. I don't share. So if you got some old girlfriends hanging around, you need to set it straight – if you are going to be with me."

He laughed some more. "Understand."

"Condoms touch you, and I don't. That leaves me a bit jealous. When we do this, I don't want nothing to be between us, no women, no secrets, and *no* condom."

"I'm with that. I'm free tomorrow – or would that be considered today? Today, later on in the morning, I'm free."

"Yeah?"

"Um hmm. Bethesda Hospital is right down the street from me. Do you know where that is?"

"Wisconsin Avenue?"

"Right, just meet me there in the front of the pharmacy around... ten"

"How about the main entrance? Let's say... ten-thirty?"

Zay

I wanted every square inch of her. I wanted to run my finger over the back of her. I wanted to feel her warm soft skin against me, flesh to flesh. I could picture her naked, and I could see me getting down and dirty with her. We could be like those models in the magazines, topless, the two of us. Her breasts exposed and pressed against my chest. I though about her some more and thought about how I've changed since I met her. It felt damned good too. This is what I had been missing. A brother had been running and playing the field for years and hadn't gained any yards. I played with many women's emotions like a full deck of cards and never once felt guilty. In the past, I have played on the generosities of trusting women, all the while wondering why I hadn't been blessed with the right spread. I asked God to forgive, and now, it's when I looked at Tammerine that I felt God already has forgiven me.

She wanted me. She wanted us to be something. That was all I needed. The sweet thoughts of her were enough to put me to sleep. Her voice stroked me until I dozed off.

Tammerine

I couldn't get caught up. I couldn't get hurt like that. I asked him – gave him the third degree. I asked him how many kids, how many ex-wives, how many sexually transmitted diseases. I even asked him how many crazy ex-girlfriends he had. These were all important questions that a woman should have the answers to. Mr. Stevenson's answer to all the questions was no. I could go with the crazy girlfriend because I'm a woman and I know that we all got a little *crazy* in us when it comes to men – especially if he fucked over our feelings.

I was so scared of dating. My heart was too delicate, too sensitive. I had a problem with contracting diseases HIV and AIDS. I had a problem with casual dating – fucking on the first night and booty calls. Sure, I had a freaky side, I mean, I love sex, but I wouldn't ever compromise my self-worth or my life for it.

Nyza Stevenson had to be good to me. I didn't know what I'd do if he weren't. What I did like about him so far was that he was ordinary. He had been a celeb, but now he was just like anybody else. We might go out and people might ask for his autograph, and he was so cool about it. I looked at him and sometimes felt bad because of why he had to give up what he loves. It must have been hard for him to live everyday. My family would say that everybody loves you when you are on the top, but they forget to love you when you drop. That was why I stayed true to myself and didn't rely on fame for identity or definition of self, because when it's gone, it's gone; what else do you have to fall back on when the love is gone?

Even when Zay was a professional athlete, he didn't act like a celeb. He always seemed to be an average brother who could relate to the average brother, so when I thought about it, I could see myself with him. From day one, he treated me like a person, a lady, and that is who I am. I had this one guy who loved to showcase me. When I would talk with him about it, he would laugh it off like I hadn't said anything. He had to go. When I thought about it, that was how most of the men I met acted, and if they didn't, they would make a big deal out of the fact that I was a female who boxed. There were so many men who couldn't embrace that fact. They would baby me up, or they would tell me that boxing was a man's sport and would usually end up doubting my womanhood as a result. That was why I had been off the dating scene for the past year. Brothers scared me in terms of relationships, but I couldn't keep running from it. I was hoping that Zay would be different. Why wouldn't he be? I mean, he used to box, and he loved the sport, so wouldn't he respect what I did?

The fight in New York was a test. I had to take him to one of my fights, and I had to have him ringside so I could have my people to keep an eye on him. I would steal glances between rounds just to check his reaction. Would he look sympathetic or would he cheer me on? And at the end of the night, would he look at me as anything less than a lady? Glad to say that by the end of the night, I was still his lady.

Zay

·

She had on her sweats and Adidas that day. She had to make it to the gym later to train. But still, I was able to convince her to grab some lunch before she left.

There was this banging soulfood restaurant. It's a little mom and pop joint over in Tacoma Park. It wasn't too far from the subway station. I was getting tired of the separate car thing. I don't think she rode in my car more than twice. We had different schedules. Usually, it was under conditions like this, where we both had separate places to be at the same time.

Our time was well spent – when we spent it. We could have spent more time, but I wouldn't push her. Baby was so cute in her pink sweats with the white stripes sweeping the sides of her arms and legs as she walked. Her shoes even matched. She had that soft booty that shook a little when she walked – kind of like a semi-firm Jell-o mold.

I loved to watch her walk. Her ponytail bounced as she stepped out of the door.

We two walked back to the street where we parked our black rides. Standing in front of her roadster, I took my free hand and patted the bend of her arm where she got punctured earlier. I smiled and handed her her box of food.

"Seven days," she said, and looked down to my pants.

I walked up on her, kissed her on the cheek, and said, "Yep. Seven days."

For about two years, I'd been saying that I was going to have this tree cut down, but I hadn't done it yet. The tree added so much character to the property, so I often reconsidered having it cut. That's probably why the tree was still here. In some kind of way, I'd grown attached to it, though it made a big mess every year during the Fall season. It shed so many leaves. I hated this tree this time every year. People would say pay somebody to rake the leaves, but this season comes only once a year, so it wouldn't kill me. I wasn't above work; there were just so many leaves to police.

Must have been out there for two hours or more, and I was still raking in cargo pants and a thermal tee-shirt. I was down to my last few piles when my boy pulled up. He hadn't been over my crib since he tied the knot. Judging from the look on his face when he slammed his car door, it was trouble in paradise.

I kept raking and looked over to Ms. Benson's, my next door old white lady neighbor's yard. She had not one leaf in her yard. Her dog ran about the front. I couldn't stand that bitch of hers. All she did was bark. She barked at everything. Any thing that moved, she barked at it. I thought about opening Ms. Benson's gate so that her dog could run out into the avenue traffic. I smiled at the thought... but I wasn't that kind of person.

Trace walked up and looked at me. It was Friday, and I hadn't gone into the shop, so I hadn't seen him all day. Judging from the way he was dressed, he hadn't been to work that day either. Tracey stood with a gap in his stance, and both hands were in the pockets of his sweats.

"You didn't come to the club last night," he said.

I leaned over to pick up a trash bag and said, "I know it," on the way up.

"Well, what's up? I thought you would be there."

"That's a trip. I wanted to talk to you about that."

"Talk about what?" Tracey asked.

Keeping in motion, I responded, "I'm looking to sell my half of the club."

Tracey pulled his hands out of his pockets and said, "What the fuck?"

"Yeah," I said, like it was no big deal.

"How you going to leave me hanging like that?"

I stood up and leaned on the rake handle. "I said 'sell my half'. So how is that leaving you hanging?"

"What's up with you, Zay?"

By now I had both hands wrapped around the top of the rake handle. I was cool. I wish I could have seen my own expression. I was feeling so good. I had been feeling overwhelmed, but the last week had been cake. This time, I felt like I owed no explanations. I did know that when I rendered my decision, my facial expression felt free and undefined.

"We've been doing this for a while," Tracey reminded me.

"I told you I didn't want to do the club thing anymore."

Tracey didn't say anything. I shaped my pile of leaves with the rake once more before dropping the rake to pick up more leaves. Trace bent at the waist and grabbed the sides of the hefty sack. We were silent for a couple of seconds.

"So, what is going on with you?"

"Not much." He looked around at the yard. "Wow, you *have* been working, huh?"

"Yep."

"Thought you were going to cut down that old tree?"

"Yeah, I'm getting around to it," I said. Something was on my friend's mind, and I was being patient. I was waiting for him to talk about it. I wasn't going to push him. We are boys, but it was rather odd for him to be showing up like this right now. I knew how it was when he came to shoot the breeze. He was making small talk to allude to the real talk. I kept doing my thing, thinking that he would come out when he got ready.

"Hey, man," Tracey began.

I looked up. "What's the deal?"

"What's up? I need a place to crash for the night."

I placed my finger on the tip of my chin and looked up like I was in thought. "Well, let's see… there's the Holiday Inn down the street… and then there's the Sheraton – "

"Stop playin' man. I'm serious."

"She put you out?" I asked.

"Hell no, I put myself out."

I laughed right in his face. I couldn't help it. That was the first time I heard someone say that they put themselves out of their own house. "Put your self out of your own shit?"

"Man me and her ain't vibing right now."

"Damn Trace. It hasn't been two months yet."

"It's not like that, bruh."

"Come on, you have been my man most of my life.

I know you. It's got to be serious for you to leave the house."

"Just need some time to think. So, you going to let me stay or what?"

I tapped Tracey on the back. "I got your back. You know that. E casa is Tu casa or some shit like that."

He slapped me five and said, "Thanks brother."

"It's cool. Now help me take these leaves to the curb."

He smiled and went to the untied bags. I caught him before he tied them. "Hey. Wait."

My friend looked at me like he did something wrong.

"Don't do that."

"You don't want me to tie the bags?"

"No. Leave those alone. Just take the ones that are already tied."

"Okay," Tracey said as he walked over to the other bags. He loosened up some and was ready to start talking. "So man, we get into it about this girl that called my cell. You know we – *I* – am trying to get that new female group out of Atlanta to perform in the club – since you don't want to do this anymore."

I didn't say anything. I barely paid his comment concerning me any attention. I wasn't going to let him make me feel bad for wanting to sell my half.

"You know that isn't my personal cell. I use it for the club?"

"Right," I co-signed.

"So why did this chick call about the gig and now my wife thinks I'm sleeping with this chick?"

"Cause she's probably fucking around herself," I said.

I pushed my glasses up on my nose when Tracey said, "Fuck you."

I looked at him with a frown on my face. "Now, was all that necessary?"

"I mean it, Zay. You are still the same selfish motherfucker I went to school with."

I grabbed a few trash bags and looked him in the face again. "We were little then. You can't hold me for nothing I did before 18."

Trace picked up a few bags and followed me to the curb. "You know what I mean."

"Really?"

"Yes. You know what I mean when I say that you are still selfish."

"So why are we still friends then, Tracey? I mean, if I am so messed up, then why would you want to stay friends with me?" I was smiling the whole time I questioned him.

"'Cause we're friends," my boy argued.

We were at the curb, and he was still holding on to the bags.

I dropped my bags. "Well, I don't know about you, but I couldn't tolerate a selfish-ass person who calls himself my friend."

"No, Zay that was some fucked up shit you just said about my wife, and it was disrespectful."

I licked my lips and said, "You think so."

"I think you owe me a fucking apology."

I smiled. "I'm going to get some more bags. You can help me or you can go in the house and make yourself at home." I threw my hands up over my head and dropped them quickly. "It's up to you. Like I said, you got a place to sleep if you need one."

The man wearing the wedding band stood in the defensive position waiting for the apology that he wasn't going to get.

"I ain't playing with you, Zay."

"I ain't, either. I'm not going to apologize for being a friend. You've always been a sensitive tittie baby. You asked me a question, and I gave you my honest opinion."

I stood in the middle of the yard while Tracey remained at the curb with his arms folded. "Look man, we messed with a lot of women – a lot – and based on my experience, if you are on the up and up – and I know you have been on the up and up – and she accused you out of the blue, then she just might be creeping or looking. Don't get mad."

"I guess you would know. You had a couple of sweet honeys that only wanted to be with you, and you would get paranoid when you called them and they wasn't home. Shorty could've been in the shower, and you swear she's on the creep. You were trippin' on them because you know what you do when you go out."

"You're right. I'll admit my shit. And that is why I am saying when you are out there creeping, it is natural for you to think that the other person could be out there doing the same."

"But that's my wife, Zay."

I held my hands up. I was surrendering. "Okay, you got it, baby."

"Thank you," he said.

I lowered my hands and told Tracey that I was about to grab some more bags. We stood over the tied bags, and Tracey pointed to the driveway. "What is up with those bags?"

"You'll see." I said.

I walked over to the fence after all the other leaves were taken to the curb. Trace followed me, eager to see what I would do. I grabbed a couple of bags and instructed my boy to grab the rest. We walked across the dying grass towards the fence that separated my yard from Ms.

Benson's. Her damned dog was keeping up a bunch of fuss. I hated that dog.

I smiled at the dog and grabbed a bag of leaves. Tracey figured it out. He knew what I was about to do. "That's fucked, Zay."

I lifted the first bag of leaves and took a look at Ms. Benson's clean yard. The dog was on the other side of the fence at my ankles, barking at me. He started jumping at the fence. I was giggling my ass off as I dumped the full bag onto the dog. Tracey was laughing, too. "Give me another bag, Trace."

"You still fucking with that old lady?"

"Nah, man, she be fucking with me."

I took a few side steps to the left before I shook the second bag into her yard. Tracey was still laughing. I explained some more. "Nah, man, that is a mean-ass old lady, bringing her dog – I watched her bring her dog over here to crap in my yard. She started laughing and walked off. So forget her old ass."

"One of you will have to quit."

"See, you think you know that old lady, but you don't. You think that she's nice and stuff. Besides, it's not fair; everybody around here has leaves to rake but her."

Tammerine

I hadn't talked to him in about two days. I had business to take care of. He was very secure, I could tell. He wasn't hunting me down, asking where I was, either. I liked that. This was another test. Maybe I shouldn't test my men, but I do. I'm scared of new relationships because I require 50/50, and a lot of brothers just are not capable of this. 50/50 is necessary for relationships to make it past the 6 month stage. Not many relationships make it past the 6 month mark. People aren't dedicated to too much of anything any more. That is why AIDS and STDs are rampant. People don't seem to practice self-control, let alone safe sex. Sex has become a competition sport. How many can he get? Or who can knock it out the hardest? Society got sloppy a long time ago, having multiple unprotected sex partners.

I required a sex test, because I am just that careful. I

believe everybody should request one when they decide to engage in a serious relationship, because you never know. What I liked about Nyza was that he was so willing and actually thought that it was a cool thing to do. Maybe I had figured him wrong. I remember the first time I met him. We got off on the wrong foot, and I hated him. But in some kind of way, his arrogance made me horny. His immature wit rubbed me the wrong way, but I found that he was very mature as a man. Most importantly, he was ready to settle down. His agreeing to have the HIV test done and being willing to wait for the results was confirmation. I thought I had found the man for me.

Nyza was willing to wait, but I didn't know how much longer I could. I only had two more days, but I really didn't feel like waiting. I broke down and called his ass. I wanted to go over to his place. Yeah, it was only day 5, but I had a box of condoms for desperate times like this one. I wasn't playing. I love my body, and I had to protect it.

Zay

He was surrounded by beer bottles. I drank about two. You know how some people don't like to drink alone. I couldn't drink too much beer. I liked hard liquor. Beer always did something to my stomach; gave me gas.

Tracey had been up for the last three hours sounding like a sick puppy. I was trying to get his drunken ass to go to bed, but he stayed up talking. I was a bit vexed. Tammerine called – she wanted to come over. I knew that we had two days left, but on the real, I just wanted to see her. I could control myself a couple of more days. I just wanted to touch her hair and smell her citrusy setting lotion and I think I could've been cool with that.

I had to say no to her. This drunk fool was getting into all kinds of stuff. He came back into the living room drinking from a bottle of Belvedere Vodka. I was bothered at first but chilled out quick; I knew it wouldn't be long before that vodka would put him to sleep. All I wanted was for Tracey to go to sleep.

Two-thirty, and this fool was downstairs laughing, watching *The Terminator* in full surround-sound. I heard every explosion, stage whisper, and dramatic note. I got out of bed and walked to the top of the stairs. "It's time to go to sleep."

"I'm watching *The Terminator*," Trace said, like a kid that was looking for permission to stay up later.

"Tracey, turn off the fucking movie!" I yelled. Right then, the phone rang. If it was Tammerine, I was going to get in my car and straight go over there. Before I picked up the phone, I could hear the volume decrease as Tracey yelled, "It's her dog. Don't answer it."

I ignored him and pressed the talk button. The person on the other end sounded wide awake though it was early in the morning.

"Nyza?"

"Yes," I returned.

"Sorry to bother you, but I am looking for Tracey. I haven't seen him all day."

I didn't want to sell out my boy. I was trying to figure out what to say, when he picked up the other line. "Don't tell her nothing," he said.

I laughed and sat the cordless on the charger. I could hear him down stairs doing the Keith Sweat – apologizing and begging. He got what he wanted. He wanted her to be worried about him and his whereabouts. I guess this was his test to see if she really cared. I was glad that she called. They would fuss for a minute then grow apologetic. He would get up and head for the house, or he would ride the night out, but either way, it would be quiet and he'd be gone. I rolled over with a smile and pulled the covers over my head.

"Fucking traitor," Tracey called from downstairs. I continued thinking, I hadn't even touched her sexually, and I was ready to trade in my player's card. I was a vet. I've had way more than my fair share, but was I really ready for retirement. Man, this was serious. I hadn't even seen another woman since I met Tammerine. She wasn't promised – we weren't promised to each other just yet. We still had to wait on the results. I was avoiding other women left and right. I couldn't believe that I even quit smoking. I laughed to myself. I hadn't had a cigarette in weeks, nor had I thought about having one. Maybe I had already put in my retirement papers or maybe God put them in for me. The more I thought about Ms. Phillips, the more I felt ready for retirement from the game. I don't do well with change, but maybe change was good for me in this case.

Tammerine could be selfish. I picked up on it, but I could be selfish too. She was funny. She wanted what she wanted when she wanted it. Whether you were ready to give it or not, she was willing to give it and she wanted to get it in return. At first, I labeled her demanding, but learning that she was an only child put everything in perspective. She wanted to come over that night, but I told her that my boy was over. I was surprised she didn't tell me to put him out so she could come over.

Tammerine

He had a cool but reckless personality pattern. I pulled up behind his Benz, and I could hear him playing Go-Go music. He was playing some old-school Rare Essence. He didn't look like a Go-Go kind of person. To me, Go-Go was an immature type of music. Though I knew it as a concept of accepted music, it was a unique sound that I could not get into. I once had a boyfriend from DC a few years back, and he only listened to Go-Go. That was how I was introduced to it, and after hearing the music, I never wanted to hear it ever again.

What Nyza was playing sounded classic. I didn't mind it too tough. It was mellow compared to today's Go-Go sound. Zay was standing in the door waiting for me, wearing his glasses and with his little boy haircut. He dressed appropriately for his age. He was right at a level I could be cool with. He was stylish, not faddish – of age, but not too old. I spent a moment looking at this man and his Allen Iverson-sized earrings that seemed to match his cufflinks. He had on a dress shirt with a pair of jeans. I dug the whole cufflinks with jeans look. It was a turn-on for me.

He turned the stereo down and told me to make myself at home. He had this deep black rug in the middle of the living room. It was forbidden to step on the carpet with shoes on. He made sure that I knew it when I walked through the front door. A part of me was thinking that he was just trying to satisfy his foot fetish by telling me to take my shoes off. He told me from the jump that he liked my toes. He didn't know I was going to mess with him. Sister got her feet done on the way over here. I had that French tip look going on. I was a naughty girl, and I knew it. I came over here with intentions of enticing him. Sister was wearing the low-rise capris and a blouse cut low in the front.

I loved the way it felt between my toes. I could have lain on this rug and probably have gotten a great night's sleep. The black carpet was so soft. It looked expensive, like the rest of his house. His sofa swallowed me when I sat down. When I looked up, I saw a large picture of Nyza from his boxing days. He still looked the same, except for the glasses that he wore now. He was all cut-up and chiseled. After I finished admiring the picture, I looked down at myself and pulled my shirt down to tease him some more. My lips were glossy, my makeup was lightly applied, and I made sure I'd put on the sweetest, most seductive perfume I had. He walked in, and I glanced at the picture then looked at him. He still had his body. There was no mistaking that. I had started fantasizing already. I was going to fuck him tonight. I had my mind made up. That was my mission.

He put his hands together like he was about to say grace when he asked, "Ready?"

"Umm, hmm," I hummed with a smile.

The CD changer was loud when the discs changed. His old-school Essence changed to this guy from D.C. named Raheem DaVaughn. I hadn't heard the CD, but I liked the song that radio station would play everyday.

I was five or six steps from Zay when he reached for my hand. Finally, I was close enough to him to smell his cologne. It had a citrus hint to it, but it still smelled very masculine.

"I remember that you like crabs, so I got a few pounds of Dungeness crab legs."

"I knew I smelled seafood."

"Yeah, a little something."

"You think you are a cool old man, don't you?"

"Oh, now I'm an old man?" He asked.

He pulled the stool out for me like a gentleman would. He didn't seem his usual self. I know I wasn't myself. I was nervous because usually I don't do this, coming over to man's house like this, confiding in him. But after a while, I caught the urge to look sexy, as sexy as I could for him. I didn't want to appear desperate. I didn't want to startle him with my forwardness. I can be too forward sometimes, and even I know that some men don't handle that too well. It intimidates some, and turns some of the men off. Zay hadn't seen that side of me just yet. I wanted to trust him completely. I already trusted him with my feelings, but I didn't know if I was ready to trust him with my insecurities. Not sure if I was ready for him to point them out or show them to me. Granted, I knew it was a part of the relationship regulations, but it had been a long time since my last relationship.

There were two beer bottles sitting on top of about five layers of newspaper. The paper was spread all over the island that he had converted into a conventional eating area. He then came over with two vanilla-colored packages. The packages looked a lot like the ones the Jews at the corner store would wrap our lunchmeat in. The Jews' packages were only bigger and thicker. When he unwrapped the seafood, I lost myself in the aroma of ocean water and Old Bay Seasoning. The retired boxer placed the two opened packages before me.

"You don't know how much I love crabs."

"Yeah, most women do."

I dropped my crab leg. "What the fuck is wrong with

you? Whenever I think things are cool, you say something stupid."

He looked at me, smiling.

"What did I do now?"

His smile was pissing me off – like he didn't take me seriously. I wanted to throw the crab at him.

I mean-mugged him before I asked, "What did that shit mean?"

The smile remained, like he was trying to keep from laughing. The funny thing is, I felt like laughing myself, but I didn't.

"I said, 'what did that shit mean.'"

"That means you need some. You need to get tossed up, need a stiff one, need to get tore out the frame, need somebody to bang it out."

"So are you gonna give it to me?"

"We got one more day."

"I got some condoms in my car."

"I got a box upstairs."

I hopped off the stool and said, "Takes to too long. I'll run to the car."

I was so excited, and he hadn't laid a finger on my yet – hadn't even touched me. He was right. I needed some dick, but what would happen if he just straight put it on me? Would I know how to act? Would I trip out like some other females I know?

He was at the front door when I came back. He had

his arms open, ready to receive me. I jumped at him. He cupped my behind. My wrists were wrapped at his hips. Our tongues were instantly engaged in a wrestling match. My mouth was wet. I had a strong appetite for this thick man. Ooh, damn, he was a good kisser. I could feel it trickle down into my jeans. Even though I came over without a panty line, it had been entirely my intent to spend a sex-free evening with him. But there I was, running my nails up his tattooed back.

He pivoted and slammed me up against the wall. I dropped the condoms in my hand. He was a little rough. Usually I like it in-between, but I wanted it rough tonight. I was in the mood to get my ass tore up. Found myself kissing and licking his earrings. I wrapped my legs around tighter so I could kick my shoes off. He was breathing heavy onto my neck. Before he lowered me to the carpet, he lifted my shirt. He softly kissed my stomach like a baby while he teased my nipples.

I couldn't take that shit no more. "Where is your bed?" I breathed.

"Upstairs."

I gave resistance, rolled over, got up and ran upstairs. The man of the house wasted no time in giving chase.

"To the right," he instructed.

Once we got to the room, he grabbed the rim of my low-rise jeans. I shrieked as he pulled me to him. I felt like he was in charge. I wasn't going to fight. Whatever

Zay

"What the fuck? 'Where are the condoms?' You really know how to deaden a mood," I said to the woman on the other side o the bed.

"We had sex nonetheless, didn't we?"

"Yeah." I let out a cynical, "huh."

She sat upright in the bed and looked down on me.

"One more day, right; what was the agreement," she asked as she poked me in my chest with what seemed like her longest fingernail.

"The agreement – you broke the motherfucker already."

"No unprotected sex until we get the results," she argued.

"No. The agreement was no sex until we get the results back."

"Whatever."

"Look, that's not the point. I know what we agreed to. I got experience, I mean what did you want me to do, *verbalize getting the condoms?*"

"Why is every thing so funny to you?"

"You are funny to me. You are crazy as hell."

"Because I asked where the condoms are?"

"I told you downstairs that I had a box upstairs. I was going to get them. You didn't even give me a chance. Matter of fact, you went outside to get yours. What happened to them?"

"Don't make a difference, you said you had some and I wanted to make sure before we got busy."

"I used one, didn't I?"

She looked at me like she didn't have anything to say. I knew better. The way her mouth ran was unbelievable. I got out the bed and faced the mirror on the wall.

She kept on talking and was getting on my nerves.

"Why don't you shut up," I said.

"Why don't you go and shave your chest?"

I went to the bathroom, scratching my head. "This heifer is crazy", I said in a low tone. It was always something with her. We always seemed to argue and disagree more than anything else. But when I thought about it some more, I discovered it made her more attractive at times. She was a challenge. When I thought I got her figured all out, I found out more that I didn't know. When I left the bathroom, she was smiling. Her long, dark, healthy hair with honey brown highlights waved as she shook the unused strip of condoms.

"Are you tired?" She asked. Her lips were slightly puckered. I could see hints of her front teeth. Her lipstick was smeared across her face, and she looked like she was still perspiring.

I stood there laughing. She couldn't be asking me to get back in the bed with her. She was truly amazing. Well, I wasn't falling for it. Thinking that if she threw some pussy at me, then I would do what she wanted and put up with her stuff. She had the wrong brother.

I looked her right in the eyes when I told her, "I'm going downstairs to eat my crabs. I am hungry."

***

"You have this weird effect on people."

"Yeah, so do you." I smashed the crab leg with the beer bottle.

"Don't you have the little crackers so we won't have to use these bottles?"

"I do. They are somewhere around here. What's wrong with doing it this way?" I asked her.

"It's stupid," she replied, "Especially when you have the things to crack them with."

My mouth hung open as I looked at her with a bottle in my hand and a crab leg in the other.

"Aye. It's obvious that you are not having a good time, so why don't you get dressed and leave. I don't know, maybe we can try this another day or something."

"Are you going to look for the crackers or not? I am not going to break all these shells with a beer bottle."

I looked away from her like I couldn't believe her. She was serious. She didn't care about anything I just said.

"Did you hear what I said?"

"What's all the bass in your voice for, playa?"

She got up, and I knew what she was doing. She was still naked. There wasn't a stitch on her. She walked over to the sink and started pulling out my drawers.

I walked over and stopped her. "Look, put your clothes on and get up out my crib."

****

"You kicked Nichelle T. Phillips out of your house?"

"Tracey, that broad is crazy." Tracey started laughing and tapped the counted top. "I'm serious, man. Something is wrong with her."

"That's not why I'm laughing, Zay. I thought you

changed. I though this one would be different. I mean, you stopped smoking. You have smoked for the last 13 years, and then you meet honey and quit – cold turkey."

"It's not really that bad. I mean, baby got a good heart." I looked up to the ceiling and told him, "And the sex was off the heazy."

Tracey's look got serious when he asked for confirmation. "Off the heazy?"

"Off the heazy fuh sheazy. And you know I don't say that unless it was presidential. I mean we clash but I still like her – like her a lot. We stay arguing over stupid stuff, though." My friend continued to listen as I complained. "And you know what else, Tracey? Everything is boxing with her."

He laughed some more as he pointed out. "That is what she does, man. She's a boxer."

"But some of the things she does is like a dude."

"Maybe she's a dyke."

"Nah Trace, she ain't gay. She loves men. See, that's what I mean. She's sweet, good-hearted, and real sensual. It's like she wearing a defensive front – for whatever reason."

"Maybe she's been hurt before," Tracey said.

"Maybe she has been hurt before. I was thinking that, but who hasn't been hurt? When you fall off your saddle you get back up there and ride right?"

"Well buddy, you better get ready to start riding again."

I turned around, and who was on the way inside but that crazy-ass woman. I thought about it. It was day number zero. We should have had the results to our HIV tests. This was the first time in a long time that I thought about hiding. I just didn't want to see her right then. I thought she was coming to apologize for last night, but she had an envelope in her hand. I wasn't worried in the least, but I did want to know what the paper read. She didn't smile, and she barely spoke to Tracey, who walked off anyway.

She walked up on me and stared at me like she was ready to steal on me. I looked at her and was quiet, too.

Tammy slapped the envelope on the counter. "Negative, playa," she announced as I reached for the envelope to open it. She slapped her hand down on top of my hand. "Where's yours?"

"I haven't been home yet. I'm getting ready for these poets that are coming tomorrow night." I tried not to look at her as I thought back to last night. I tried to be mad at her, but all I could remember was banging the solid oak head board against the wall and her screaming like she was being taken for bad. I was softening up. Before long, I turned to butter. She kept her hand on top of my hand.

"Look Zay, last night was kind of different, but I enjoyed you," she said in a humble tone.

I couldn't believe what came out of her mouth. If I didn't think it before, I really thought it then – she's crazy. She was gone, but I dug it.

"Look, baby," she started, "Let me come over tonight. Let me make it up to you." She took the envelope and gave me that sexy, carnation-painted smile. "We look at these together."

Her soft voice melted me some more. I felt like a sucker. "I'll be home in about two hours."

She held her hand out. I looked at her. "What?"

"Your keys."

"My house keys?"

"Give them to me. I told you, I want to make it up to you." She motioned me her way with her index finger. I leaned across the counter as she leaned in with me. She put her hand behind my head and whispered in my ear, "Besides, I got some steam to release."

I smiled at her tempting ass and reached in my pocket for my key ring.

****

I stood there, looking at her in disbelief. "And you are serious?"

"Yes," she said. "Now put your gloves on."

She stood there in her gear: sports bra, trunks, and

booties. She told me to change, but I didn't see where it was really necessary; I was still laughing on the inside. The female boxing champ gave me a quick jab to the chest. I barely felt it. I laughed at her before another came. This jab was more solid.

"Come on, glove up," Tammerine insisted.

"I'm not dong this, okay." She threw another punch that sent me back a couple of steps.

"Just like I thought, you've lost it." She was still in her stance, wearing her dogface soldier look. She swung again, and reflexes took over. I leaned back and was ready to swing on her. Finally I gave in. "Okay. If this is what you really want, I'll be back." She closed her stance.

Brother returned in some nylon sweat pants and some Adidas with ankle support straps. I put my mouth guard in and didn't even get to glove up before she stole a cheap shot.

"That's for my shirt. That shirt cost me three hundred dollars."

I danced around her in my basement. With all the equipment downstairs, we weren't looking at much space to move around in. I planned to take it easy on her until she threw a combination and caught me square in the face.

"Put your guard up, playa... and that was for kicking me out last night."

"You're crazy." She swung again. I stepped out the way and countered with a right that caught her in the chest.

"Good one," she said.

I was getting upset and began to forget who and what she was. Old habits were reforming. My reflexes were sharpening. I threw a couple of combos at her. She was accurate. She landed almost every punch she threw. We were trading blows like war stories.

"Are you playing with me?"

"Are you playing with me?" I returned.

"You are full of shit." She caught me with another left hand. I returned the favor. It stung her, but that's what she wanted. She wanted to fight.

"How am I full of shit?" I asked with my guard up. I was bobbing and weaving to avoid her. I was getting short-winded. It had been a while for me. I swung hard, releasing some of my own frustration.

"You want to know me, Zay?"

"I want to know you, but you won't let me," I said with inflection. She started dancing and breathed a little heavier. "Every time I think that you and me are making progress, it's like you shy away."

"How do I know I can let you in, Zay?" Her hardened look began to soften. She was borderline emotional, and I could tell that baby was scared of this. She was scared to take the next step. She was a woman who took commitment seriously. She was all or nothing. If I did this, the relationship thing with her, I had to be for real, and I had to try hard. She loved like she fought: with all her heart. I could sense this as I stared at her. I was thinking about my player's card really hard, but then again, I didn't have to. I didn't need it anymore. She was standing there like a straight soldier. There she was, putting on this act like nothing bothered her, when I saw through her whole façade.

She swung again. "How do I know I can let you in?" she repeated.

"How do you know you can't?" I was mad. We were throwing swift blows at one another like we were trying to hurt each other. We were bussing off heat rounds. It felt like rug burn every time the leather raked across my face. Still swinging, and by this time we were yelling at each other like strangers.

"Come real with me."

"I can't. You don't know what to do with it," she yelled

"You don't know me."

"You don't know me," she screamed.

"How can I," I yelled, dropped my guard, and turned my back on her. I was walking off slowly.

She began to whimper. I wanted to turn around, but I didn't feel like it. She had me messed up. I had to get my own head right. I was emotional, too. There was something sexy about a strong woman especially one who knew how to defend herself.

She hadn't moved. She could be heard from the same spot I left her in.

"Do you want me?" I heard her ask.

"Stop playing with me, Nichelle." I turned around slowly to see blood from her nose. My eye felt swollen. We stood there looking like a new mess, but we didn't care. This session was vital. We needed this.

"Do you want me, Zay?"

I was taking 20-inch steps in her direction, when I admitted to her that I wanted her.

"Nyza. Don't hurt me." The sprinklers came on, and her face crumpled as she laid her head in my chest.

"Please don't hurt me, Zay."

I thought I was going to cry, but I didn't. We met each other with acceptance. And a solid embrace. I sealed it with a kiss on her left cheek. I kissed her bleeding wound. And she kissed my eye.

"You okay?" I asked. I could feel her let go. Her body almost went limp as I held her.

"Now I'm okay."

I smiled.

"Are you going to take care of me?"

"Huh, the way you fight. You don't need nobody to take care of you"

Her voice was muffled. Her face was lost in the crease

of my chest. "I got you," I told her. "I can definitely take care of you."

"I'm not perfect, Zay, but I will be honest with you. Being in a relationship is recognizing and respecting the individuality of the person you are with. You have to accept what comes along with the other person – even their imperfections."

"Even their imperfections," I agreed.

Tammerine

He said that he would take care of me, and he was getting a head start. Mr. Green-Eyes-Like-Donnie-Simpson had me laid in steaming bath water that he drew for me. The lights were out, and candles burned on all four corners of the tub. I trusted him with my heart. Within minutes, I felt free. My hair was pinned up in the back, and I had one leg up as the handsome man supported the weight of the other leg with one hand. He used his other hand to scrub my toes with a soft bristled brush. I closed my eyes and began to feel like I was someone else – someone I wanted to be but had never been. Sister was in her own paradise. I could call Mr. Stevenson my man as long as he loved me. I wasn't thinking about money, bills, boxing, or family. I was thinking about myself. I was getting the treatment. I was getting the attention I deserved. Yes, I would say I was definitely getting mine. He was giving it to me, and I couldn't wait to reciprocate.

Zay kissed me on the face over and over. He kissed my eyes, neck, elbows, hands, and went down to my knee caps. He came back up to my neck. He had bubble in his moustache. When he asked me to stay with him, I didn't say anything. He looked at my breasts, which were partially hidden by the jubilant suds.

"I don't want you to go home. I want you to say with me tonight," the sexy man repeated.

I smiled because I knew something he didn't. He smiled waiting for me to respond. I stuck out my tongue and licked his dimple. I ran my hot, wet tongue to the base of his neck and inhaled it. I sucked soft enough to feel good without leaving a mark. I knew I had him when I felt the muscles on his right side relax. I leaned over and left a wet spot on the other side of his neck. I motioned for him to lean in farther.

I grabbed the back of his head and confessed. "My bags are in your closet."

Zay laughed. "Get the hell outta here. You planned to stay the whole time?"

"Do you want me to go?" I asked, innocent-like.

"No. Hell no!"

He gave me full service. He dried me off as I stood on the bath mat. The heater was blowing, but I was still a bit chilly after being in that water for so long. The man did it right. He wasn't rough with the towel as he dried me, but he wasn't a punk about it either. Some men want to pat you dry like they would a baby. I'm not a baby. I wanted to be Nyza's though. I loved it when he rubbed my breasts with the towel, and I loved it more when he squeezed my ass before drying it.

I was getting so horny and wet when I decided to take the towel from him. It was obvious that he had the evening planned, so I didn't want to jump the gun by being anxious. I wanted to fuck him. I can be an aggressive girl, but I didn't know how he would take it. Most men who I ran across didn't do well with my aggressive ways. It made some feel less masculine. I looked at him and tied the purple towel around my waist.

He took me to the bedroom. I felt his naked chest, rubbed it, dug my fingers into it. It was hard but somewhat pliable. To my surprise, he'd shaved it. I was getting so aroused when I pushed him towards his bed. I pulled his pants down and started to massage his dick. He was so long and already erect, but I wanted to tease him first. Like second nature, he secured my waist as I made him think I was going to saddle up. He wasn't slick by trying to undo the towel from around me. I moved his meddlesome hand. "Uh, uh," I breathed to him passionately. I ran my business over his hardware. I was so wet. My lips were smacking as I moved. He tried at the front of the towel again as I leaned over to breathe and lick on his nipples.

Nyza grew anxious. He dug a finger into my waist and before I knew it, he threw me onto my back. I didn't know what to do this time. I was actually scared of him tonight.

When he first went inside me, I made noises like I was going to cry. It felt like we were having sex for the first time. We'd had sex last night, but this night what we did felt so pure and innocent. The brother took his sweet time with me. He wasn't racing and he didn't hit me off with those short fast strokes. Goddamn, I was just trying to take all that dick in and really enjoy it. He hit me with deep, long strokes. I was afraid that he would pull out too far. I would have been mad if it fell out. He maintained control. He never lost a stroke and didn't pull back too far. He was making a statement, like he not only wanted me to feel him, but he wanted to make sure I would remember that he was inside me. I felt so secure, so liberated, as he grabbed me and continued with his business. I let out shrieks and dug my fingers into his back. He kept knocking against me. I began to move with him. I didn't want to get into it so fast, but I couldn't but help call his name. He answered to his name but I didn't know what to say. I wanted to get a little of his attention, so I called on him some more. He did me so good until I wanted to tell him that it was his forever. I couldn't believe that he was making me come so fast. It had been a long time. I thought I would lose my fucking mind. My body tensed up at for a couple of seconds and deep emotion ran through me fluently. I didn't want to be loud, but I had to let it out. I didn't give a damn if his neighbor heard. I know I hollered loud enough for her to hear. I tried to push him off but I didn't want him off. I wanted him to slow down. My body was beginning to tickle. I wanted to call on God, the sex was so good. I didn't know what I would do if he broke my heart.

As promised, I made him dessert. He had strawberry shortcake. He took his time with the whipped cream. It was melting, and I could feel it running off my stomach and onto the sides of me then onto the sheets. He ate the strawberries with pieces of cake off my stomach and licked the remains of whipped cream. I was still aroused, and him licking on me did no justice.

Nyza was a good listener. We were in bed naked for hours talking. He was good conversation.

I lay vertically. He lay horizontally. His legs were dangling off the side of the bed. My legs were flexed with the heels of my feet planted in the creases of his stomach. "So, what's up with you and the lady next door?" I asked.

"The old white lady next door?"

"Yeah, yesterday she rolled her eyes at me and I saw her shoot you the finger earlier."

"She's ornery. You saw me, all I did was speak and her hateful ass flipped me off."

I grinded my feet in his stomach. "Come on, baby. You did something to that old lady. When I came over, she said something about some leaves in her yard."

He laughed and clapped loudly. He didn't say what he'd done, but I was concerned with something else. I looked at him once he calmed down and told him I needed to ask him a question.

He put his arm around me tighter. "What's up baby, what you need to ask?"

"Why did you really quit boxing?"

***

My personal trainer looked at me while I stood on the scale. She was not pleased. I knew she wouldn't be. I hadn't weighed myself, but with all the food I'd been eating lately, an increase in body weight was no surprise. My target weight was 146. My trainer, Nataline, still disgusted, made me get off the scale.

"Six pounds over," Nataline said.

I didn't know what to say. I didn't smile, but I wasn't worried either. "I'll get if off, Nat. Don't worry about that."

"That means we have a lot of work to do." The short woman folded her hands on top of her head. She kicked her feet out as she paced. It kind of looked like she was preparing to sprint. The trainer's body was as tight as glove. No wonder she was a fitness trainer. She pivoted on the balls of her feet and stared at me.

I smiled. "Nat, don't look at me like that. I told you, I will get it off."

"We have two weeks before Asia, honey."

"It's six pounds. We have enough time." Any other time my trainer would have caught major attitude from me, but this time I didn't care – as a matter of fact, Nat hadn't been able to get under my skin with her undermining tone and fat-girl comments. If you weren't the weight she thought you should be – even a pound over – she called you a fat girl. I thought about my new relationship. It was getting off to a really good start, and I was comfortable. I remembered what my aunt told me about relationships. She would say, "Girl, look at you. You are in that comfortable relationship, you are feeling good, and you are eating good. I can always tell when a woman is in a good relationship."

Nat continued to bitch, but I smiled and told her that she was the best personal trainer and that I knew she would have me ready for the big fight in Asia. Nat didn't look as hard at me after the comment I made. I looked over my shoulder and grabbed my butt. I chuckled. It felt bigger for some reason. I was in front of one of the large mirrors. I liked my ass.

"What are you smiling for?" The way Nat acted reminded me of a pint-sized drill sergeant when she raised her voice.

"What, I can't smile?"

"You have always been under."

"I've been eating more; so what?"

She continued to pace back and forth. She shook her pointer finger at me. "It's that man

you've been seeing, isn't it?"

There it is, I thought. She was hating – or I should say, man-hating. Some man must have messed over her real good, because if anyone brought up the word 'man' she would go into attack mode. There was a great amount of skepticism before making the decision to hire Nat. I'd never seen her with a man, and word was she dated the chick who came to all my fights. I even saw them kiss on the cheek, but that wouldn't even have been enough to provoke suspicion. A lot of women kiss on the cheek. If Nataline was a dyke, I didn't want her to work with me until I thought about it good. Someone like her would be focused on her work first, and besides, I knew how to protect myself. I was strictly dick-ly. I knew how to shut 'em down.

I had to have Nat for a trainer because she was damn good, and she was tough. When we did sessions we *did* sessions, and if it weren't for her, my body wouldn't have looked as good as it did. Whatever her sexual preference, it didn't matter. I looked to Nat and said, "Let's get to work."

She shook her head. "We do have a lot of work to do."

I clapped my hands, "Well, let's get to it then."

****

I got out my car, and I felt barely conscious. I was so tired. That had to have been the longest workout I'd done in the past year. I guessed she was trying to make me pay for putting on a few pounds. I got broke off. Like I said, I was exhausted. My arms felt like rubber. I didn't even feel like closing the car door. My stomach was tight. I could feel it when I walked up the steps. I looked back into the drive way and remembered my gym bag with the funky clothes in it. *Forget it*, I thought. I'd get it tomorrow.

I was hungry. I couldn't wait to eat. My momma even warned me about the healthy appetite you pick up when you meet a man. She would say that if the sex is fulfilling; so would the meals be. Must be true; my usual diet was a joke since I'd met Nyza. I'd been eating at least three full meals a day. When I went to see him, he always cooked for me. He piled it on just like he did the love. He had such a sweet heart, but every now and then I caught him drifting. Sometimes he was in another place but with me at the same time. It's hard to explain. There's a song that says, "Your body's here with me, but your mind is on the other side of town."

I think he missed boxing. The doctor said he needed reconstructive surgery, and even if he got it, he could never box again. I saw him shadow-boxing when he didn't think I did. He seemed happy when he did his thing. This man had a box full of recorded fights. He would watch from ten years ago and critique the other boxer's judgment and untimely strategies. If there'd been some way to help him, I would have in a heartbeat. I knew that he lost a big part of himself when he had to quit. He seemed so helpless at times. I still saw the desire and the passion in his eyes when he watched the fights. Everybody has a gift, something in this world that they are naturally good at. He was a gift to boxing. I remembered only a few of his fights, but I remember the hype in California. They called him Zabba-Zay. Though his career was short-lived, he'd been on his way to being the best pound-for-pound fighter in the heavy light-heavy weight division. Zay said that he could box again, but doctors said that his shoulder could give out at any time. Even if he got pins and screws, his arm would never be right again. He injured it really bad while boxing.

I'd thought about Nyza long enough. I could move on with my night. My bed was calling me. I was still hungry, but if I went to sleep, I'd forget about being hungry. If I let Nat tell it, I needed to skip a couple of meals any way. I picked up the phone and looked at the display. It showed two missed calls from Zay. I was sure he called the cell, too, but I'd left it in the car when I was with Nat. I was so tired when I left the gym, I forgot to check it. That girl really whooped my ass. Thinking about earlier made me tired all over again. I began thinking about the shower, and then I thought about food again. I wanted to call Zay, but I knew if I called him I would want to see him. Surely, he would have come, but I didn't want to bother him. He'd left one of his signature messages and wished me good night.

I kicked off my shoes in the living room and went straight to the kitchen. I squeezed my thighs and buttocks as I leaned into the fridge. Ooh, I was so tight. I thought again about skipping dinner and climbing into the bathtub. The way I was feeling, I was liable to fall asleep in there. I stood up and thought, *Nope, don't do it. Get your ass in the shower and call it a night.*

I got upstairs, and I was thinking about Zay once more. The more I thought about him, the more I wanted to call him. I needed to rest. If Zay came over, my physical attraction to him would surely take over, and we would end up fucking. I never thought I could find a man with a sex drive as vivacious as mine. As I thought of him, I could feel his strong hands caressing my body, caressing and rubbing my ass to sleep.

The phone rang. I didn't want to be bothered. I kept digging through my panty drawer. The phone stopped ringing, and it was so quiet in the house – but I heard a distinctive chirp from outside my window. I closed my panty drawer when the door bell rang. I damned near tripped trying to get to the window. When I looked out my bedroom window, I could see into my driveway. I was on the side of the window, so I could see without being seen.

I was giddy. I started giggling like a child as I ran down the stairs, skipping some in between. When I opened the door, I didn't know whether to kiss him or take the white plastic bag from him. I knew what was in the bag. I could smell it. "Baby, how did you know?" I asked.

"Well, I knew you were training and I called earlier. You weren't home so I figured, unless you stopped on the way home, you'd be hungry.

I grabbed him and squeezed him. His hands were full, so he couldn't hug me back. I wondered if he could tell how happy I was to see him. I could smell the greens and catfish. Zay smelled good too.

"Are you that happy to see me, or are you just that hungry?"

Of course I was happy to see him. I was glad that he

could tell. I pushed the door shut behind him and relieved him of the bag that I took straight to the kitchen while he locked the door.

After I tore the food up, I wasn't as tired any more, and I was ready to tear him up. I still needed to take a shower first. When I got upstairs, I reached for the clothes that I had laid out for the night when Zay insisted that I lay down – but he wanted my shirt off, and he wanted me on my stomach. He straddled me and went straight to work on me. How in the hell did he know this was what I needed? He was massaging deep, and I had to fight the urge to fall asleep. Yep, I was comfortable; I was eating good, and I was being loved good. Zay's back massage was firm but easy. I couldn't remember when I crashed out, but when I woke, I was on my side of the bed and Zay was on his. I lifted the lavender sheets from my naked body. Nyza slept like a baby and I hated to wake him, but I wanted some so bad. I reached for him. I was smooth like men try to be when they are sneaking the goods from us in *our* sleep. I stuck my hands between his legs and ran my finger under a leg of his boxers. I felt him – he was still asleep, but not for long, I thought. I massaged, and slowly but surely, he was rising. I moved to his balls and rubbed them softly. Zay's legs began to move a little. I fondled his genitalia some more. He was almost at attention. I turned on my right side so I could feel on him a little better. He grunted and turned over to his side. I snatched my hand away and immediately tugged at his waistband. He pulled his boxers down, and I could see the whites of his teeth in the dark as he got on top of me and dug me out; then he turned me over. I got on my hands and knees and stuck my ass out like I was in the club. He gripped my ass and rode me like a Kawasaki, full throttle. I reached for the headboard so I could brace myself. We women would like to think that we possess the stronger mind, but the truth is, good sex makes a big difference.

"Dammit," I said to the heavy weight. Brother had control of his manhood. It wasn't that premature ejaculation, two minute bullshit. He had stamina, no doubt. He pulled back and slammed it in me. I thought I would lose my breath. A few more shots of that and I emitted screams of pleasure and slight pain. I was cussing between screams, but I didn't want him to stop hitting me with that long dick. I swore he was wearing me out, and I thought I would lose my fucking mind when he pulled my hair. We had been going for at least 20 minutes. I tried to control my muscles. I clamped down on him and was coming all on his dick. I felt stress-free. My muscles continued to spasm and my legs were shaking. He was in steady rhythm. I moaned and reached behind me to slow him down. I bit down on the pillow when I felt him jerking inside me. I let the pillow go and wasn't ready to stop. I ordered him to make some noise as he came inside me. Most men are quiet and don't want to reveal their inner feelings, scared of being called a bitch, but the truth is, real men confide in their women. They can be so sensitive and secure at the same time. In my opinion, security comes with experience, and Nyza had plenty of it.

He released me and rolled onto his back. I fell on my belly. I was ready to go back to sleep, but I had to make it to the bathroom.

When I returned, there was a wrinkle in the bottom sheet where he'd just lain. I was wide awake. I could still smell the sex in the air. I inhaled it and couldn't wait for him to return to bed. What was I going to do with him, I thought. The room was still dark, though I'd left the bathroom light on. I was rather fond of his body, and frankly, I think I left the light on just so I could see him in the raw. He was still stark naked, and I knew this because his jeans were on the chase, and his boxers were still in the middle of the bed. Right then, I had an idea. I ran my exposed ass to the closet, stood on my tippy-toes to reach the black case on the top shelf. I left the closet to face Zay, who was wearing nothing but a smile. He was holding a plate and had a mouth full of food.

"Bought you some sandwich," he said. I'd figured he'd be attending to his appetite. I set up my project. I pulled the device out of the black case, flipped the switch, and pressed the red button. I still hadn't satisfied my appetite. I was still hungry too, but not for food. Zay walked to the bed' I followed him with the video camera. I had to get that sexy ass on tape.

"Eat up baby. You will need your strength. We ain't done."

He smiled and said, "Baby, I need some time." The brother looked down as if he were shifting the blame. I understood that he needed some time to get it up and he was getting his time. I went over to the dresser and positioned the camera so that it could capture my bed in its view. I walked over to him. "Do you need time, or do you need incentive?" After sitting on the bed, I scooted back. My long legs were opened as I faced the camera. I had the camera display aimed my way, so I could see myself. I was hoping that he was watching, and he was. I rubbed my legs from my knees up to my crotch. I massaged myself and looked at the camera display – Zay was looking, too. If he needed incentive, that was what he was going to get. I ran my fingers over my pussy until I got wet. Keeping my legs apart, I flexed my knees and stuck my fingers between and touched, rubbed my dripping lips some more. I spread my lips apart for him. I looked at him, and he was the same size. I fell into my role. I felt my heart beating like I was nervous, but I wasn't. He looked at me, and it looked like he was getting aroused. I was so moist and wet all over again, sticking one finger inside of me, and then another. Carrying out a steady, yet easy motion, I was breathing heavy, licking my full lips, making sex noises. In and out, I was fucking myself, hoping it would turn him on some more. The red light on the camera was still lit. I was just starting to get loose. I spread myself more for him and indulged in myself, whispering words of anticipation, calling on him, waiting on him to finish that goddamn sandwich so he could finish the job. When I opened my eyes, he was holding the camera on me. He was at attention, long and erect once again.

I liked being on top. It made me feel sexy, like a stripper or a private slut. I would never be seen like this in public, only for my man. I was living out my fantasies; I feel like every black woman wishes she could be a stripper for at least a day, a sexy stripper at that. Maybe she wants to strip for the crowd, or she could just strip for that special one. Zay's comments always confirmed my thoughts. He didn't always call me sexy; it was his body language that said it sometimes. My eyes were closed, and I wondered what he was doing. Was he still watching me? I went deeper inside of me, frowning and smiling at the same time. Just when I thought he was still enjoying the show, I felt his warm hands on top of my supple breasts. He squeezed and kissed my nipples. The sensation alone ran messages to my inner thighs. He took his hands off me. He braced himself on each side of me as he opened his legs to straddle me; he pulled my wet fingers out me and inserted them into his mouth. I didn't think I was going to make it. He told me to turn sideways, and I looked at him. He sat the camera on top of the dresser. The red light was still on. I could see movement in the display, so I knew we were still on video. It turned me on even more. I couldn't stand it. I was so horny. My head was once again pointing to the headboard when he ran up in me. I dug my nails into his back; I didn't want it slow. I didn't want it soft. I wanted to get fucked. I wanted my pussy torn up and given back to me. Fuck it. He could put it in his pocket if he so desired; as far as I was concerned I had given it to him anyway.

Zay

My little knockout was out like a light. She bore a slight smile on her face. I didn't want to wake her, but I had to. There was little time for me to get dressed and to top it off, my clothes were in the trunk of my car. Spending the night wasn't in my immediate plans, things just fell that way. My momma always told me to keep three things in the car: a coat in case the car breaks down, a change of clothes in case she puts you out, and a condom for whatever may happen. Momma would have been proud.

Even though I didn't want to, I had to wake the baby. I looked over to her alarm clock. *Oh shit, I got to get the hell out of here. I have somewhere to be and if I don't hurry I'll be late.* With an instinctive yawn, I took an elongated stretch before I woke Tammerine. To my surprise, she awoke on her own. Tammerine opened her eyes with a smile. When she did, I jumped and almost fell out of the bed. Tammerine jumped at the same time. Before I knew better, I spoke before I thought. "What the fuck," I exclaimed, surprised.

The two of us were on opposite edges of the king-sized bed. Tammy looked at me so innocent-like, with the covers pulled up to her neck.

"Something wrong?" She asked.

Hell yeah something is wrong. "Where are your teeth?"

"These two are missing," she said, pointing at the same time.

"I can see that."

"Problem?" She asked.

It was obvious that either she didn't know how to tell me, or she felt really comfortable with me. I hope I didn't sound insensitive, but that caught me off guard big time. Who could blame me.

"No, it's not a problem, but you could have told me."

"I thought that everybody knew that my teeth were missing in the front."

I swung my legs out of bed. The whole time I was trying to get myself together. The more I thought about it, the more it didn't matter much. "Baby if you are missing teeth, don't you think that you should make sure that I know this so there is no misunderstanding?"

She could tell that I understood the whole thing. She apologized.

"You never took your teeth out before," I said.

"Yeah I have. I take them out almost every night that I am with you." *I just get up and put them back in before you wake up.* "Usually I get up before you do, and when I get up, of course, I put them back in."

She did have a point. She did get up before I did in the mornings. "This is true, but when I go to sleep at night, you have your teeth in. So what do you do, wait until I go to sleep to take them out?"

She looked at me shyly and nodded. She started to giggle, though I didn't seem to find much humor in the secrecy of the cosmetic prosthetic. Tammerine was nervous. Her secret was out. She wondered if withholding the information was enough for me to change my mind. Carefully, I leaned over to her and gave her a soft peck on the cheek. "It's all good." Deciding to laugh the whole thing off, I stretched again as I came to my feet. "Hate to run, baby, but I got to go."

I heard a long, drawn out, excited "I-i-i-i-i-i-ts Fr-i-i-i-i-i-i-i-i-i-i-i-i-i-i-i-i-i-d-a-a-ay" on my way down the stairs. The WPGC news report followed. If you lived in the District of Columbia, Maryland or Northern Virginia, you could always look forward to David Bruce Haynes and his distinctive voice as he delivered the day's news and weather. On Fridays, it was his tradition to announce to everyone in the listening area that it was the end of the week. It was definitely something that lots of us in city looked forward to.

Tammy was so amazing. It was so hard to believe that a person so violent in the ring could be so beautiful. She was so nice to look at. I had always thought that. She was just the type of lady who you wanted to explore sometimes. I had yet to explore every opening and ending of her.

"Hope you're hungry, baby."

I patted my stomach. It was kind of hollow-sounding. "Only if it's to go."

Tammerine looked up from the stove. "Did it bother you that much that you have to go?" She pointed at her teeth.

I smiled. "No baby." I walked around the island, stood behind her and wrapped my arms around her. I kissed her on the side of the face and inhaled the scent of her hair lotion. "No, baby, remember? I am picking up my sister today." She nodded after a couple of seconds as it came back to her.

She turned her head and said, "That's right. Your sister does fly in today."

"Yep. I look forward to you and her meeting."

"We met already."

"On the phone doesn't count," I said.

"Well, in that case, I look forward to meeting her in person then."

What is the quickest way to Regan Airport, I thought. Last night, I'd mapped out the route I would take in my head, but I didn't count on leaving from here. I was going to leave from the crib, so of course, I didn't count on the traffic. I was leaving from Annapolis on route 2 to 97, and from there I would hop on 695 towards Glen Burnie. Surely, I would catch the traffic from Baltimore towards DC. If I took 97 towards Ellicott City, I would get the traffic from the B/W parkway. I could take 270 and still be stuck. I needed to be on 95, and either way I went, I would have to hit one of these highways to get there, and I would hit traffic no matter which way I went. I could hear Vette's mouth already. Sitting in traffic, I began to think about Tammerine again and the incredible sex bout we had the night before. The fellas would call me puss whipped. I was wondering if I was or if I was in love. She put it down on me. I mean, she had the sweetest pussy – and she was so damn sexy the way she moved. I couldn't lie, thinking about it made me want to curl up in the fetal position when we finished loving each other. She liked variety, and I could tell. As long as she kept giving me that ass, I would switch it up so much she'll think she's in the Matrix. Fast or slow, hard or fast; we could go from straight fucking to slow love in no time at all. We never lost a stroke, either. I felt this strong connection when we entangled under the sheets. The pillows smelled like her setting lotion, and the sheets smelled like Dior Perfume mixed with Secret deodorant. That woman had my head so far into the clouds that I almost missed my exit.

****

I was late already, so I wasn't going to park, but I hated to circle, too. Knowing my sister, she would have a bunch of bags. I circled once when Vette called me and told me that she and her bags were at the baggage claim. I had to come off the ramp and had to be careful using the cell phone without an earpiece. DC cops would give you a big ticket for that.

"Where are you, Zay?" My sister asked.

"I am passing the sign that says arrivals. Bring your bags outside to the curb and I will pick you up from there."

She didn't say anything, just hung up the phone. My older sister hates to wait. I don't know who made her queen of the east coast but that was how she had acted since we were little, like she couldn't wait on anybody, but they all had to wait on her. She had dudes eating out of her hands left and right. It's like they were scared of her. Them boys did whatever Vette told them to do. I thought it was funny. She had this one boyfriend named Steve; he was a straight up yes-man. One day, he asked my sister to the movies. She said okay and then called him back and told him that her girlfriend Felicia was going with them. He said it was cool. Me and Tracey were rolling. Tracey said, "That wouldn't happen to me. You tell me some shit like that and I'll tell you to go with her and y'all be together." I think that deep down, Arvette dug what Tracey said; moreover, I think she dug Tracey. She said that he was too young for her. She was only four years his senior, but she acted like she had him by 10. I could see her just making it to the curb, setting her Louis Vuitton luggage down. My sister was lighter than me. She was as yellow as a banana and her features weren't as prominent as mine. She had a button nose, small, raised cheeks, and a small cleft in her chin. She had a cute mole on the left side of her upper lip. Sis had her hair in a short and neat hair style. She was a real estate agent, and she looked like one. I loved the fact that my sister was such a professional. She was good at everything she did.

I leaned to the right and flipped my hazards on. She raised her hands up like she had been there waiting for a while.

I released the trunk and swung my legs out of the car. My sister walked around to the back of the car to meet me with open arms. We hadn't seen each other in a year and a half, but we squeezed each other like it had been longer than that. I kissed my older sister on the face before I dropped my arms.

"That's enough emotion, scruff-face. Help me with my stuff. We are in DC; they love to give tickets."

"Thought you would have got a tan being in that Florida sunshine," I said. Leaning at the waist, I reached for her bags when she popped me in the head.

"Watch it, big head."

She pulled her purse up on her arm and got into the car. My sister said she was staying for a week, and she packed like she was staying for a month. If I knew my sis, she had nothing but shoes in one of those suitcases, one full of sleepwear and make-up, and an empty one so she could go shopping. I never knew my sister to leave her work behind, so I was surprised when I didn't see her laptop case on her shoulder. She said that she packed it in one of the suitcases after she claimed her luggage.

"So, you are settling down. I couldn't believe it."

"Yep." I looked over my shoulder and pulled the nose of the car out of the space. Police were directing traffic and monitoring the people that were double parked. My sister adjusted herself in the seat and looked around inside the cabin of the ride.

"Nice ride… Not bad… Not bad."

"Trying to keep up with you."

"So you are finished ho-ing, huh?"

"You're calling me a ho?" I asked. "Everything I learned, I learned from you." My sister and my aunt were the biggest pimps. We have different mothers, but of course, we have the same dad. The older we got, the closer we got. She came to live with us when she started 11th grade. I was only in the 7th. She transferred from Eastern to H.D. Woodson high school. She was running game. She had men doing everything from buying her clothes and shoes to taking her out to lunch everyday. She had a lot of men, but people had mad respect for my sister. They knew her, but her name wasn't around. They called her nothing less than a lady. They knew that my sister was stingy with the ass, but they all thought they had a shot, and my sister would let them think it too. She used this to get what she wanted. When I used to box for Highland, she would come up to watch me fight, and they would try. They heard about my sister, and they knew she was fine by word of mouth before they saw her for themselves. She was so opinionated. I don't know if it was a turn-on or a turn-off for most of the dudes. Some of them wanted a woman who they could control, and others wanted a woman who liked to stand up and speak her mind. My sister definitely spoke her mind at all times, and she knew how to run game. I never thought she would settle down until she met that tired-ass cat who she has a kid with. I love my niece, but I can't stand her worthless father.

I looked at my sister and smiled. I was glad to see her. She smiled too and asked me about my mother.

"Momma is fine."

"I would like to see her. Well, you could give her a call. Sure she would love to hear from you."

"That was my girl. I loved the way she used to mother all the kids on the block."

I laughed. "You ain't lying." My mother was what you would call the community ass beater. It didn't matter who the kid belonged to, if my mother knew the kids and they were showing out, she would correct them right where they stood.

"Momma would beat anybody's kid."

"Hell yeah," my sister agreed.

"Remember that time she caught you and Tracey throwing rocks at the metro bus?"

"How can I forget? Momma was driving up the street. She saw us rocking the bus. She stopped, hopped out the car, and left the car door open and the engine running. Man, I looked over, and all I could see was the look on her face. I can't even describe it, but you know those crazy looks that mom gives."

"Uh, huh."

"Yeah, when I saw momma I told Tracey to run."

My sister started laughing. "That's right, you did tell him to run, and his ass took off, too. He started running, and she went after him first. She did a football tackle on his ass."

I laughed because Arvette was telling the truth. Vette

called it a football tackle, but I preferred to call it a combat roll. She dived on Tracey.

"Do you remember the time she caught you and Tracey jumping out of the swings?"

"Sure do. You were visiting for the summer."

"I think she whooped everybody who was swinging. Then she took them to they momma."

We laughed a little more. I had the windows cracked, and by this time we were on M. Street. Arvette clapped her hands. I looked over to the passenger and asked, "What's your problem?"

"You're taking me shopping. We are on M. Street."

"I got things to do, Vette. I'm not taking you shopping." I glanced at the clock on the dash. "You just got here, and you are talking about shopping already."

"Come on now, brother, you know that there ain't no shopping in Florida that could compare to the shopping in D.C."

"I noticed that one of your suitcases is in damn near empty."

"Act like you know, Zay, you are taking me shopping; matter of fact, I want to go to New York while I am here."

I laughed. She was crazy. I didn't have time to go to New York. She wasn't serious any way. She was just talking; I bet that if I gave her a minute she'd be talking about Atlantic City next. Arvette is the true definition for

"Shop-a-holic", which kind of concerns me because most shop-a-holics shop out of boredom and/or unhappiness. Vette seemed stable and sufficient to me, but at the same time, I only talked to her once a week and I only saw her about once a year, so she could have been hiding anything. There could have been a lot going on that I didn't know about. I looked over to my sister with her short, yet rounded face, and I smiled. She has always been the materialistic type. What I liked most about her was that she never asked a brother to hook her up. She was always the type to pay her own way. She never asked a man to buy something for her; they offered to buy it. It would have been too easy for Vette to get men to spend money on her, but she preferred to buy and do for herself.

I looked down at Arvette's ring. It had my niece's birthstone in it. "Where's my niece?" Arvette seemed nervous upon my asking about her daughter. She smiled and told me that my niece was doing just fine. I loved that little girl. She was my first and only niece. Arvette didn't say that much. I didn't pry. My sister was a very good momma.

"You know she is in school now?" Vette asked.

"That's right," I sang.

"So, what's going on with this female boxer you are with?"

I smiled. I couldn't help it. I had been away from Tammy for about an hour, and I could hardly wait to be at her side again. With the more time I spent with her; the more time I wanted. I subdued my smile and prepared to answer my older sister.

"She is cool. Man, she is as cool as a fan. She is a little different, but that is what I love about her."

My sister busted up with laughter as she clapped her hands. "That is what you love about her. You said the words love and her all in the same sentence."

I tried to clean it up real quick. "No I said, '*that* is what I love about her.'"

"Brother, it sounds like you are trading in the card."

I switched gears on her. "You are older than me. Shouldn't you be somewhere in a kitchen cooking for some old dude with a heavy gut?"

Vette held up her middle finger and snickered.

"Come sis, I know you got cats sniffing your dross. Why are you playing with me?"

"You know what? You men ain't shit. Y'all don't know what you want out of life."

"I got my shit together, thank you."

"You got a coffee shop."

"Sorry, I'm not a realtor like you, but I still make good money."

Vette got serious on me. She started asking me about my health and the condition of my arm. I told her that I am good, that my arm is good as long as I limit my physical activities. "Doc told me to chill on the free weights. You know me though, I still got my thing but I take it easy."

I was a bit agitated with my sister. I knew something was up with her. She wasn't herself. I knew something was up that she wasn't telling me about. We were so much better than making all this small talk.

So, we were cruising down Georgia. I made a right towards City place and looked for a parking garage. We were in the heart of Silver Spring, about two blocks from the subway station. I stop here damned near every morning. I'd get my Starbucks some mornings, and from there I'd sometimes go to Barnes and Noble. Depending on the mood I was in, I would pick up a book. In the springtime, I liked to walk the square just because. It was a different kind of place here. People seemed to be so carefree and happy every day. People were always on the go. They might be talking on their cell phones, having negotiation luncheons, meeting for that secret rendezvous, or they might be like me, just picking up something from the cleaners. Sometimes I came here just to get that mental break and other time I just wanted to clear my head of all the superfluities of life, only to refill later.

That day, the women were pushing baby strollers, and the ones who weren't strolling were carrying one in the womb. Their bellies were sticking out. I wondered if these young girls knew what to do with a baby. I was wondering if they'd even started college or finished high school. *We have got to start taking better care of our kids*, I thought. I thought about the young fathers to these little babies, and I thought about how me and my sister came about; how we are from a house divided. Daddy was with my momma and made a family with my sister's momma. I talk about the young men, but I guess sometimes, the older ones don't know that much more than the younger ones. Arvette was taking care of a baby who the father doesn't support. I was still looking for him. If I ever found him, I swore it'd be over for him.

Arvette said that she wanted to get something to eat, even though I only came down here to pick up my stuff from the cleaners. It was only 10:45. It was cool. "Chik-fil-A cool with you?" I asked my sister.

"Boy, you know how long it's been since I had some Chik-fil-A?" I smiled. I was happy to be with my sister. Out of all the family that I had, she felt the closest to me.

"In Florida, we have Crystals."

"I know. Y'all got that fake me out White Castle down there."

She laughed and I led the way to the fast food joint. This Chik-fil-A was different from all the others ones I'd ever been to. When you first walked into this one, there were some stairs. We walked down the stairs and to one of the lines so we could order. Usually, there weren't many people this early in the day. Then again, it was Friday. My sister was excited and anxious to order. She acted like a little kid. It took her a minute to order. I knew exactly what I wanted. I got a number one with lettuce and tomato most of the time, and other times I got the number five. I told Vette to order for me while I went to wash my hands.

I worked up a good lather, and I looked for the paper towels, but there were none. All I saw was one of those damned blowers. I hated those things. Sure, I know that they save the owners money. I know that the blowers are cheaper than buying rolls of paper every few days, but I hated using those things. I did what I had to do to get my hands dry. When I cracked open the door, I couldn't believe what I saw. Sometimes, you think you see someone that you that you know, but when you get close enough you realize that it's someone else. I was hoping that this was one of those times, except I didn't plan to get close enough to make sure I was seeing the person I thought I was seeing. I stepped back. I knew I looked suspicious. I left a four inch opening between the door and the door jamb and hoped that no one was on their way to the bathroom. I was trying to see without being spotted. I had to know if this person was who I thought she was. It was her. I knew it was. I could spot that walk of hers anywhere. I remembered the details in her Louie bag from her last birthday. She stood about five feet away from Arvette. She was with this man who she kissed on the mouth before grabbing his hand on the way up the stairs.

Tammerine

H e said that he had a lot of errands to run. He took all day running them and we had to be at the Howard's in a matter of hours. If that man didn't have a type A personality, I didn't know who did.

I was looking forward to meeting his sister face to face. I talked to Arvette on the phone a few times. I had one long conversation with her one night. She was schooling me on her brother and his funny ways. She was cool. We could be shopping buddies. I heard that she loved to shop.

I heard a noise outside. It sounded like the chirp Zay's Benz makes. I got excited. I started combing through my hair with my fingers. I brushed over my eyebrows with my index fingers. I took a deep breath and just waited. For a few seconds I got scared. I was getting used to Nyza. I was getting used to having him around. I was getting used to his everyday normal schedule. Maybe it was the pipe talking. God knows I'd never had the pipe laid like that to me before.

They came through the door. I looked at him and couldn't help but smile at him, with his little boy shape-up and distinguished glasses. I pushed him straight out of the way and reached for his sister. I hugged her and we both laughed. Zay stood off the side and looked at us like we were both crazy.

"Well I guess I'll skip the intro. It seems like you know each other already."

"Good to finally meet you," I said.

"No, girl, good to finally you meet you. You got my brother on lockdown."

We laughed and high-fived each other. "Come on girl. Take off that coat." I waved her in my direction.

My man looked at his wrist. "We ain't got time for this. I brought her by to see you, but I still got to change and shower."

Something was wrong with Zay. I didn't know what it was, but I knew it was something. He wasn't acting the same as he did earlier. I doubt he was still tripping about my teeth. Arvette said before that her brother was moody. She said that he had been like that all her life. "One minute he's laughing and the next minute he's quiet." So maybe his existing mood was nothing to worry about. I tried to keep all things in mind when it came to Zay. He was different from any other man that I had ever met. He had been in the house for only ten minutes, but it bothered me, and I had to know if he was okay. I asked him to meet me in the kitchen before he left.

He did his thing. It took longer this time – longer than it usually took to meet with me whenever I said I wanted to see him. I touched his youthful face and asked, "What's going on, man?"

He smiled, but he answered my question with a question. "What?" He asked.

I lifted his head. "Tell me what's up. You have been too quiet." He was ready to tell it, whatever it was. He was acting the way a man would act when he wanted to break it off with his woman. Zay would have to wait until tomorrow. I couldn't take it this night. I took a deep breath and was ready to ask again when he answered my question.

"I saw Nichole today with another man."

I didn't understand. *Who in the hell was Nichole and why would you care?* "Am I supposed to know Nichole?" I asked in the simplest tone.

"Nichole is Tracey's wife."

My heart fell for Tracey. I didn't know what to say. We were supposed to go over there for dinner. "Baby, are you sure? I mean, it could be somebody that she works with." I smiled, hoping to make light of the situation.

"Well, this person that she could work with had

his hands all over her ass, and she kissed him on the mouth."

I didn't know Tracey well, but as far as I could tell, he was a sweet person; he didn't deserve this. I could see why Zay was acting the way that he did. Now I was sure he was feeling the pressure. He had to tell, or maybe he felt like he should. I was sure he felt responsible as a friend to tell his friend what he saw. I asked again to make sure that he wasn't jumping the gun. Maybe it wasn't as it appeared.

"Yes, I'm sure," Nyza said.

"So, what are you going to do?"

"Tammy, it was her. I mean what do I do? That is my boy. I have to tell him."

"You're not thinking of doing it tonight, baby?" I could feel my face wrinkle as I asked him that question.

"Well, when else?"

I didn't know what to say. He was more than right. How could he call himself a friend and not tell his friend that his significant other is seeing someone else? My father used to cheat on my mother, and since then, I have always despised cheaters.

"I don't know Tracey all that well, but I don't like what you saw. At the same time, Zay, I know he's your friend, and I know you want to tell him, but do you think she will be honest – do you think he will believe you?"

"You are right. If you ask him, she can do no wrong. But I'm just looking out for my boy. If I don't tell him, I will feel bad later. If he doesn't take my word, it's cool. He can never say that I didn't tell him. You know what? Maybe we won't go to the dinner tonight."

"So when did you see them? When you walked in?"

"No."

"How long were you there before you saw them?"

"'Bout four or five minutes, why?"

"I'm trying to figure out if they saw you or not. Because if you show up at their house tonight, she will know what's up."

"So, what does that have to do with if they saw me or not?"

"Well, baby, when you see a person and they say they didn't see you, most of the time they are lying; they saw you, they just didn't want to be seen. It's kind of a psych-out, if they pretend they didn't see you then they think you didn't see them – if they didn't want to be seen."

He laughed. I knew it sounded twisted, but it must have made sense to him. I looked at the kitchen wall, and I thought about how rude I was being to Zay's sister. We left her alone and I was beginning to feel bad. I wanted to finish hearing my man out though.

"She could've seen me, maybe, maybe not."

I stood behind him, put my hands on his fully-developed shoulders, and squeezed. "I know you will do what you think is best, baby. But if you are thinking about canceling this evening, don't."

He turned around to face me. He smiled and wrapped me tight in his arms. This was what I had been waiting for all day. Lately, this is what I'd been living for.

Arvette was on the sofa with her shoes off and her feet tucked underneath her thighs. She was all into the TV. I could tell what she did with her spare time by the way she held the remote. She was a professional channel surfer. Zay didn't want to snatch her from the TV, but he'd already communicated his schedule to me and he was ready to go. He always stood with his arms folded when he was ready to go. We kept talking, though. Meanwhile, Zay made these noises like he was trying to clear his throat. He did this two more times before Arvette said, "Don't rush me. We will go when I am ready." I laughed. I couldn't wait until I could have more control. I couldn't wait to understand all his signals. I looked at the comfortable sister. She acted like she was at home. I wasn't mad at her. She was one of the closest people to my love interest. I was glad that I could share something with her. I was glad that she felt comfortable.

Arvette looked at Zay but pointed at me when she said, "When that lady over there tells me I have to leave, then I will leave. Zay, you don't run shit around here."

I was loving it.

Zay unfolded his arms and leaned over his sister. "I'll

leave your ass here, then you can walk your ass home. How about that?"

"I got money, fool. I can find a cab. My sister here might even take me home."

"Look, Vette, come on. Get your ass in the car. We got some where to be later. You two have plenty of time to talk and hang out."

She turned around and looked at her brother.

"Where we got to be? Are we going shopping?"

"No. I told you that we are going to have dinner with your boy."

Vette stopped smiling. "Who is my boy?"

"Tracey."

"Tonight?"

Zay chuckled. "Yes, tonight. I have some things to do and I still have to swing back out this way to pick up Tammy."

"I'm not going," she said with a thick hood twang.

"Why not?"

" 'Cause I'm not. Y'all going to be couples. There are four tires, Zay, and dammit, I ain't trying to be the spare."

"I already told them that you are coming," Zay said.

"I got plenty of time to see Tracey. His big peanut-head-ass ain't going nowhere."

"That won't even look right. Besides, he wants you meet his wife."

"You don't even like his wife, so why does it matter if I meet her or not?"

Vette had a good point. I began to wonder why Zay disliked Tracey's wife so much.

"Nah little brother... I think I am going to sit this one out."

Zay breathed hard and pulled out his keys. The sister didn't say anything more. I didn't know what to say as she put her feet on the floor and slid into her sandals. My man looked at me.

"Are you wearing what you have on?"

I looked down at my clothes. "No."

"Well get your clothes. You can get dressed at my house. We can just leave from there."

I didn't argue with him. I went upstairs, got my stuff, and met them at the car. Arvette was ready to hop in the backseat, but I told her it was cool. It wasn't every day she got to see her brother. It was a quiet ride. Zay had stuff on his mind, and his sister was quiet too, like she had something on her mind as well. It wasn't right in the car. I didn't say much. I was thinking about what Zay told me, and I was wondering what might go down that night. I was hoping for a good night. I didn't know Tracey's wife, but I wanted to get to know her. After about 15 minutes of road noise, I decided to make small talk. I asked Vette about her daughter. The driver stepped on my question by asking his sister a different question.

"What's wrong with you, and how come you don't want to see Tracey?"

"Didn't you say that he has a wife now?"

"Yeah but you knew that. You tripped out when you found out he was getting married."

I was in the backseat waiting for the seat to heat up. It was pitch black in the car, except for the dash display. Zay's windows were so dark. To me, it was obvious why she didn't want to see Tracey.

***

It was dry at the dinner table. I wasn't so hungry. The silence kind of killed my appetite. Zay didn't like Nichole as it was. He was holding out on his friend, and I knew that was hard for him. Tracey was trying to get to know me, and I could tell that he and his wife weren't vibing. She seemed a bit snooty and uppity, but I wasn't one to judge. Sometimes, people turn out to be different than they appear. I was always told not to judge a picture by its cover. I didn't know what Zay had against Tracey's woman, but if he told me that her attitude had something to do with it, I wouldn't be surprised in the least.

I should've stayed home with my sister-in-law. Yep, my sister-in-law. Zay was going to be mine, whether he knew it or not. He was already mine, but I was going to keep him, and I was going to make him marry me. He was what I wanted in a man. Even if he wasn't ready, I'd give him some time. He was my husband. I had already named and claimed it. I smiled on the inside at the thought of us being totally committed and in love. I should have stayed home – we should have stayed home. He went where I went, so if I would've stayed at home, he would have too.

Me and Vette could have gone shopping, but instead I was here at this boring dinner. It was quiet except for the sounds of the flatware scraping against the plates. I didn't have much on my plate to begin with. My trainer had told me to cool it so I could keep my weight down. Zay was unsettled. I didn't like to see him like that. I stared at him long enough to get him to notice me. I crossed my eyes and made these childish faces. When he refused to smile, I used the tip of my tongue to push my partial forward. He tried to keep his food as he laughed at the same time. The newlyweds looked at Zay, who was wiping the smile off his face.

"You okay, Zay?" Tracey asked.

He smiled and said, "Yeah, I'm cool. I was thinking of this joke I heard earlier."

Nichole put her fork down, folded her hands and said, "A joke, let's hear it."

I started to giggle myself. The lady of the house

glanced at me and looked back at Zay. She was waiting to hear the joke.

"Nah, I'd rather not. It's not the kind of joke you tell at the dinner table."

She didn't say anything else. But I watched her. I watched how she looked at Zay. Some people give themselves away with their looks. Looking at her, I couldn't tell if she'd seen Zay earlier or not. I was willing to bet that she didn't know that Zay was at the Chik-fil-A earlier. Zay told me when we first got to the Howard's that Nichole had on the same outfit when he saw her that morning. He would shake his head from time to time. I knew that holding his secret was killing him. He wanted to say something, but I didn't want him to. A part of me didn't want him to get involved, but when I thought about it some more, telling Tracey was the right thing to do. I guess I just didn't want to be around when he did it. I did, however, want to know how she would respond. Would she admit to it or would she lie about it? Would Tracey know if she was lying? The fact is, we women know how to hide better. We are naturally better liars than men. Something could be wrong with us, and the man would never know unless we wanted him to. While the man thinks that everything is cool, we are plotting. Men are different. They are more confrontational. If they got something to say, they are going to say it. If they have a problem, they are going to make sure that you know it – just like right now, Zay wanted to tell what's on his mind. He wanted to talk.

I stared at Zay some more. *Yep, he is going to be my husband.* I smiled. He smiled back. *I don't care what it takes. He is going to be all mine.*

Zay dabbed the corner of his mouth with his napkin. He looked at Tracey. "Man, you will never believe what I saw today."

I looked Zay in the face and shook my head. He was silent but waiting for someone to ask what he saw. I guess they took too long to say something, so Zay started.

"I was in Silver Spring today, over there by City Place."

Tracey frowned. The wife kept poking at her salad.

"Yeah, I was over there at Chik-fil-A."

The look on Nichole's face was priceless. I wanted to kick Nyza from my side of the table. I couldn't believe he was doing this. Nichole shoved more food in her mouth. She kept her head down and wouldn't look at any of us. Zay leaned back in the chair. That is when I jumped in. "Zay, you are not at home. Stop rearing back in that chair."

"And you are not my momma, and this ain't your house."

I was surprised by his comment, but it turned me on at the same time. That is what I love about Zay; he puts it down, and he doesn't have to do a lot of cussing to get a point across. His masculine tone and pitch is enough.

"So, like I was saying–"

"–Doesn't have to be my house."

"You know what, forget it."

I squinted and gave him the evil eye for the bold stunt he pulled. By this time, Nichole looked up from her plate and quickly changed the subject.

"So this is your lady friend, Nyza?" Nichole asked. She had this look of approval on her face. I mean what the fuck was I, his first girlfriend? I didn't know he needed momma's approval. I dabbed my mouth as she went on.

"And Nyza, she is cute. She's not like the other women you meet." She focused on me and said, "Let me tell you, it is good to know and see that he has finally met a good woman."

No she didn't. We had been here for thirty-five minutes and this bitch ain't said nothing to me. She spoke to me and that was it. *And she got the nerve to serve this dinner out the goddamn can. Serving us this microwave mac-and-cheese out of the box, Learn to cook, bitch.* I was being nice. I didn't want to insult her in her own house, but I felt that she was getting back at Nyza at my expense, treating me like a pound puppy that was found and cleaned up. I changed my mind. I hoped Zay would tell all her business, bust her out right here at the dinner table. She didn't know me. I would kick her fake Chanel-wearing ass. Zay wasn't happy either, and his poor friend was in the dark. Hell, I wanted to snitch. I wanted to tell what Zay saw just to piss his snotty wife off. I tried not to look her in the face, but I couldn't help it. I was mad. When I looked at her again, she had just put her glass down and she dabbed her mouth with her napkin like I had just done. *Is this bitch mocking me?* Ooh, Zay better tell this bitch. He better tell her, because I was about to lose it around here. If he didn't tell, I had it in my mind that I was going to reach across the table and snatch that weave off of her head.

Tracey excused himself from the table, and so did Miracle-Gro. They went in opposite directions. Tracey went upstairs, and she went into the kitchen. My man scooted himself from the table and told me he'd be back. He said he was going to straighten her out. Momma told me a long time ago that you never leave your man with another woman, but I decided to let Zay do what he needs to do. I wanted to follow, him but I didn't. I knew that I was going to fuck her up if she said one wrong word to me.

Nyza

"**W**hat's your fucking problem?"

"This is my house. I do what I want to do," Nichole said in a low, but minding tone.

I looked around the kitchen, paranoid. I didn't need anyone to come in while we were having this conversation. "You are fucked up, you know that?"

She stood there with her hands on her hips and looked at me like her shit don't stink.

"How am I fucked up?"

"You know I saw your ass today."

She smacked her lips and poked out her hips a little more like she was all that. "You saw me today with whom?"

I laughed and looked around some more. I was losing my patience.

"You know that I saw you with some dude this morning. You had on the same overpriced outfit that you do now."

She laughed and said, "You mean you saw me today with one of my co-workers."

I leaned against the refrigerator so I could be close enough to her without looking suspect if some one walked in. I had to make sure she heard everything I was about to say. "Play that role if you want to. When I say I saw you; I saw you." I looked around again before I whispered, "Nichole, I saw everything."

"Whatever."

I didn't know how long Tammy could hold Tracey from coming in – if she could hold him at all – but I wanted to tell Nicole about herself.

"How are you going to do that to my boy?"

She took her hands off her hips and asked, "What are you going to do about it Zay, are you going to tell him?"

"That's my friend, Nichole, and he loves you."

She got in my face close enough for us to kiss. "So, big man, if he's so much your friend, then how come you didn't tell him about us?"

I frowned up.

"How come, Zay? Did you tell him how you fucked the shit out of me and that I liked it?" She smiled.

I took a step back. "That was old," I whispered in a stern tone. "You know that is old. We did that before you and him hooked up, and way before you and him got married, so don't throw that shit in my face."

"Okay, so why didn't you tell him then? You know, since it was before we hooked up?"

"I should've, but I'll tell you this; I told him not to marry your ass because you are a ho."

She raised her voice. "A ho!" By this time, Trace and my date had walked in. They were both in a defensive position, trying to figure out what was going on with about two inches between me and Trace's wife. I put a message inside my look before I gave it to Nichole. When I walked off, Trace and Tammy stood still, looking confused. I didn't know what to say, and I didn't know what card to pull. I wasn't really concerned, either. I had a feeling about tonight. It wasn't the best– and it was about to get worse. I would have more explaining to do than I cared for. For the first time in years, I felt like I owed someone something.

Walking past the table, I took my napkin and threw it on top of my plate. I took a swig of lemonade and told my lady to get her purse.

I threw up the deuces and yelled "Be easy," to Tracey. He threw deuces back. Tammy was at the front door before I knew it. Tracey didn't ask why we were leaving. He knew something was up. He and she needed to talk, and me and mine didn't need to be around when that happened. We let ourselves out and left them to be.

Tammy's heels clicked against the concrete. She was walking fast towards the car.

Tammerine

"What the fuck was that?"

"What?" He asked as he looked in the rearview to back out of the Howard's driveway. I had my arms folded. I was ready to cry. I was fighting back the tears. When I'd sat down at her dinner table, I'd had a premonition. The way she went tit for tat, I knew something was up. I wasn't concerned with the cheating ordeal; there was some underlying issue, something unresolved, and I was taken right back to my premonition. I was still struggling against tears. My face was warm and my eyes burned. I had to know for sure. I looked straight ahead to the traffic in front of me. It was burning me up so I asked him.

"You fucked her, didn't you?" I tensed up so I wouldn't fall apart upon receiving an unpleasant answer.

"Where did that come from?" He asked.

I felt the water pool in my lower lids. "Nyza, I asked,

151

did you sleep with her. All I need to hear is a yes or a no."

"Yes."

The tears were rolling down my face, but I was calm. People think that I am so tough because of my profession, but I'm one hundred percent woman. I can be just as sensitive as the next. I was crying and talking at the same time to him. I sounded like a five year old that just got her feelings hurt by her favorite relative. "I knew it." I yelled, still boo-hoo crying. I knew something happened. Nichole had taken things too personally for there not to be a history there.

Zay glanced at me and looked back to the road. "Baby."

"Take me home, Zay."

"Baby, that was long before I met you."

"So?" I turned to the side so I could look him dead in the face. "So what. I don't care when it happened. You take me to some bitch's house that you used to fuck."

He reached out to put his hand on my leg. I pushed his hand out the way.

"Like I said, Tammy, that was before you."

I gritted my teeth together and said, "Take me home. Take me home."

"Baby let's talk about this. Let me explain."

I didn't want him to explain. *What was his real reason for wanting to tell Tracey about what he saw? Did he really care about his boy, or was he just trying to get Nichole in trouble.*

"Zay, listen. I don't want to hear your explanation. I mean, how would you feel if I took you to dinner to meet my friend and his wife, and then you find out that I used to bone my friend? Whether it was before you or not, Nyza, I know you wouldn't feel comfortable and you sure as hell wouldn't be cool about it."

He didn't say anything.

"Did you love her?" I asked.

"Love her, whatever."

"Did you love her?"

"What difference does it make?"

When he asked me that, I wanted to haul off and slap the shit out of him.

"Answer the fucking question, Zay."

"No. Hell no! She was just someone I met. I hit it off once and that was that. We didn't get along, and she wasn't my type. She was crazy."

I rolled my eyes and said, "Oh Lord. The typical male thing; y'all think that six inches makes all the difference in the world." I couldn't believe this mother fucker. "It was that good, huh?"

The driver smacked his lips. He was getting frustrated as well. I thought, *maybe I should listen to him.* He had a look of sincerity on his face. But he had better talk fast.

"I don't mean crazy like that. I mean, her ass is really crazy. Some of the shit she does is unreal."

"She is crazy, so that makes it cool for you to pass her off to your boy?" I started to chuckle.

"Shut up!" he yelled. "I'm trying to explain. If you want to go home, then I will take you. If you want to know what happened, then listen."

I sat there frozen. I didn't know what to feel, but I did know my feelings were still hurt. I won't lie, his tone scared me.

"I met her; we slept together the same night. I tried getting to know her, but it didn't work out. Four months later, I'm at the shop and Tracey shows up with his new girlfriend and it happened to be her."

"Does he know?"

He sighed and said, "She asked me not to. She said, 'hey, me and you was a fluke, no hard feelings, but he doesn't need to know.'"

"Are you serious?" I questioned.

"Baby, I've been kicking myself everyday for not telling him. That is why I got mad when I saw her today with that dude. I know what kind of woman she is, and I didn't want someone like that for my friend."

I was still mad at him for not telling me about him and her. I did feel a little better with his explanation, though. I wiped my face and allowed him to continue.

"So I was like, no biggie, they are just sexing. How

was I supposed to know that they would get serious and then get married?"

"Right, but that's your friend."

"Tammy, it was a mistake – maybe one of the biggest mistakes of my life. Tracey is family to me. I should have told him… and I should have told you that me and Nichole used to see each other."

I wanted to smile. That had to be the cutest apology I'd been given in a long time. I popped him on the arm and said, "You damn right. You should have told me."

"But look, I swear she doesn't mean anything to me. Nothing else happened, except for what I already told you." He held up his right hand. "That's my word, Tammy."

I turned into mush. I believed him. People do make mistakes.

"So what are you going to do?"

"About her?"

"Um hmm."

"I don't have to do anything, I guarantee you that Tracey will know after tonight. She is going to tell him."

"Because she is afraid that you will tell him."

"I should have told him and known that. I'm not hating on her, but she's not good enough for my boy. When I met her, she had a bunch of dudes sniffing after her, but she didn't seem to mind. It was like she enjoyed the attention too much – like she wasn't used to getting it."

I became empathetic towards the whole situation.

I could understand Zay's position and not wanting to complicate things. That was so understandable. I wondered, then, why it was so hard to do the things that you really needed to do and why it was so hard to say simple things to people that mean so much. If I could answer that, it wouldn't be a mystery. It happened all the time. I felt bad. I felt bad for him, and for reasons that he knew nothing about. I got mad again.

"So you didn't think I should know that, Zay?"

"Look, I told you that I am sorry. I met her ten months ago. What do you want me to do?"

I got mad again. But it didn't last long. We were riding, and I noticed that he went down 95 towards Baltimore. He was going the wrong way if he was going to I-270. He was trying to be slick. I knew I'd told him to take me home. It was all good. I pressed the power button for the stereo and relaxed in my seat. The quiet storm was on WHUR. I listened to the soothing sounds until we pulled into Zay's driveway.

The lights were out, so I assumed that Vette was sleeping. She had a couple of long lay-overs, and she hadn't seemed to be feeling well when we left.

Once we got inside, I was startled by my sister-in-law, who rose from the couch. She had been lying under a blanket. "Y'all scared me," she said.

Zay told her to go upstairs to the guest room. I liked the guest room myself. To me, it looked better than the master bedroom. Arvette was a bit groggy. She collected the pillow and blanket and made her way to the stairs in her pink pajamas. She dragged the blanket across the tile and slid her feet as she walked. Right then, she reminded me of Linus from the peanuts.

"Your niece says to tell her favorite uncle hello."

"Favorite uncle? She have any other uncles I don't know about?"

Vette didn't say anything; she just kept going up the stairs.

"Tell her I'm still looking for her daddy."

I popped Zay on the arm.

Nyza

I drove my future ex-wife home. She'd had extensive training that day. There were only two weeks left before her big fight in Asia. I told her that we needed to pat our brakes for the next couple of weeks. No going out to eat, lying around, and being lazy like we were used to. I didn't want to get in her way. I wanted her to be fully prepared – physically and mentally. If she wasn't prepared when the time came, I'd feel responsible, so I insisted that she take the time for herself and take full advantage of every minute. I had to be careful how I presented the whole thing to her. Some women would have taken that as a way of asking for space. The last thing I wanted from her was a break. I wanted my little champ to stay champ.

My sister didn't have much to do that day, and of course, she wanted to go shopping. I left the Benz for Vette in case she wanted to go some place. Tammy had been riding in luxury for so long, I didn't know how well she would take to riding in my Nissan, even though I kept it in good condition.

I dropped my woman off and went the opposite direction. I was going to holla at my boy – that is, if he would talk to me. I had to go and see what was up. My heart wasn't right. I felt like such a hypocrite, the way I talked about some people. Tammy had been teaching me a lot about friends, love, and relationships. I had to laugh, because I'd never thought this would happen to me. I'd settled on the fact that I could be by myself for a long time, if not for the rest of my life – until I met her. She stressed the importance of good people and how to treat them. I think I had been bitter for a while, and I needed something I thought could never be mine. I guess I looked down on others and what they had to make me feel better. I was looking in my rearview now. That was all behind me, and it felt good, too.

When I got to the shop, I looked for Tracey's car to be in the parking lot. It wasn't there. I went inside. He wasn't there, either. This was serious. He must have taken it hard. So much was going through my head, but I still wanted to talk to him. Maybe he needed some time to himself. The cats at the shop were waiting for their checks when I asked for Tracey. It was 11:40 in the morning, and no one had seen him yet. I hung around some more to see if he would show. When he didn't show by two o' clock,

I called his house. There was no answer, so I decided to call his cell.

Tammy called me to see if I talked to him. She told me last night that if I truly valued Tracey as a friend, I would talk to him. When she calmed down, me and her got cool again, and she used the most unique set of adjectives and nouns to describe Trace's wife. I thought she would bring up what happened last night, but she didn't. Even if she had, it would've been cool, just because that would have meant I was able to hear her soft voice.

Tammerine

As I hit the Heavy Bag, I envisioned that bitch from last night making faces at my man, using me to get back at him. I knew nothing was there between them, but she tried to make it seem like it could have been a possibility. *Game recognizes game.* I continued to rock the bag back and forth. My first mind told me to hit the bitch in the jaw last night, but I went over there as a lady. A scandalous bitch like her would probably try to sue me for that. I could see someone like her pulling some shit like that. I would have to beat her ass good then. I would have to make sure I got my money's worth. *Ole bitch.* I socked the bag hard. Zay said she was a gold-digger before she hooked up with Tracey – broke, aint have no money, and last night she had the nerve to act like she'd always had the finer things. I knew her type. She wasn't used to nothing but projects and police sirens. Tracey'd given her everything that she had. I rocked the bag that much harder when I thought about how close they stood to each other last night in the kitchen. I let out all my aggression on that bag. If I knew Tracey better, I would have told him about his wife last night. I bet she didn't even tell him about her little dude. If she told him, I couldn't see her telling the whole truth. She'd tell the story to her benefit. I told Zay to make sure that he told Tracey everything when he saw him. It was only right *and* I wanted to make sure that bitch gets in trouble.

Nat was on the side cheering me on. "Good, darling, Fuck her up!"

It seemed like she was in my thoughts. Maybe if I pretended that the next opponent was Nichole, I'd be sure to win. Funny thing was, I hadn't stopped swinging, and I wasn't tired. Zay should've have told me about her. I punished the bag some more as I thought about what else he could be hiding. *What else has he kept from me? Don't think like that girl. Don't let your insecurity get the best you.* But I couldn't help it. Men are always so suspect in the way they pick and choose information to share. Talking about 'it wasn't none of your business'; 'I didn't tell you because it was old and I didn't think it mattered.' Men do some stupid shit. I want to give them the benefit of the doubt but how can I when things start off like this. How can I? Then they want to play the role like they don't know what you are talking about. When a woman is serious and lets you in her bed, ninety-five percent of the time she's considering a relationship.

"Time out. Take a break," Nat said as she handed me a towel.

"Now if you hit like that in Asia, you'll knock that big dyke bitch out."

"How do you know she's a dyke, Nat?"

She handed me a bottle of water and said, "Trust me sweetie. I know."

After taking a few swallows, my trainer asked if I was okay.

"You say tunnel vision is good."

"Some people never get tunnel vision, and when they do get it suddenly," she held up two fingers, "One of two things will happen; you will fuck up or you will get fucked up."

"Reassuring, Nat, that is why I pay you so much."

Tracey

Who really needs friends? Even the Lord said, one of you will betray me. I felt betrayed by my friend, but the story seemed off. Some thing wasn't right. I wanted to know the whole story. Most importantly, I wanted the truth so I could move on. When it came down to it, I wanted to hear it from him personally. I thought, *If I get confirmation on this day, there is no telling what I am going to do.* Down like pimps without hos, we would say. This time, I was down and it was because of hos. Both of them are hos, Zay and Nichole. That was why he didn't want me to marry her. He slept with her and still had feelings. I banged the steering wheel just thinking about it. I was feeling like a punk. I got hoodwinked and bamboozled by the two people who I trusted the most. I had a long talk with the woman they call my wife, and the more she talked to me, the more I wanted to Ike Turner the bitch.

You know it's bad when you blame yourself, and I was doing just that. It wasn't all Zay's fault. I knew what Zay has always been and always will be. He won't change. I knew this, and I still chose to be friends with him after all these years. Dog-motherfucker. He fucked over so many women, he became paranoid – didn't want me talking to his sister because he's afraid of the boomerang. He was scared because he knows, what goes around come back around. When we were kids, we had boomerangs, and mine would always come back to me while his would never return. His boomerang always seemed to stop short. I couldn't figure it out until one day I realized: Zay didn't try to make the boomerang complete the motion and that is why it would fall short. He just knew that one day his boomerang would find him at the right time, no matter how it was thrown. Today was the day his boomerang would back.

I figured he'd be at the coffee shop, but his Benz was in the driveway. I pulled up as close as I could get without hitting his rear bumper. I got out and it hit me all over again. I was hurt. I let out deep breaths in succession. Deep breaths didn't help me much. I walked up the steps. The old lady from next door looked at me with a frown.

Arvette opened the door, stood there smiling so big until I forgot what I was mad about. I grabbed Arvette and she grabbed back. I gave her one of those long-time-no-see hugs, but it felt a little more personal.

"Haven't seen you in a long time, girl."

I stood back to take a good look at her. She was still a sexy motherfucker. When Zay used to box, I'd see her ringside, and she always seemed to sit across from me. She looked like one of those models for Black Men magazine. I noticed all the changes about her. My happiness was temporary. I remembered why I was there. "Where's your brother?"

"He's not home."

She continued to walk ahead of me barefoot. I watched her walk in those cute capris. I guess she thought she was still in Florida. I followed her into her brother's study. She sat in front of the laptop and put her glasses on.

"You cut your hair."

Vette perked up. "You like it."

I walked up on her and I began to reminisce. I rubbed her ear and said, "It's different."

Vette took one hand off the keyboard to move my hand. "How's your wife?"

I laughed.

"She know you are over here?"

"I came to see Zay."

"Zay said he was going to the shop. This doesn't look like the shop to me."

"Why do you want to go there on me?" I asked.

She didn't say anything. She kept typing. "What; because I asked about your wife?"

"Why are you acting funny?"

She looked me dead in the face with one of those angry, black woman looks. "Why are you fucking acting like nothing ever happened?"

"How would that have worked, Vette?"

"We don't know, do we? You were so damn scared of my brother and what he would say."

"How come you didn't tell him? You're his sister. I recall you creeping around him too."

"If you weren't scared of Zay, how come you couldn't tell him about us?"

I leaned over the desk and got right in her face. "Just like a fucking woman. You talk about me and my wife; where is your husband?"

The tan sister with short hair got up on her feet and folded her arms defensively.

"He left, didn't he?" I asked.

She didn't look so mad, so hard anymore, though she remained in her defensive position. Something was wrong. This was the part where she was supposed to withdraw and I was supposed to figure out what's wrong. She wouldn't ever tell me where it hurt for sure, so I would have to find it.

"Why would he leave a woman like you?"

She was quiet. It took her a while to answer. I waited patiently. I wasn't going to repeat the question, but I was sure she would answer. I thought she would cry. It wasn't my intent to salt old wounds.

"Do you really want to know why he left?"

"Yes, I do."

"He couldn't stand to take care of a child that wasn't his."

She gave me this look that told a story. I'll be dammed if it didn't hit me like a speeding car. I pointed to myself, and she nodded slowly. I dropped my keys on the floor. Everything made sense, from the jealousy to not showing up at the house last night. "What the fuck is wrong with y'all? How are you going to just keep some shit like this from me?"

Sounding apologetic, she said, "Look, Tracey, like we said, it was not going to work. I was in Florida, and you live in Maryland – then to top it all off, you go off and get married! I didn't say anything because I wanted you to be happy, and if she did it for you, then I was happy."

I frowned up and I didn't know what to say. "You are not normal, you know that?" I walked off. I wondered why she held out on me. I wondered if she did it on purpose. Was she keeping that info from me to hurt me, or did she find out much later? I could hear her walking on my heels. She was sniffing, but I didn't turn around. I wasn't ready to cry, but my eyes burned. I was starting to get a mad headache. I couldn't take much more of this. She was still following me. They say cry when you want to laugh and laugh when you want to cry but I didn't feel like doing either one.

She stopped following me. "I thought you loved me, Tracey?"

I didn't hear what she said. I was thinking about last night and how I wanted to fuck Zay up when I was no better than he'd been. I put my hands over my eyes and applied pressure. This was bad. How could I explain this to Zay? How could I tell him that I used to see his sister behind his back; how do I tell him that I'm still in love with his sister – that I never stopped loving her? How could I tell him that I was his niece's father? This shit wasn't fair. I didn't know what to do.

I turned around and walked up on her. "So, what are we going to do?"

"We have to tell him."

I though aloud for a moment, "I made a mistake."

"Being with me?" she asked.

"Not being with you."

By this time we were holding hands. It was like a normal reaction. We embraced and reunited with a kiss to signify our enduring passion. I was still confused. I didn't know what I was doing, but I liked it. I missed my little red Arvette. I couldn't help but think about how she was the one I let get away. This time, opportunity was knocking twice. This could be a second chance for me.

I knew that I could never love Nichole the way I loved Arvette. I guess Zay was right; I was settling.

"Vette, I have to take care of our daughter." I looked down at her bare ring finger. She should have been mine. Vette started to cry. She didn't have to say it. I knew that she was scared. I knew I had to tell Zay, but I wasn't in the mood for his stank-ass attitude. I wasn't scared of Zay, I just wanted to respect his wishes. All those years before, he'd had everything his way while others stayed out of his way. He would like to think that he changed, but he was still the same selfish motherfucker he'd always been. He always had to have the girl before me – even my wife. But with this woman who was standing in my face, I didn't care about my wife. I could never love my wife like a husband should. We weren't equally yoked, but what couple really is? Time and time again, I wondered if it was possible to have it all at once in one woman. Could I really be happy every day that I looked in Nicole's eyes? When I looked at Arvette, the answer was 'yes'. I could truly be content. but I'd traded my chance at happiness for appeasing a friend. I think that is the one thing I regret. I made a big mistake.

I couldn't resist her. She stood before me the, the mother of my child. Nikki didn't even want to have kids. Me and Vette stood close to one another like high-school sweethearts posing for a prom picture. She still had it. She still had that nice shape, though she'd put on about thirty pounds, and her complexion was as smooth as ever. She looked up to me and asked, "What are we going to do?"

"We got to tell him."

"I mean about us," she said.

"I don't know."

"You don't love her, Tracey. You think I don't know that?"

She was right. If I really loved my wife, I wouldn't have fallen all over Vette the way I did. Vette was the only person who seemed to know as much about me as I knew about myself. Zay was always the player, and I have always been the one in relationships. That is just how I am made. I was always the homebody. Zay was the wild one. I would spend a lot of my time keeping him out of trouble. I would keep him anchored. Looking at baby girl, I knew she could keep me at home, and I would love every minute of it.

Vette hung her head. I raised her chin and said, "I can never love her the way I love you. So you tell me what we can do."

"I don't like to share. You know that."

"Share?"

"Would you leave her?"

"I already have," I said softly as I put my fingers in her hair. She smiled and put her arms around my neck.

"Do you remember what you used to call me?"

I smiled too. "Little Red Arvette," I answered.

She giggled. "Yep, like the Prince Song."

When I first got interested in girls, I looked at Vette. I didn't mess with her, but I thought she was so pretty, so I tried to figure out what made her that way. I loved her eyes. They were shaped like almonds. She was a Prince fan. Back then, we had records, and she must have had every Prince record made at the time. When "Little Red Corvette" came out I would sing it to her, but I would replace Corvette with Arvette. She thought it was the sweetest thing at the time.

Zay

I was from South East. I was there all throughout my childhood. Tracey moved to Wheeler Road from Benning Road. We went to Simon Elementary School. He was the new kid. I knew what it was like to be the new kid in the class. I never liked to see people get take advantage of, plus he looked like he couldn't fight. They teased him and messed with him one day, and I took up for him. At 3:00, this dude named Mark and all five of his brothers were waiting for me outside. Now, I never ran, but I never had to fight six dudes before, either. So, I was trying to think of a way out. I hoped that they wouldn't jump all over me in the meantime. When they rushed me, Tracey ran over after he found out it was me. To my surprise, the new kid could throw the hands pretty good. You could say he owed me for looking out for him in class. Then again, he didn't owe me nothing. I made the choice to stick up for him. Every since then, me and Tracey have been boys. We both went to Charles Hart Junior High School, and with things being as bad as they were back then, my mom heard that Ballou was worse, so she got my Aunt to enroll me in Eastern Senior High. By using my Aunt's address, me and Tracey were inseparable. Since I was going to Eastern, Tracey went too.

All I could think about was how bad I felt about last night. I felt even worse when I pulled into my driveway and saw Tracey's car. He was parked behind the Mercedes, so I parked on the side of the two cars. I got out, pressed the automatic lock button, and closed the door. The Benz hadn't moved at all. Then again, how could it move, as close as Tracey had parked to it?

When I walked in the house, he and my sister were standing in the hallway surprised, like they got caught doing something they shouldn't have been doing. Maybe they got finished talking about me. Tracey hadn't been anywhere. He had on a Chaps T-shirt and some sweatpants. He hadn't even shaved, and Tracey shaves everyday. It's like a ritual. The way he acts sometimes reminds me of a white boy.

Vette greeted me first. "Hey, Zay."

I didn't return the greeting. I thought about making small talk with him before I confessed what he already knew. Tammy's words echoed in my head, *tell him everything... tell him everything.* I looked at my sister, who stood so close to my best friend. I had butterflies in my stomach, and for the first time in a while, I was about to do something I was afraid to do. I valued Tracey's friendship, and I didn't want to lose his trust, but I had to do what I had to do —and I had to do it right then.

"Can we go and talk some place, bruh?"

"Nah, let's stay here," Tracey said. He didn't seem as defensive as I expected him to. When I looked at him good he looked guilty as hell. I had a feeling that he was about to come out the box about some shit.

Tracey took a deep breath. I was preparing myself. He always had this look when he was in trouble or did something wrong. I can't explain the look exactly, but I knew it when I saw it on his face. When he took a deep breath, it meant he was about to tell you something.

"I need to tell you something." My sister grabbed Tracey's arm and stood closer. All I could do was brace myself. "Well, you know, I've been… well me and Arvette were seeing each other and…

"He's the father of my child," Vette chimed in.

Tracey turned around and looked at her, like *why did you do that.*

Arvette

"Oh." Zay chuckled. I knew my brother better than he knew himself. He was speechless. He felt betrayed. It was all my fault and I knew it. I came between two friends. I felt like a slut for it, but I wasn't going to apologize for loving Tracey. I knew he had his own agenda. The pregnancy wasn't planned. I was seeing someone else at the time.

I stepped to my younger brother with the whole truth. "Zay, it's my fault."

Zay started walking towards Tracey.

"You got my sister pregnant and didn't tell me."

"He didn't know… I didn't tell him. I just told him a few minutes ago." I defended Tracey.

My brother looked at me before the doorbell rang. Zay wasn't going to answer it, and I didn't want to leave the two of them alone.

Zay shook his head and smiled. "I don't believe this."

"After what you did to me, I don't owe you shit," Tracey said.

"Zay, are you going to answer the door?"

Zay kept on arguing with Tracey. I felt bad. When I opened the door, they were still going at it.

"Girl, I told him," I whispered. Tammerine ran inside.

"You heard me. I don't owe you shit. You slept with my wife." Tracey said, pointing in Zay's face.

Zay smacked Tracey's hand away. "You sound like a fucking fool." Zay raised his voice. He was mad. It's rare that he uses strong cuss words like that.

"You were messing with my sister behind my back, and you still want to tell me that you don't owe me nothing?"

"I don't. How can you stand in my face every day when you know I am about to marry a woman you had sex with?"

"Pot calling the kettle motherfucking black! Looking me in my face every day when you know you got my sister pregnant, and I'm thinking some other cat did it."

It was getting heated. Tammerine stepped forward and tugged at my brother's sleeve.

"He didn't know, Zay."

Me and my brother looked at Tammerine. "You knew, too?" Zay asked.

Tammerine dropped her head. I could tell that she didn't intend for that to slip out. She was just trying to diffuse the situation. She'd said the first thing she could think of in Tracey's defense.

Zay threw his hands up and his head back. He turned around and looked at the front door. He chuckled again and looked at his lady friend. "You knew about it, too, and you didn't tell me, either?"

"Baby, what did you want me to do? Y'all are family. I couldn't get in the middle of that."

He looked at me. "I'm your brother. Why would you keep that from me?" My little brother always seemed like an older brother, except for the times I schooled him on women. I would help him to understand women better. That is what men want to understand most: women. I stood there at Zay's mercy, not sure what to say. I decided to tell him the truth.

"You always overreact, how could I tell you?"

"You got a baby, he ain't around, so was it worth it?"

I ran up on him and slapped him dead in the face. "You ain't no better, Zay."

"You are right. We are all fucked up – all these fucking secrets around this bitch."

"See how it feels, Zay?" Tracey asked.

"No, that's different."

He was walking towards his own front door, bumping Tracey on the way. Tracey grabbed him.

"Hol' up Zay, what's done is done. We all lied to each other."

"I thought we were friends."

"Back at you, you selfish motherfucker. You were supposed to be my friend."

"I am your friend. I told you not to marry her. I am your friend – that is why I went over last night to tell you about your woman."

"If you are talking about Chik-Fil-A, she already told me."

"And you are cool with that?"

"You are always reading into shit, Zay. That was one of her co-workers."

"So I guess its business etiquette to slob down your co-worker huh?"

Tracey's expression changed suddenly. I could tell that he hadn't heard the whole story. My heart dropped for him.

"Are you saying that you saw them kissing?"

Zay's expression changed too, so did his tone. "I saw 'em, Trace."

"Why should I believe you?"

"Fuck you Tracey. Check your wife. The first time that I saw you with Nichole, I stepped to her and told her who you were and I told her that I was going to tell you about us. She told me not to. She told me it was better if you didn't know. She asked me not to say anything, so I didn't, and I have been regretting it, but I wouldn't lie about some dude kissing your woman."

The curly-headed friend tried to move forward, but he was stuck.

"So you are telling me that you actually saw them kiss?"

"She didn't tell you, did she?"

"No. I fucked up. I didn't want to be like you. I didn't want to be forty years old, still living by myself... How close do you get?" Tracey looked at me. "How many chances do you get?"

Zay looked at Tracey, but he didn't say anything.

"I had my chance at love and I didn't want to waste my time waiting for a second chance because they don't always come back around." Tracey grabbed my hand while looking my brother in the face. "Now, I'm being honest when I tell you that I didn't know about the baby. You can be mad at me if you want, but I love your sister and I got a second chance... I can't let that go, Zay."

Nyza Stevens turned and walked out of his own house.

Tammerine

"Wait, Zay." I ran after him. He was in the driveway, cussing. He was blocked in on both sides. He best friend parked his Saab right on Zay's rear bumper, and I was parked behind his Nissan.

"Move your car," he demanded.

"Just wait, baby."

He pointed towards the house and said, "You knew she was fucking with my boy, and you didn't say anything?"

"I didn't even know your sister like that. She wanted to talk. I guess it was becoming too much for her."

"So she tells a complete stranger? That don't make sense."

"I don't know Zay, maybe she felt like she could trust me or something."

"Move your car."

"No." I stood up to him, which is what others are

afraid to do. I was pacifying him by running after him. He couldn't go anywhere unless I moved. He was going to have to face this and deal with this.

"Tammy, I need some time to myself."

"So, you are going to leave your own house with all of us still in it?"

"You are right. Tracey is about to get his ass out my house."

I shook my head. It was pitiful. He wanted me to leave, too, but we were partners. You couldn't leave your partner when they needed you most. Zay was used to walking out when he didn't want to deal with things – like the time he put me out.

I walked to the driver's side door, where he stood. I raised my hand slowly and touched his face. "It's a shame, Zay. I see you that you are hurt, but running out isn't going to make things better. You've gotten so used to running, until you were ready to leave your own house."

The man walked off in the direction of his home. I could see the lady from next door peering out the window. Zay flipped her off and marched up the steps. In an instant, I heard the lady's window open, followed by obscenities. I trotted up the steps behind him to keep an eye on him. I didn't know what he would do once he got back inside. Sure, he might tell Tracey to leave, but would Tracey leave?

Tracey and Arvette stood in the same spot he'd left

them in. Zay pointed over his right shoulder with his thumb when he said, "Out, Out, Out!"

"What?" Arvettte said.

Zay looked at his sister. "I'm talking to him." He looked back at Tracey. "Get out, Tracey. Just get out of my house."

"So, that's how it is, Zay."

Zay nodded. "That's how it is." He motioned for the man of equal size to leave once more. "Let's make it."

Tracey's forehead was wrinkled. He let out a deep breath, looked at Vette, and turned towards the front door. He bumped Zay this time. Arvette stood with her head drooped. When she realized what was happening, she perked up. "Wait," she called. Tracey stopped on command, but he didn't turn around. "I'm coming with you," Arvette said. Tracey waited outside in the car while she went upstairs. She returned shortly with her large Fendi bag. She had some t-shirts hanging off the side of the bag. Her over-protective brother asked where she was going. She bumped Zay too and started laughing. "Sheee-it. I'm a grown-ass woman… asking me where I'm going. You got to be crazy." Zay watched her walk out the door. He looked like he wanted to tell his momma when Vette slammed the door.

***

Tracey and Vette went to a hotel that night. I stayed at home with Zay. He told me to leave, but I wouldn't. I wasn't going to make this easy for him. Running was all he knew how to do. It was time for him to man up.

"Why do you want me to leave so bad?"

"I told you an hour ago, and I told you an hour before that: I want to be by myself."

"Why, so you can run into a room, close the door, and pretend that today didn't happen?"

"I just don't feel like talking."

"So what? You can sit here in this house with me and be quiet. You don't have to say nothing," I said.

"Well, stop talking to me. I can't be quiet if you keep on damn talking to me and expecting me to answer you."

I tapped him on the knee. "You're a big boy, Zay. You can be mad and be in the same room with me at the same time."

He got up and started walking off. I snatched his arm and broke it down to him. "That is what I am talking about. Don't walk off from me. Stay and talk to me. You know it's bothering you, and I know it too. There is nothing wrong with being upset. Get it all out. After you get it out, then you can walk out."

"What's the difference in walking out now and walking out later?"

He refused to look me in the face, so I lifted his head.

"I meant it when I said I'm your partner, baby. We are in this together. If you are mad or we are mad, then we are going to have to learn to work through our frustrations."

"Maybe I will, but maybe I need some time to get my head together without your nagging."

I laughed. "Zay, sweetheart, if you were a regular person, then I could understand that. If I leave you alone, you will never fix the problem. You will just sit back and pout like a spoiled-ass brat."

He couldn't help himself. He started laughing. I smiled. "Zay, it's okay to be mad. I'm not saying that you can't get mad, but don't get in the habit of turning your back on me."

Nyza

I couldn't let her know that she touched the soft spot of my heart. She was right, though. I smiled. "Don't turn your back on me either, then." I grabbed her hands. She wasn't the enemy. I felt my smile diminish. "It's just that I never had to trust anybody as much as I have to trust you."

She touched my face. "I know it, baby. I want you to trust me. I want you to trust me with everything." As fast as I kissed her, I slammed her to the wall. Didn't know my own strength, I guess. But it was a pretty hard slam. She grunted on impact. Her grunt was so feminine, though. She sounded half-hurt and half like she didn't mind. I had her in my clutches. "If I can trust you, then how come you didn't tell me?"

"She told me yesterday. That is when I found out. I didn't know before that. I'm sorry, but I'm not getting in the middle of that. I didn't ask her for the information, she volunteered it. I had no idea that she had the slightest interest in Tracey. It was a total surprise to me."

I looked at her and didn't have anything to say. I was mad at her for not telling me, but at the same time, I guess it wasn't fair for be mad at her. I could respect her reason for not telling me. I'm sure that put her in an awkward position. I leaned in and kissed her neck. I let her go. "You're right, Tammy." I walked off and she followed.

"We are supposed to get our first snow tonight."

"I heard."

"I love the snow. In California, I never saw snow."

"No wonder you are so crazy."

She laughed and popped me on the shoulder. "What does snow have to do with anything?"

"Every kid – I mean every kid – needs to see snow. That is one of the prerequisites to becoming an adult. If you don't experience some things while you are a young, your mind won't be right."

She popped me on the shoulder again. She was still laughing. "Shut up."

I walked over to the stereo. She hopped up to me playfully. I pressed number two on the CD changer as Tammy stood, waiting for me to give her all my attention. Right away, there was a thunderous boom. I reached to turn the volume down when the lady stopped me. "Leave it up. I like it loud."

A feeling came over me, and I wanted to talk about it, so I turned the radio down. "I acted kind of retarded today, huh?"

Tammy looked and me and smiled while shaking her head. "No, not at all. The way you reacted was totally normal."

"I don't feel normal, baby."

She touched my face again. I loved it when she touched my face. "You just have a few things to learn."

"I have a few things to learn; what does that mean?"

"It means that you can't write off people when you get mad at them, and you can't stop loving a person for making mistakes."

Tammy always had a way of saying things to me in way that they made sense. Things were always better put when Tammy arranged them. Her philosophical lines and theories made me appreciate her that much more. Sometimes there was reasoning in her voice, and sometimes she had authority in her tone.

"Zay, I love you, and I'm not going anywhere because I want to be with you."

"I need to hear that."

"I will tell you something else, too. If two people want to be together, you can't stop them because they will always find a way to make it work."

"You're talking about Tracey and my sister, right?"

"That's right, baby."

"I guess you are right, but I don't like it."

"They respect you and yeah, they kept it from you but after seeing you today – how you react to things – I understand."

Normally, something like that would have messed with me. But that day, I felt like I grew up. She was right, and I couldn't agree with her more. Tracey called me selfish and I guess in my own way, I really am selfish. I want things my way, and I am just accustomed to that. Was that really my fault? I am used to people appeasing me. I don't like it all of the time, and I think that was why I am so attracted to Tammy.

"They are seeking your approval. They want you to bless off on this thing of theirs, and it's best that you do… because if they decide they still want to do this, then they will."

I exhaled deeply. "But, she is my sister."

She cupped my chin with her hand and made me look her in the eyes. "And that is your friend. If you don't trust him – I mean truly trust him – then he's not your friend."

"But he lied."

"Zay, I don't know anybody that tells the truth all the time. I love my Grandmother, but she lies. I lie, I'm sure that you have lied, so, if you are looking for a totally honest person, you will be alone forever."

I wanted to laugh in her face. She didn't treat me

like others, she didn't placate me, and she gave it to me straight, no matter what. I dig that shit.

"Do you trust him, Zay?"

I nodded.

"So, can't you trust him with your sister?"

I was about finished with the subject, but I was still a bit angry over the fact that she knew before me.

"Still mad at me, playa?"

She had those doll-baby eyes, and I couldn't resist. I grabbed her titties and felt them up good.

"Ooh," she breathed.

I wasted no time. There would be no foreplay tonight. I quickly undid her pants. She reached over and grabbed the master volume knob on the stereo. "I love this song," she said. As she worked my belt buckle she kicked off her Pro-Keds. Her pants were at her ankles, and she shook her ankles out of the bottoms. When she was free, she turned around with her plump ass sticking out. She held on to the front of the floor speaker, and I rammed her aggressively, enough to make her feel it but not enough to hurt her. Her pussy was so wet. I just wanted to take my time a little and enjoy it, but at the same time I just wanted to fuck. A brother was so anxious. I was knocking it out, and her hair was flopping wildly in different directions. I could smell her hair spray and perfume as she rocked. I could feel the vibration of the bass through my body. Tammy dropped her head some. Her eyes were closed, and I didn't want her to hit her head against the speaker, so I grabbed her hair and lifted her head. "Goddammit, Zay, you motherfucker, you know I like that shit. Fuck me baby," she urged. I wanted her to shut up. That shit was arousing me more than I was ready for at the time. I slowed it down and start hitting her with those long, slow strokes. She was making it so hard for me to contain myself with all her sensual noises. I was ready to put my hand over her mouth when she found my hand and placed it against her ass. I squeezed that ass too, like a roll of Charmin bathroom tissue.

She said, "Spank me."

Was she for real? Did she want me to play smack that ass or did she want me to Bad Girl spank dat ass? I was down for whatever.

Again she said, "I've been a bad girl, spank me, daddy."

Baby was getting down like a real freak, and I was with it. I backed off enough and started spanking her. "Harder," she said. I spanked her some more. I came off her ass and came back to smack it at an angle. "Harder," she demanded. My hand stung on that last one, so I wondered how it felt to her. She didn't want me to stop, so I didn't. She was shaking that ass to the beat. I was still taxing that ass. "So Hot," by Charlie Wilson, was playing. She asked me to turn it up some more. I pulled out and reached for the remote that lay close by. I turned up the volume and slapped her ass some more. She grounded herself to the speaker more as I got back into the groove. I could feel the bass vibrate through her body. It seemed the vibration along with the spanking turned her on that much more. She had done this before. I'd said it before to myself: she was no amateur when it came to sex. She asked me to go faster. I sped up for a couple of minutes before she slowed me down. She said she wasn't ready to come. I could understand, because neither was I.

I pressed a button on the remote to change the track. I wanted to slow it down some. Track number five was an old, pimped-out groove. It had a killer base line and I was feeling it. I knew I was in love, and I felt the words that Charlie sang. It described an unappreciative man who gave time to everything more than his woman. It described me and the way I treated all the women I had been involved with, even the ones I thought I was serious about. It was nothing like this – what me and Tammy had. Charlie Wilson is an O.G., and I knew that he knew what he was doing when he wrote this song. He sang "Just show me you love me and you won't have to say a word." That is how I wanted to love Tammy. I wanted to love her so good that no matter when she saw me, no matter what time she woke up, she could feel the touch from my hand and she would always know. She would always know that I loved her. My touch and my expression would say it all, and I wouldn't have to say a word.

I rubbed her back softly. I took my time working her. I hoped that my touches spoke for me.

***

"My momma was the community ass-beater."

Tammy cracked up laughing. As we lay in the bed fully exposed, I ran down memory lane, talking about my momma and the things that she did when me and my sister were little. It was a beautiful. She didn't have her front teeth in and she looked like a little girl. For the first time in our relationship, I felt totally comfortable, and for the first time ever, I felt it was okay to be in a relationship. I felt that we both knew the worst of each other, and if we both could live with that, then things would be just fine.

I kissed Tammy's forehead and continued with the story. "I don't know about where you grew up in Cali, but in DC, we had those neighborhood watch signs posted all over the place."

Tammy smiled. "Um Hmm. I used to be scared of that sign. Our sign was a picture of a black silhouette, and the only things that were white were his eyes."

"Yep, sounds like ours. But anyway, picture that same sign, but instead of a man, picture a lady with an afro with a belt around her neck."

"Zay, you are silly."

"I'm serious, that was my momma. I called her the

community ass-beater because that's what my momma did. She beat the community. If you were doing something you weren't supposed to be doing and she caught you, that was your ass. She'd whip your ass in broad daylight in the middle of the street; then she'd call your momma and tell her what she did.

"Wow."

"She didn't play when it came to kids. She didn't care whose kid it was, either. I used to think that whipping kids was a hobby for her. You know, she done beat me for long until that got boring. It wasn't the same to her anymore. She had to go out and find something new. She had to go out and find some new kids to beat."

Tammy was smiling, but she had that look on her face like I was stretching the truth a little.

"See, you don't believe me. Ask my sister. I'm not lying, girl. Once, my momma took the strap off her purse and whipped they asses with it."

"Oh come on, Zay."

"Like I said, Vette can tell you – matter of fact, *she* was seventy-five percent of the reason me and Tracey would get in trouble. It was always Vette running her big ass mouth."

"Well, that's what sisters do. They are supposed to get their brothers in trouble. They wouldn't be good sisters if they didn't do that."

I knew she was teasing, so I didn't respond directly to

her comment. Instead, I went into my story. "There was this time when my momma whooped Tracey, and Tracey's momma was ready to fight my momma."

"What?" Tammy's eyes were big.

I nodded. "Yep."

"For what?"

"Over some Kool-aid."

Tammy started laughing. "Zay, over some Kool-aid?" He mouth was wide open as she waited for my confirmation.

"Listen." I pulled her body in closer to mine. "We loved Kool-aid, so momma would buy a lot of it. She would buy all different flavors. You know, red, purple, yellow."

Tammy tapped my stomach. "Baby those are colors, not flavors."

"Well, you know, we didn't care about flavor because it was all good to us." She still had a smile on her face as I continued. "So anyway, Vette made this Kool-aid. I was never allowed to make the Kool-aid because my momma said that I put too much sugar in it, so Vette was the only one allowed to make the Kool-aid. So one day, she came to me and asked what I did with the Kool-aid. I was like what? I didn't do nothing. You make it and I drink it. Now this broad, my sister, counted all the flavors."

"She counted them."

"Right, she counted them. She could tell you how

many packets were missing. Three packets were missing every day for about a week, and Vette only made a pack a day. The next day when Tracey came over, we were doing our homework when I noticed that his fingers were purple."

Tammy tapped my stomach and started laughing.

I put my pencil down and got ready to ask him about his fingers when Vette came into the room with two empty Kool-aid packets with sugar in the bottoms."

"He was eating the Kool-aid, Zay?"

"Hell yeah, and he had been doing it for a while. That was what Tracey's momma didn't understand. She thought my momma whooped him for drinking Kool-aid. She didn't understand that he was opening the packets and eating it."

"What did his mother say?"

"She said, 'Marlene, I don't mind you disciplining my son if he does something wrong, but how you gon' whoop Tracey for drinking Kool-aid? How about I go over there and whoop your ass?'"

"Didn't your mother tell his mother what happened?"

"Well, my mother told her, 'Jackie, I jus' wanted to let you know that Tracey was over here and I got his hind-parts for eating my Kool-aid.' And you know what, baby, my momma told her what Tracey did, but I don't think it registered with her until my momma told her the whole story."

"He liked Kool-aid that much?"

"Yeah, that fool used to buy those dipping stix all the time."

"Yeah, I remember that. It was candy that kind of tasted like Kool-aid."

I folded my arms behind my head and rested against the head board. I was reflecting. We had some good times, me and my sister. I looked down at Tammy, who had just rested her head on my stomach.

"Are you ready for the fight?" I asked.

"Yeah." She looked up and me. "You ready for Asia?"

"Yeah, I guess," I said.

"Have you ever been?" The snagged-tooth lady asked me.

"I've been there. I fought in the Olympics in 1988. It was at the Seoul Sports Complex."

"That's right, it was in Korea, huh?"

"Yep, went there in the summer. I heard it was good shopping there. I didn't care about shopping and clothes back then. So later on, me and Tracey went back there to do some shopping."

"So, the shopping is good there?"

"Yeah, it's pretty good there. It's even better in China.

You can get DVDs there for a dollar, and you can get handbags for about ten or fifteen dollars a piece."

She smiled. "You know I love purses, right?"

"For sure," I said.

"I don't know, though. I like my bags, I don't know about all that swap meet shit."

I laughed. I felt her on that. I was a wristwatch junkie. I had to have them, and the knock-offs wouldn't do. I was sure that we could go over there and find some things that would tickle her fancy.

"So, you ever went there to Korea in the fall?"

"It's December, might as well call it winter. I heard that is what it's like this time of the year."

"Yeah, that is what my trainer says." There was silence. Something was on her mind. I could tell. I had come to terms with things real quick and was beginning to learn that some things need to be left alone. All that you can do is have faith and trust that they will work out. Tammy let out a deep breath, and that was when I knew it was time to ask her if something was bothering her.

"I'm a little nervous about the fight."

I stroked her hair. "Why?" I said with confidence.

"Well… because she is good."

I chuckled. "Is that all? She *is* good, but you are the best, baby."

She smiled. "Listen, baby, when a person is good at what they do, he or she can be a little intimidating. Don't be afraid to learn from her. Take what you can from this experience and use to your advantage. Just think of this as another opportunity."

Tammy grabbed me tight. I feel her cheeks raise as her face was pressed against my chest. "You know what, Zay, you are the most amazing man I have ever met. You always make me feel good about everything that I do."

I let go of her and scooted up in the bed. "I got something for you."

"Right now," she asked.

"Yeah. You are going to like this," I said as I stepped over to the dresser. I opened the top drawer when she told me that I should be her trainer. I thought about it, but I figured, if I can't box, then I don't want any other parts of it.

"I mean it, baby. Whenever I take your advice, I always come out on top."

I pulled the box out of the drawer and made my way back to the bed. "You've always come out on top. You don't need me for that." I got in the bed and of course her eyes were glued to the small white box. She had eyes like a kitten. They could be devilish like a Siamese cat's, or her eyes could be soft like a tabby's.

"I want to get serious on you for a minute, baby." Tammy was quiet, yet attentive. "You have done some things for me since you have been around me. You help me do better – be a better person, and I just want to say thank you. I have never fully trusted anybody except Tracey and my sister. You are right to me. You have to be."

My lady looked at me like she was about to cry. I liked bringing out that soft side of her. I had my own way of doing that at the right times. She liked to walk around like she was so tough and like nothing bothered her. I took the diamond necklace out of the box and showed it to her before I placed it in her hands. They say the right expression is priceless; I would have to agree. She was choked up when she finally spoke.

"Zay, baby, this is really nice, but it's too much."

"Nah, this is for you."

"It's beautiful." She held the diamond-encrusted necklace between her finger tips. She was checking out the charm. I'd had it made especially for her. I thought I would explain the meaning behind it. "The chain belonged to me. I had the charm made just for you. The boxing glove represents the toughness of your love, and the crown on top of the glove represents your real title – what you are to me."

"And what am I to you?" She asked.

"You are my queen." She smiled. I took the chain from her and opened the clasp so that I could give her the crown she deserved. Tammerine swung her legs to the left side so that her back was to me. She lowered her head, excitedly snatched her hair back, and quickly lifted her hair up and out of the way. After I draped the chain around her neck, she spent a couple of minutes just looking down towards her breasts. I hadn't given Tammy anything that she couldn't get for herself. It was just the fact that I gave her something. I liked giving her things.

I got up from the bed. "I'm going to go and brush my teeth. You know, you could get a better look if you went to the mirror."

Tammy

I looked at it in the mirror, and it was beautiful. I couldn't believe him. He hadn't boxed in years. He had an unbelievable house, nice cars in the driveway and yet, he still came with the most expensive presents. It was good to know that he was an investor – and a very wise spender. There are some people who go broke when their careers end. Not Nyza, he took his money and immediately invested and secured properties. I like a smart man. Just the thought of him made me want to fuck him. I looked at the shadow box that hung on his bedroom wall. Inside the box was a picture of Zay when he won his first championship belt. He stood so proud with the belt draped across his right shoulder.

The water was still running, and Zay was rinsing the bristles of his tooth brush. I stood leaning against the door jam with my bare left foot on top of the right one.

"Baby," I said. He looked up. When I had his attention I continued. "I can't take this."

"Can't take what?" He asked.

"I can't take this chain."

"Why not." He looked concerned.

"Because it's yours and you've had it for a while. I know it must mean a lot to you. I looked at some of your older pictures, and you had this chain on."

"You are right, I liked it a lot, but I want you to have it. That was me back then. That was my present to myself when I won my first prize fight. I don't box anymore and now I am passing it to you."

I didn't know what to say, so I decided to thank him and let it be.

He dried his face and turned to me. "It brought me lots of luck. Maybe it will do the same for you."

"I don't need luck. I got you. You are my luck," I confessed.

Zay

Tracey was at every after-party. We'd do it up right. I put all the ladies in the VIP section so that they could get in for free. They could do what they wanted to do. They were groupies, most of them, and I knew that. It didn't matter, they'd put on a show for me and Tracey. Some of the ladies were out of character. I could tell that they were doing things that they wouldn't normally do. There were others that were just nasty like that. They were just being themselves. I was careful but happy. I'd never stop them from expressing themselves freely. I mean, some of the things that the women were doing was probably considered illegal.

But those parties were the best. Women of all shades and colors would come through to check us out. They were all coming to see me. I knew a lot of the big names in television, movies, sports, and music. They would come to town and party with me. They loved to come through so they could party with the champ. My name would be up in lights. I would shake my head like it wasn't a big thing. My entourage would follow me everywhere I went. I liked it, but there were sometimes when it was too close for comfort. They were good for me. They kept me out of trouble. I think the thing that we really had to watch out for was the under-aged girls who would try to get in. My staff would go out of their way to protect me.

VIP was the shit. It made people feel special – made them feel like a big shot. Everybody would be sipping on something. The bar was open all the time, so they were drinking for free. All drinks were on me. They liked me. They would be calling my name; chanting it, almost. I felt like a big shot. I liked being a big shot. They would call me undefeated, because that is what I was. I would just go through the crowd and pick my flavor for the night. I would choose young, tender woman to slide with for the night. They never said no. If they would have, or if there was any hesitation on their part, I would smile to show no hard feelings and move on to the next one. Usually I'd walk up to the finest young miss, slow-sipping a glass of Chardonnay with her friend. I would extend my hand and she'd look at me like I was just another Joe. That was cool with me. I liked it when they didn't know who I was. Whether they knew me or not, it didn't matter. I usually got the dross anyway. I knew that the life would get old after a while, but at the time it was the life everyone wanted to live – and I was living it. I knew that it would stop one day, but that day came a lot sooner than I thought it would. A deep muscle injury and a dislocation put a stop to my whole career just like that. I lied to myself and everybody else. I told them that I would get back into it. I said I would get back into professional boxing, but I never did. They forgot about Nyza Stevenson. That life was long gone, but I still had the dreams of the good life. I didn't miss all the groupies and table dances, but I did miss the spotlight at times, and I will always miss being the champ. I still dreamed of my VIP parties that I would hold on the 30th floor of some of the finest hotels. Everybody loved me, and everybody who was anybody to me was VIP.

I dried the last glass, replaced the coffee beans, and cleaned off the bar about fifty times. Tracey didn't say much to me, and I didn't say much to him. It wasn't that I didn't want to talk to him; the time was never right. We were short-staffed but long on customers. Just when I thought things would slow down just enough for us to get a break, we got more coffee and espresso drinkers.

Don't get me wrong; when we sell coffee, it's good – that is what we do, sell coffee – but on a day like today, I wasn't in the mood for the constant rush. I didn't have the jazz playing on this day. There was a whisper of R and B coming through the speakers. Like I said, that was even at a whisper. I had the TV on to keep me company, since my partner wasn't much for conversation. I knew that he had to be really going through it. I mean, what would his wife say when it was all said and done?

Around three o'clock, we were still getting the heavy pour of customers, but our talk was long overdue and I didn't care how short we were. I was tired of the silent treatment. I don't think I would have given a damn one way or the other, but after last night, it mattered. We needed to talk. For the first time, I didn't like the uncomfortable silence between me and my boy. I wasn't trying to avoid this conversation; I was just waiting for the right time. While waiting, I thought about what Vette said about my personality, and things were making sense to where I could really apply it to my life as I lived it. She said that people walk around on eggshells around me because they never know how I will come at them. I smiled. It was true.

Tracey brushed past me when I stopped him.

"Hey man, you got a minute?" He didn't say anything. "I need to holla at you."

Tracey took a deep breath and let it out slowly. "I

don't want to hear it – whatever it is that you got to say – because I know it's going to be fucked up."

"Come on, Trace. Just let me holla at you. We can go in the back. Man, we been working all day, let's take a break."

Tracey tossed the dank rag onto the counter top and pulled off his apron. I took mine off and draped it over the back of one of the chairs.

"Let's take a walk down the street."

We stepped in the back, grabbed our jackets, and we were out. It was a little brisk outside. But between the light jackets and constant circulation, we would stay warm. Tracey was on the defensive with both hands inside his pockets. He looked down most of the time. Finally, I tapped my best friend on the forearm arm and began to expel. "Look man, about yesterday; that *is* my sister"

"I don't give a fuck whose sister it is, I care about her, Zay, and that is all there is to it."

"Look, Trace, just hear me out."

"I'm tired of worrying about what you want."

I chuckled. "Damn, can I just get out what I wanted to say?"

Tracey stopped walking and looked me straight in the eyes. "What is it, Zay? Just what the fuck is it?"

I looked Tracey in the face as well, to be sure that he was paying attention to me and what I wanted to say to him. "Look man, you know how I feel about my sister."

Tracey rolled his eyes. "I love my sister. She is my baby… and I trust you." Tracey perked up some. It wasn't as bad as he thought it would be. I continued with my delivery. "Look, I kind of understand why you didn't tell me before. I wish you would've told me anyway, but I can't change that. Like I said, I do trust you with my sister. I know you are a good man."

Tracey smiled and said, "I love your sister. I have known that for a while. I didn't know how to make you understand. I tried to avoid her out of respect for you, but it only worked for so long. You don't know what it was like for me to avoid her and resist the urge to be with her."

I nodded while Tracey continued.

"I always knew that she was a special kind of lady – even when we were little and she would snitch on us."

I clapped my hands before I gave him a pound. "Yeah, I remember those days."

"They were some good days, weren't they?"

"You know what, Tracey, I mean what I am about to say. You got the green light." I quickly held my hands up. "Not that you need my permission, but I'm on board if you two are going to be happy."

Tracey canted his head sideways and stared at me for a few seconds longer than he normally would have. "You mean it, Zay?"

I looked down, and I could tell that I'd really changed. It seemed to have happened overnight. I knew that if I was going to grow, I would have to leave the past in the past. I had been selfish. What happened was a product of my selfishness. No one wanted to tell me anything out of fear of how I would react or over-react. I looked at Tracey, held out my hand and made a fist and said, "Pimps without hos."

Tracey smiled and held hand out to make a fist too. "Since second grade," he finished.

We started up our walk back to the coffee shop.

"What about your wife?" I asked.

"Zay, don't be judging me."

"Nah, baby boy, I'm not judging, I'm just curious."

"Well, I'm serious about Vette, so it won't be nothing for me to sell my house and downgrade to an apartment. I have a legal appointment with an attorney – want to see about getting the whole thing annulled."

"Whoa! You sure about that, baby?"

Tracey smiled. "Nichole is not my kind of woman – never has been, I know that. I don't even know why I married her, plus she don't love me – out there running with other dudes."

"Okay, okay, but you are sure you want to do this?"

"You been telling me from day one not to be with her, and now you act like you are having different feelings on the whole thing."

"I'm just saying that this is all of a sudden. Have you had enough time to think about this?"

"I've had plenty of time. I'd been thinking about the whole thing long before Vette came to town. I just didn't want you to laugh at me or say 'I told you so.'"

I tapped my friend on the back.

"I'm glad things turned out the way they did. It gave me a chance to really see for myself what I got myself into."

"We all have to learn, buddy," I said.

"Yeah, last night I was in the room by myself with no radio, television and no one else around. It gave a chance to sort everything into their own separate piles – put things into perspective."

"But sell your house, Tracey?" I repeated.

He smiled like he felt really good about the whole idea. "Sell the house," he affirmed. "I'm going to be with your sister, your niece – my daughter. How does that look – me kick one woman out and then move another one in."

I shrugged my shoulders.

"Come on, Zay, you know I don't roll like that. I want to do it right."

"I hear you." I frowned and asked, "Where was my sister last night, if she wasn't with you?"

"I checked her into a hotel, made sure she got in safe, and went back home. I told Nikki everything. She didn't want to stay in the same house with me, and I wasn't going to stay in the same house with her." Trace was quiet and after a couple of steps more, he stopped in his tracks. He looked me in the eyes. "I swear to you, Zay, I didn't know about Zimorah."

I put my arm around him and started walking. "My niece is in good hands now. She is still young, and she has a good man for a father. You'll make it right."

"I didn't know, Zay."

"I know. There is nothing you can do about it now but be there for her."

"I told Nikki that it was over between us. It wouldn't work."

"You cool now?" I extended my hand. Tracey extended his.

Tammy

I'd heard the locks click earlier in the morning, but it wasn't Zay. I stood at the top of the stairs and spoke to Arvette.

She looked up from the front doorway and smiled. "I was hoping you'd be here."

I went downstairs and asked her if she was alright.

"That's my little brother, and he acts more adult-like for the both of us put together."

I looked at Zay's sister. "You know what I do when I'm not feeling like myself?"

Vette smiled. "What's that, what do you do?"

"I go shopping. Didn't you want to go shopping while you were here?" I didn't give her a chance to answer. "I'll go and grab my credit cards and check book. We can talk all about it on the way."

***

We came back to the house about five or six hours later. Sister girl could shop – and she spent big money. This shopping trip was on me, but she still insisted on paying for some of it. I knew that shopping was her therapy. Some women clean when they are upset; most of the times they clean because they don't have the money to shop. We both needed to blow off steam. I couldn't think of a better way to do it than spending money. We went to Saks, Bloomies, and Neiman's. I think that was the best time I ever had shopping. Vette is naturally funny, and she didn't believe in holding anything back. We had a lot of time to do our girl talk. She felt like the sister I never had. She was older than her brother by four years, and she had me by 12 years, though it didn't feel like it. She was wild, silly, and carefree for the most part – until we got close to her brother's house. I could tell that she was nervous and didn't want to face her younger brother or have to justify anything to him. But I knew that things might work a little smoother than she thought. We had to wait and see.

I looked at the clock on the dash, *Nyza should be home*. Arvette was still quiet. She talked, but didn't say much. She wasn't as jovial as she had been. I felt the difference in the ride as we hit the corners. The car didn't ride the same with all the weight in the trunk. I mean, we had the trunk loaded down. I couldn't wait to try my new clothes on for my man. I knew I would look sexy in all that shit. I loved it when Zay would shoot me that sexy look over the rims of his glasses – sexy-ass man.

I flipped the blinker. Vette hadn't spoken one word in the last seven blocks. I looked over to her quickly as I waited for the light to turn green.

I looked over to Vette. "Baby, you know you are not doing anything wrong. If you love Tracey, then you have to hold on to that. Don't you worry about Zay. I know he is your brother, but I'll handle him." The lady with short haircut looked at me and smiled.

"You know, girl, I been meaning to ask what you did to my little brother. Do you got fire in your pussy? I ain't ever seen him like this."

I winked before I pulled into the driveway. "Well you know, girl, *I do* know how to work that pole."

Vette hollered with laughter and clapped at the same time. "Do you cook for him too, girl," Vette asked.

I looked her dead in the eye and answered, "Naked."

Vette howled again. "That's right. That's what I'm talking about, girl."

"Yeah, then maybe you will do the same for his friend. You know that you and that man have a lot to talk about… and I think that you and Tracey have the potential to be something great. Just don't forget to keep it interesting. Keep him guessing, girl, you don't want your man to ever get bored. Men get bored easy." Vette winked at me like she knew something I didn't; that was when I put the shifter in park. It was then that I realized that I was parked next to Tracey's Audi and right behind Zay's Mercedes. I could feel it. Vette was nervous. I didn't know if I was filled with more of anxiety or fear. Those two were in the house together, and there was no telling what was going on in there. I could almost see the green-eyed man squinting over the rims of his shades, telling his friend where he could go. Zay always squinted when he wasn't looking through his glasses. When he got excited, he often squinted. The way his teeth were made, I fell in love a little bit. His teeth were perfect. He didn't have an overbite, and he didn't have an underbite; his teeth were just straight. It looked like his tops and bottoms would click together when he would talk, but his teeth didn't; that's how perfect they were.

I snatched off the seatbelt from around me. I was ready to jump out of the car. I had to get inside to make sure everything was okay. Vette walked around to the back of the car. She stopped at the trunk. I had forgotten just that fast that we had clothes in the back. I almost suggested leaving the bags, but I went ahead and opened the trunk.

I swear, I will wring Zay's neck if he's been in there mistreating Tracey. We grabbed the bags. I couldn't wait to close the trunk. I stepped it out down the walkway in my high-heeled Timberlands with bags in each hand. I looked at Vette, who stayed a couple of paces behind me and hoped that everything would be fine. Part of me wanted to believe that Zay would be sensible, especially after having the talk that we had previously. *Yeah, he would be cool… But then again, with Mr. Stevenson, one can never be too sure.*

Vette was stressed, and it was obvious that she knew her brother a lot better than I did. I was sure that she didn't know what to expect from her little brother. When Vette went to insert her key into the key slot, I reassured her. I told her that everything would be fine. *I hope.*

I went inside, walking like I owned the place. Vette gathered some attitude as well and marched behind me. There was talk coming from the kitchen. I couldn't make out what was being said, but the voices were loud. We slowed our walk. Arvette looked at me. I was prepared for anything. I was ready to drop all of my shopping bags to play referee if I had to. The two men got louder. I looked at Arvette and said, "I knew it." She nodded. We both dropped our bags. "Let's go break this up, girl," I said.

After we busted inside, the two men wore extreme looks of surprise. They greeted us and resumed their talk. Neither man seemed upset, their expressions were neutral, and they both had green coffee mugs in their hands. They seemed to be doing just fine. I was so relieved until I started smiling. I looked at Vette, and she didn't look so pleasant.

Vette walked away from me and got in her brother's face. Zay didn't budge. He held onto his coffee mug and remained silent.

"Look, Zay, I'm a grown woman and you are not going to tell me what to do. You are not going to tell me who I can and cannot see." Vette looked over to Tracey. Tracey smiled but had a weird look on his face. Right then, Zay turned away from his sister to sit his coffee mug down. Both men looked at each other and started to laugh hysterically. Vette was there with her arms folded still. She didn't understand what was going on. The boys continued to wail. When they began to simmer down, Tracey walked towards Vette and opened his arms when he got close enough to her.

"Come here, baby." Vette looked at Zay to check his expression.

"Go to him," the younger brother ordered.

Tracey wrapped his arms around her. "That's peace, baby. I like that. Stand up for your man."

Zay took a sip from his cup. "She-it, my sister ain't no punk, you better respect her, gangster."

We all laughed. Vette let go of her baby's father and turned to her brother; she thanked him by giving him a warm hug.

When I looked over my shoulder, it was snowing

outside. I didn't know if it was a sign, but I took it as such. Tracey picked up on it too. He stared laughing and pointed outside. "Damn, will you look at that, Zay forgiving somebody; it really is a cold day outside." Zay even had to laugh at that.

I was so proud of that man. I knew that it took a lot for him to do what he did. I knew how he felt about his sister, but it's all about trust when you get down to it. Zay accepting the fact that his sister and best friend wanted to be together showed how much he really trusted his friend. Tracey knew it too. Today had been a good day. I remembered something just then. I looked at Vette. "I don't know what y'all are going to do, but I got something that I need to do."

"That's right. We went shopping," Vette said.

"Oh, that's good, cause I sho wasn't ready to spend my whole day walking from store to store and driving from place to place just so that you could fill that empty suitcase."

Vette looked at Zay and said, "Huh, you don't even know what you are in for." She looked at the coffee mug. "I hope that coffee was strong enough."

I started laughing. "Come on, baby, I got something to show you." I couldn't see my expression, but I tried to give him my sexy, devil look. When my man got close enough, I grabbed him by the hand and led him into the next room. He watched me and I leaned over to pick up my bags. I held up the Fredrick's of Hollywood bags. "I got some stuff I want to try on for you," I said. I could feel it already; my panties were starting to get wet. I looked at him like he had absolutely no clothes on. I was getting so horny just looking at him. *I don't know what it is about you boy, damn you make me insatiable.* He could just look at me the right way and I was ready to fuck him. I was glad that he could do that to me.

"Right now, you want to show me?"

"Ooh yes, right now." I was still dripping, and it tickled a little. I wanted to cross my legs, but I didn't want to be obvious. Even though I liked that fact that he could make we wet so easily, I didn't want him to know.

Zay walked in closer and kissed me softly on the lips. "Where do you want to show me?"

I let out a deep breath. "Why are you teasing me?"

"Where," he repeated.

"You know where to go," I said.

"You know that we can't get too loud. We have company."

"Tell them to go home."

He laughed. "I can't. They don't have one."

Tracey

It was snowing outside. Even God recognized this day as a miracle: the day Nyza Stevenson gave in. I wouldn't have been surprised if we get a blizzard tonight. Really what was it? Had this fool had a revelation or an epiphany? Was it the serious relationship that had him faded?

I sat down most of the day trying to figure it out. I asked Vette a couple of times, and she didn't know what was up either. We both decided that it wasn't pussy. He had gotten plenty of that from many women, but then again, not all women were like Nichelle Phillips. Part of me would have liked to think that she was what he had been missing. Here this man was at forty years of age and he would have told you that he had never been in love. People who have never been in love can never understand love. They think they can but they can't. I never understood how a selfish person could really believe they were in love with another person. Love is not selfish; it is *selfless*. Zay never seemed to understand this until he met Tammerine. It hit me like freight train.

"Baby, Zay is in love."

Arvette

What had gotten into my little brother? That girl was good – damned good. I warned my brother about women like Nichelle Phillips. She would get him, and once she would get him, she would be holding the power. She would have the power to hurt or heal him. He would be at her mercy. She had the power, but it seemed that she was going to do some good with that power. Zay lucked out. The way he played with hearts was crazy. I would lecture him often and tell him that his little wee-wee was going to fall off. But I thought he was settled, finally, and it was good to see.

Zay didn't know what to do with himself, but whatever he did, he would not think of doing it until Nichelle said so. She got him sprung. She got his balls in her purse. I warned him about women like her, but I'd been beginning to believe that my brother would never find her.

I was beginning to believe that no one would want to deal with his attitude long-term. One of my fears was that my brother would die alone. I didn't want that for him.

I thought about him some more, and I was happy for him. I was glad that he was with her. She was exactly what he needed in his life. She cared about him, she didn't spare his feelings, and she was honest with him. And she never took no shit. She could be what every man wants: an all-around woman. This woman could be his momma, his sister, his friend, and, of course, his lover. She had street swag too. She very well could be the sister that I never had. She was younger than me, but she acted like she had been on this earth a lot longer than all of us. She was cool and down to earth, and I really liked her. I could see her being around forever with him. I could see the two of them waiting for the kids to come home from school. I could see us all living in the same city, visiting each other.

I laid there some more and thought some more, and then I looked at my friend. I smiled when I thought about all the things that he had ever been to me. I went back about twenty-something years when he and I would flirt and brush against each other; how I thought he was so cute and how I wanted to kiss his lips for real. Not a fake-me-out kiss. I wanted to kiss him for real like we were married. I remember when Zay would get mad because I would always be the momma and Tracey would be the daddy, and we'd make Zay the child every time we'd play house. It was a game to everybody but me. I used to call Tracey "little boy" all the time. Truth was, I'd always had a deep crush on the little boy; I never stopped.

Tracey to me was always the ideal man. I would compare him to my brother most of the time because Tracey was the only boy my step-momma would allow me to be around. But when I really studied him, I was able to notice and appreciate certain things about him. Tracey was very studious and seemed to think about what he said before he said it. He was compassionate. Zay was smart, but he spent most of his time acting an ass. He was always on joke time. Tracey was more serious and collected, while Zay was a hot-head.

Zay was the more impulsive one, while Tracey was the information seeker. Now, even with all these qualities, Tracey was never a punk; he was never a pushover. He always had this fire – a certain confidence about himself that seemed to send me over the edge. It really keyed me up. His attitude was downright sexy, but I knew that I wouldn't cross the lines. He was friends with my brother. But the more we grew, the more Tracey grew with wisdom. The more we grew, the more I burned more with desire and inquisitiveness. We were friends, but I wondered all the time if we could have been more than that.

Zay always talked about how I had game and how I taught him some of his game. I tested his theory to see how much game I really had. I went on a mission to see if I could draw Tracey out. I had to test the grounds to see if he was feeling me like I was feeling him. I felt for him a lot, but back then he didn't have to feel me like I was feeling him; if he liked me just a little bit it would have been enough for me. A girl just has to know. I was taking a chance. I was putting myself out there. I was always a good-looking woman. Men hit on me constantly. I didn't have to step to any man, but my situation was different. I knew that Tracey would never come up to me, and I would never know the truth unless I asked him. I needed my question answered: *did he like me?* Was he nice to me all those years just because we all grew up together, or was it something else?

Seven Years Ago

I was living my dreams. All those years of watching the Design Channel and reading the Oprah Home Magazine had paid off. After I finished with school, I went on to work under a broker. From there I went out on my own to sell properties. A sister made lots of money working under her own name. My company is named after myself: Arvette Chambers Realty. I made that job look easy. People couldn't say no to me. I had a way with people. The couples were the easiest. It didn't matter if they were married, dating, or common-law. I am a woman, and I knew how to make women want the house. If you really think about it, it's not hard. Women dream of living in and decorating their own home from the time they are little girls. I know that because I am a woman. To pour salt in the wound, I made the woman, whoever she may have been, envision herself cooking on the stovetop, taking a hot bath after wards. The decorating possibilities were endless. I'd draw visions of olive paint in the common areas and soft yellows in the low areas. Once I made the woman really want it, the rest was just as easy. I loved my job, and I was good at it.

My brother stayed on the road. He was undefeated – the number one contender in the heavyweight boxing association. When he would come home, people in DC treated him like a hero. With all the crime and negativity, people needed to see people like Zay. They needed something tangible that they could be proud of. I loved it when he would come home. I could look at him and be happy, knowing that his hard work had paid off as well, and he, too, was living the dream. Aside from all that jazz, I wanted to see Tracey.

This one time, it was in the middle of spring and Zay and Tracey took some time off. They had come home for a bit. I remember Zay talking about how they starved him and the bus hadn't pulled over for lunch. He complained some more before Tracey suggested that we all go out for something to eat. He said that he would pay. It was perfect for me. I had one last appointment for the day, but they canceled forty-five minutes ago.

My feet were killing me. I had on some red heels. They were *that* pair of shoes that looked sexy but hurt to walk in after a couple of hours. I had a pair of tennis shoes in my car but I was going out to dinner with Tracey, so I wasn't about to change into them. I wanted to look good for him.

We sat at the table. Zay was preoccupied with incoming calls.

"His dick is going to fall off," I whispered to Tracey, who smiled at me. I was reminded of the same little boy who would hide my Barbie dolls from me when we were smaller.

I couldn't keep my eyes off of him. I tried not to stare at him. I would steal a peek when I thought he wasn't watching, but he seemed to catch me every time. I was embarrassed when he caught me the first couple of times, but then after that I didn't care. When he would catch me, I wouldn't hide it. I would stare at him until he broke contact.

Zay finished two plates and from there he was ready to go. He didn't ask if we were ready or not. Maybe we were still working on our plates, but that didn't matter. All Zay knew was that he was ready to go, which was cool with me that day. Tracey dropped Zay off at his home and we kept going.

Tracey was cool as usual. He turned the radio up so he wouldn't have to talk. I turned it down and looked at him. "So you are still shy, huh. I peeped you out; you turned the music up so you won't have to talk to me."

He laughed. "What are you talking about? It's jazz. I'm trying to give you some culture."

"What are you talking about; you couldn't culture me, little boy," I said.

He stopped smiling and looked at me in the eyes. "So, is that it?"

I got nervous. *What is he asking me?* "Is that it? Is what it?"

"Is that how you still look at me after all these years, a little boy?"

I was speechless. Where was this going? I had rehearsed what I would say to him when the time was right. I was flirting with him, licking my lips and stuff, and I believed that I was going to call him out, but I punked out. I looked at Tracey and then reached down to turn the radio back up. My childhood friend looked at me and started smiling. We weren't children any more. He was thirty-two, and I had just turned thirty-five.

We rode downtown on Constitution Avenue past the Treasury building. The Washington Monument was in full view on the left hand side. I didn't mind riding – matter of fact I was enjoying it. I pretended that I was Tracey's woman and that we were on a date, but this wasn't our first date, no, we did this all the time. He would chauffer me around and he liked doing it. I crossed my legs and hiked my leather skirt up bit to show a little more thigh. He kept driving. By this time, I could see the Potomac River on the left side and the National War Museum on the right side. He busted a U turn and headed in the opposite direction. When he took the 11th Street exit, I knew where he was taking me. We were going to the Haines Point Park.

"Where are you taking me?" I asked.

"Don't worry about it."

I smiled.

He put the car in park and turned the ignition to the off position before he took the key out. I sat in my seat until he came around to my side to open my door for me. He reached for my hand and I gave to him. I stepped out, he looked at my shoes. I smiled.

"Damn you still have that same pretty smile."

I stopped smiling. "What?"

He didn't repeat himself. He looked at my feet again. "Look, I got some flip flops in the trunk. You can wear them if you like. I'm sure they will be a little more comfortable."

"Your dirty-ass shoes, no thank you."

He laughed. "Okay, have it your way, baby. You know you look fly in those heels, you don't need me to tell you that."

I wanted to take them off, but I was still trying to be cute. I wanted to reserve all my sexy to keep in his plain view. My feet were killing me. The time would come when I could take them off. I would be casual with it when I would take them off.

We started walking. "So, what's up with that?" He asked me.

"What's up with what?"

"Dinner."

"Dinner?"

"You know, the way you were looking at me."

"How did I look at you?" I pretended not to know what he was talking about.

"You looked at me… I don't know. You didn't look at me like we grew up together; you looked at me like, you know, like I could have been something to you."

I played it off. "Well, Tracey you have always been something to me."

"Nah, I don't mean like that, not like it was when we were kids."

I didn't say anything. My feet were really hurting. I raised my right leg up first, pulled the strap down, and took the shoe off. Tracey busted up laughing while I took the left one off.

He touched my hair and looked at me. He didn't look at me like we were friends. He looked at me like something else. "I see you, Ms. Arvette, with your realty company. You did that."

"I did. When are you going to let me sell you a house?"

"Well you know, I haven't got that far yet. You know me and your brother been doing our thing, you know, making miracles happen, and I love that. I love being your brother's manager and keeping him out of trouble. I guess when things slow down, I can think about settling down. But for right now, I'm helping somebody achieve his dreams."

"So, you are still scared of him."

"Who; your brother?"

"His name is Nyza. Why do you keep calling him *my brother*? You can't say his name?"

"Whatever. Why would I be scared of him?"

"You just sound like it. It's just the way that you talk about him."

"Zay is my friend and I respect him; that is all." He chuckled, "scared of him."

I got serious on him. I couldn't help it. "You know, you still have that same cute smile that I loved when we were kids."

He seemed to get a little serious on me too. I felt kind of reticent after making the comment, but I felt like we both had put ourselves out there so much already so what did I really have to lose?

I looked at him, and I wanted to kiss him. I was tired of playing the game with him. I wanted to know. I wanted him to know how much I wanted him, but I decided against it. Before I could finish my thought, it started raining. It started out little drops, and then I felt fat drops falling against my head.

Tracey grabbed my hand, and when he did, I felt a gentle tingle on the inside. "Let's get out of this rain," he said.

I sat on the passenger side of his car and was almost unable to contain myself. I wanted to suck on the side of neck; I kind of got the urge to straddle him as he drove, but I knew I wouldn't. My bark was worse than my bite. There were plenty of things that I said I would do, but I knew on the inside that I wouldn't do it.

I sat there, and for a while we were both quiet. Right then, I wished I could read minds. I wanted to know what he was thinking. He kept driving. I stared at him. I sunk down in the seat and looked around the car. His car was simple, too modest for him. He drove a mid-size Acura, but my brother paid him Bentley money. I liked that about Tracey. He had lots of money, but he was always cautious with it. With the money that my brother paid him, he could live any kind of way that he wanted. He would tell me when we were younger that he would rather live below his means so that he could keep money in his pocket. I was the opposite. I thought for a long time that Tracey would be the man to balance me out.

The rain seemed to taper off, but when we pulled up to Tracey's place, the rain poured like water from buckets. We looked at each other as if we were about to act on a dare. If he opened his door first, I would follow suit. I wasn't brave enough to open mine first. I lost myself in him for a minute. *This is it. Right here and right now is the perfect time.*

"Are you okay?" Tracey asked.

I was discomfited a bit, thinking for the moment that he had read my thoughts. I cleared my throat. "Yeah, I'm fine."

"I said that I don't think this rain is going to let up."

I could barely see out the window. "I guess not."

We opened the door and made a mad dash for the condo. He lived on the first floor, so that was a good thing. Once we got inside, he looked at me. I knew I was a hot mess. But he stood there looking like he wanted something. Did he feel it too? He walked closer, and right at that point, I wasn't cold from the rain any more.

"You know something; you look so sexy right now."

"Whatever Tracey, you play too much." I looked down at myself while touching my hair. "I am a mess and you know it."

"Well, why don't you go and dry off. You can shower if you like. I can take your clothes off – I mean I can take your clothes and put them in the dryer for you."

"What will I put on until my clothes are dry?"

He looked at his watch. "Well, I mean, you don't have any other plans do you? I was thinking that you could stay here with me tonight." He pointed over his shoulder,

"I got some stuff for you to sleep in – you know what I mean."

I was glad on the inside. It was about to happen. Tracey felt like I felt, so it seemed, but in his own way, he was still treating me like Zay's big sister.

"I am not the same girl I was when we were little kids," I reminded him.

His brows rose and he shook his head slowly, "I know, that's right."

"My brother doesn't tell me what to do. I do have a daddy, and Zay is not that man."

"I know."

I got out of the shower, and I was burning with desire and lust for him. My nipples were so hard. I wanted him so bad I thought I could feel him standing behind me. I looked in the mirror just to make sure that he wasn't actually behind me. I finished drying off and put on the Maryland t-shirt that he left for me to put on. *I will be taking this with me.* This was the same shirt that he used to wear when he went to Maryland of College Park. I lifted the bottom of the shirt and smelled it. It smelled so good. I reached for the shorts that he gave me to put on, but then I had an idea.

Tracey was in one room, and I was in another. The

bed looked like it hadn't been touched in a while, it was so perfect. The sheets smelled fresh, though.

I walked to the next room where he lay. I walked slowly to the side of the bed as the bottom of the t-shirt swept my legs. He was awake.

"Are you okay?"

I didn't say anything. He lay in the middle of the king-sized bed. I was careful as I got into bed with him. I straddled him.

"You ain't got nothing underneath that t-shirt," he discovered.

"Yeah, I do. I want you to reach down and touch it because it yours. It's all yours."

"Hey Vette, we can't do this."

"Tell me you don't want me."

"You know your brother isn't going to understand."

"I know it, but I know your secret. I know you want me, and I have always wanted you."

He took me by surprise when he leaned forward to grab my face. He kissed me and didn't hold back either. He kissed me like he really meant it. I made a passionate noise that might have sounded like a shriek if my tongue hadn't been locked with his. I was busy as we kissed. I rubbed his wide shoulders and brought my hands to the center of naked chest. We rolled over and he began exploring with his hands. I let him do what he wished to do to me. We took a break from kissing, and he kissed me from the top of my head to top of my feet. He came back up and kissed my kitty. It was a soft peck. "Are you sure this is for me?" He asked for confirmation.

"Baby, it's all yours. I don't want anyone else to have it."

We started making love, and it was extraordinary. "I have always loved you, Arvette, always."

The next morning, I had things to do and so did he, but not for one minute could I pretend that the night before hadn't happened. We had to address it.

"How do you feel," he asked.

"I feel... good. I never felt like this before."

"Was that the last time – 'cause I don't want it to be the last time."

I smiled then wrapped my arms around his seventeen-inch neck. "Oh, baby, I don't either."

Then there was the downer. "What do we tell Zay?"

I loosened my arms around him. I looked him in the eyes. "I don't know. What do we tell him?"

"I don't know."

"How about we don't for right now," I said.

"Don't tell him?"

"Let's not – not right now."

He kissed me and went to get my clothes for me. I was happy about what happened. I was happy that Tracey felt the same as I did.

Zay

They stood close to each other. They both looked content. If it had to be anybody, I was glad that it was Trace.

The snow was coming down, and I reflected on my actions. This new life I was living and this new way of thinking was different to me. I didn't know this person I'd become, but I was starting to like him a little bit. I had done things the same for long and wondered why I always got the same results. But things have to change sometimes.

When I looked at my watch, I was reminded that my sister was supposed to go home the day after tomorrow, and I hadn't spent much time with her. I hadn't spent any real time with her, anyway. I think my lady friend had put in more time with Vette than I had. I had to play make-up a little bit. My attitude had gotten in the way, and I almost forgot what was most important. She had planned this trip for a while, and I didn't know when I would see her again. I looked at Tracey and chuckled. He was my niece's daddy. He didn't know, but how could Vette keep something like that. Her not telling me was one thing, but not telling the father was totally different. I shook it off. What's done is done. I couldn't be mad at that now.

It occurred to me that people were looking at me. It was if I had removed myself from the conversation, but it wasn't that. I was learning to listen. "Sis, what are you doing tomorrow?"

"Well my new sister took me shopping... so I don't know."

"That's good. Don't make plans during the day." I looked at Tracey. He nodded his head.

"I got the shop tomorrow," he said with a smile.

I rubbed Vette's shoulders. "We're going to hang tomorrow."

"Damn, it's about time you stopped pouting," Tammy said.

Vette was enjoying this, I could tell. "Girl, you got it going on. I don't know what you do to Zay, but you got him all the way in check," Vette said. "Zay would get mad about stuff and be mad for the rest of the week."

Tammy rubbed my ears and looked at me. "You're okay, baby. I got you."

Matter of fact, everybody was enjoying it. I couldn't believe that I had finally decided to settle down – and

I was cool with it. They kept laughing but it didn't stop there. Tracey even threw in a couple of comments.

"So, y'all have fun tomorrow. Vette don't keep him out late. You know your brother got curfew."

"Don't worry, you are about to have one too," Tammy chimed.

Tracey smiled. "Maybe, but I'll take that. I've known this dude since single digits, and I've never seen him like this before."

"You too, Trace. You're supposed to be on my side," I said.

"Sorry, bruh, we got to mark this one for the history books."

Vette said, "You see it's snowing outside, right?"

They were making fun at my expense, but I didn't mind. It felt like they were celebrating. Right then and there, I began to look back. I wondered had I been *that* hard and callous. They made it seem like I was extremely unreasonable and hard to get along with. Maybe I had. I never wanted to be that way again. They say that it's hard to see what right in front of you sometimes. If you asked me why I acted the way I did, I would use the old alpha male response. The alpha male is the top dog. He takes confrontation well, always handles the situation but the alpha is too cool to fight. I knew that I was an alpha male, but it didn't mean anything if others didn't know it. Others had to be able to detect it right from the start. I prided myself on that. I didn't demand many things, nor was I a dictator; I was who I was, and others recognized. If you asked me, I was exuberant, boisterous, confident, and secure. Sometimes, I guess I could be loud and overconfident. But I was the top dog, and everybody knew it. When I began to think some more, that isn't what life should be about. On the other hand, the alpha male is very important.

I was always that alpha. People knew it before they stepped in the ring with me. There were floating rumors that people were afraid to fight me. I wasn't a sensation like Tyson, who knocked out half of his forty opponents in the first round, but I didn't play around either. I had a perfect record; I'd never lost a fight. Sometimes, I still missed it. I used to work out for strength training, hoping the doctor would release me from my profile so that I could go back to professional boxing. For a while, I was looking for something to fill that void, but I believed that Tammy had filled that void. The last time I'd felt this good, I was in the ring.

Tracey

I loved her, and I hated to see her go. Arvette had to get back to Florida. She had things to do. I was mad at her still for not telling me that Ziniah was my child. I thought about how much time I'd missed with my daughter; it had me heated, but I understood why she did it. She was trying to protect us both. Even though I was upset, I was still happy because of the way things turned out. We'd kept our feelings for each other locked away because of my peanut head friend. We'd deprived ourselves of happiness for a while.

While I was driving from the airport, I thought about how much I missed her, and I realized how much I needed her. I sexed the hell out her the whole time she was here. *Damn, she got some good sex.* It never changed. Whenever we made love, the shit was the bomb. We did that like we were supposed to. It felt like we were made for each other. For that same reason, we were determined to be together at all costs – even if it meant keeping it from my best friend, which we'd done for some time.

DC

Arvette wasn't the same kind of woman that she used to be when we were kids. I used to like her cute dimples. I liked every hairstyle that was created for her. I liked her fair skin color and small moles under her eyelids. I liked it when she would touch me. There were times when I would pick a fight with her just for the attention. I was young, and to me, that was big back then. Any type of attention a younger man could get from an older woman was good. She got a little older, and all the regular things that come with being in high school came into play. She was feeling herself a little more. She felt the power that she had as a woman. She was so fine. She had a long list of brothers standing in line to date her. Vette made light of all the men she had to turn down for the high school prom. She was a girl who just had it like that. I watched her though. I didn't like it when she brought other boys around. I wondered why she didn't see that I was the man who wanted to be most significant in her life. Sure, I was younger than she, but I knew what she liked. I knew what she wanted in a man; that was one of the advantages of growing up with her. It seemed that I just didn't have the chance.

I got over my jealous spirit after a while and drove on with my life. I cut her out of my fantasies. I stopped myself from dreaming about her night after night and went out to pursue other things. My best friend was hot and in demand. I was his trainer and cut man. Before his sister, Arvette, got into real estate, she worked for her brother. She handled all his finances, so she wasn't just the average girl down the street. She was a classy, rich girl who liked Gucci and Fendi. She was still a good custodian of money. Zay trusted me and he trusted his sister fully. He never questioned what we did.

We were all paid, and we were all happy. It was like old times, except something was a little different. Me and Zay went all over, but as close as he was with his sister, he made sure that we'd make local stops to see her.

It was cool to see Arvette. I would see her about once every six months. Sometimes I would see her more often. For the most part, she was available. She was into her work, and she didn't appreciate any distractions. I had always admired that about her. When I was younger, I would talk to the fellas and we would talk about women like Halle Berry, Lela Rachon, Tyra Banks, Thandie Newton, Jada Pinkett, and the chick off the Cosby show. We would fantasize when we would go to bed. To us, those women were top notch. If you were a man and you were lucky enough to have a woman like that on your arm, you were doing it big. Secretly, when I would go to bed, I would think about some of those women, but I always had reservations in my thoughts for Arvette.

I never thought I would cross the line until that day we came off the road. Vette was still living in DC. She was a senior at Howard University at the time. Me and Zay came off the road and we had to be back on in three days. I was exhausted. All I wanted was a big steak and a good night's sleep until I set my eyes on Arvette. I was revived. I had the energy that I needed to keep going. Zay was complaining about being hungry, so I suggested that we all go out together.

We went out, and I swear the whole time his big sister was looking me up and down. I couldn't understand why. As she looked at me, I tried to be good. I didn't want to undress her with my eyes. I didn't want to entertain any unclean thoughts, but I couldn't help it as I watched her lips move as she talked. I studied her pretty, white teeth. I was taken by her fresh splashes of Versace perfume and her playful, yet adult outfit. I tried to think of other things. I tried to spark conversation, but Zay was so tired until he wasn't much for words. All he really wanted was to get to bed, so I dropped him off and proceeded to take his sister home.

Something came over me as I drove. I passed her exit and kept rolling. She was well-relaxed in the passenger seat. There was silence about the vehicle. I could hear the road noise as I drove, but after a while I ruled out all the distractions, and I promise I could hear her breathing. There was silence still, but it was a good kind of silence. I could feel anticipation inside the cabin. There was something she wanted to say. I knew there was something I wanted to say to her, but I deemed it best to keep to myself.

Downtown DC was one of my favorite spots, and if I remembered correctly, it was one of Vette's favorites too. She wasn't ready to go home, just like I wanted to save the night. What was I doing? I knew damned well that I should have been taking her home. I told myself that the whole thing would be an innocent time between two friends who hadn't seen each other in a while.

It rained that night and somehow or another we ended up at my place. We were soaked, but we were happy. She was so sexy to me, as she stood in front of me dripping. Her hair had fallen and her clothes stuck to her. I was trying to behave but I couldn't help but want her. I could see through her white blouse. She had no bra. Her breasts were perkier than I had remembered last. Her nipples were hard. She knew that I was looking at her, but she didn't seem to mind at all; it was as if she wanted me to look. She wasn't ashamed. If I hadn't known better, I would've said she stood there like she was ready to give herself to me. Quickly, I asked to dry her clothes and offered her a room. I didn't plan on taking advantage of anything, but I just wanted her to stay with me. The road was lonely. For a change, I wanted to be around someone familiar.

I stretched across the bed in the guest room while she occupied my room. As tired as I should have been, I couldn't sleep. I didn't really want to. I was on my back with no shirt on. My hands were folded behind my neck when she walked in.

"Are you okay?" I asked.

She didn't say anything. She got on the bed and climbed on top me. She was wearing one of my old college t-shirts and that was all. She sat right on top of my stomach. She had no panties on. Her lips were so wet for me. She felt so good and warm. She wanted me to feel her. I could feel something wet run down my side. I got hard right away for her. I felt like we were about to do something wrong. It felt like we were sneaking around in the basement while our parents weren't home.

"You ain't got nothing underneath that t-shirt," I said.

"Yeah I do. You can't feel me?"

"I feel something," I said sheepishly.

"I want you to reach down and touch it because it yours. It's all yours."

"Hey, Vette, we can't do this."

"Tell me you don't want me," she said.

God, I wanted her so bad. "Tell me," she demanded. "Tell me you don't want me." She smiled and reached around to grab me. "Oh yeah, Tracey, I knew you wanted me," she said passionately.

"You know your brother isn't going to understand."

"I know it, but I know your secret. I know you want me, and I have always wanted you."

I did. I wanted her from the first time I saw her. When I was old enough to understand women, I possessed her in my mind, but I never told anyone. I was staring opportunity in the face, and I knew that it would never come this close to me again, so I took her face in my hands before I engaged her in a kiss. That shit felt so good. I felt relieved, rejuvenated. Life made sense all in those few seconds. I did whatever was natural. At once I took my childhood sweetheart's face in my hands and kissed her like it meant everything to me. I wanted her to feel the weight of my heart in that kiss. I wanted our first kiss to be the best kiss. A brother started reaching in separate places. She let out so much emotion with each breath and I loved it. Her noises were erotic as she gyrated on top of me. She hit me with a devilish grin that made me feel like it was okay to do whatever we wanted. I blinked my eyes a few times to make sure that it was real.

Vette started tugging at my shorts. "Are you sure," I asked her.

"Take your fucking pants off and stop asking me questions. I want you – I want this."

I rolled her over. I was still enjoying the foreplay. I liked the way she kept her hands on me. I started kissing her all over. I kissed each part of her body at least once.

She told me that she was for me and no one else. She said that she didn't want anyone to have her goodies. I didn't take it lightly. It was so intense every time that we locked lips. This was what I had been waiting for. I enjoyed the act of making love to her. I wanted it to last because I just didn't know what would happen with us.

The morning after was awkward for me. We stood before each other with nothing to say. We were both thinking about the same thing. It was great, and we were glad that we had done it, but there was an underlying issue that we knew was there. I looked into her eyes without blinking. I felt brand new, and at that moment I didn't care about what her brother would possibly think, but I had to bring it up. I couldn't pretend that I didn't have feelings for her. I couldn't pretend that the night before hadn't happened to the both of us.

"What do we tell Zay?"

"I don't know. What do we tell him?" Vette asked.

"I don't know."

"How about we don't for right now," she said.

"Don't tell him?"

"Let's not – not right now."

I kissed her. There was nothing left to say.

Miami

It was always cool to visit Arvette. I mean, she was in Miami. Miami, Florida was so many things all at once. Among other things, Florida was hot and humid. But you couldn't beat the nightlife. I couldn't lie; I had this love-hate thing going. I loved the District of Columbia, but I hated that fact that it could never be like Miami. DC also offered a good night life, but in Florida I could have it all. The beach was right there; you would meet more stars in Miami than you could dream of meeting in DC. They flossed so hard, it was ridiculous. I had a little change in my pocket, but the South Beach, Floridians were big fish in and out of water. When they were in the water they cruised the waters in yachts. When they on land they drove Bentleys, Ferraris, Lambos and Maybachs. They sped down the coastal strip, and nobody would mess with them. I didn't envy their status, I could have lived that way if I wanted, but it was good to be around people with money. It made me feel like my money was actually longer than it was.

The second time I ever went to Florida, we were there to, of course, see Arvette, but we had passes to the American Black Film Festival. We had to be there; Zay did a cameo appearance in a film. The director wasn't one of those that were highly celebrated, but his first work surprised millions. He requested that all acting persons and affiliates attend. Secretly, Arvette was my date but, of course, we couldn't let the Champ know.

The Festival and Celebration were held at the Nikki Club. I was told that there were at least seven of these clubs on and around remote beaches and lakes. We rented a Phantom Rolls Royce for the event, and I was glad we did, because every car in that parking lot cost three hundred plus. I stepped out in De la Renta, while my girlfriend stepped out the backseat in one of those Dior dresses. I looked at her and then looked at Zay. I couldn't wait to get rid of him so that our evening could really start.

I grabbed her hand, and we walked towards the entrance while the valet proceeded to park the car. Zay smiled as we held hands. He thought I was merely playing the role for the cameras. To walk hand-in-hand in front of an important crowd made you look even more important. It was the right thing to do, but, little did Zay know, I had other reasons for taking his sister's hand. She smiled at me and stole a kiss while her younger brother smiled for the onlookers. I guess I blushed a little bit. No other woman had ever achieved that. She always had what it took to bring out my emotions, whether I wanted them to be known or not.

The three of us walked towards the entrance. We got a swift break from the heat while we walked between mist from the small pillars. There was water falling from the twin pillars. There were blue and purple lights that seemed to add ambiance and sensuality. The falls gave a simple relief from the humidity. Cameras flashed constantly. I remember the first time that I went to an event with my boy – I felt star struck. I wasn't the one in the demand, my boy was. I just shared the light with him.

The cameras followed us. Members of the press ensued, asking Zay questions about his career and cameo appearance. They wanted to know if he saw a future in acting. Zay waved them off with a smile and kept going. His sister and I followed. I was checking the whole place out. There were tepees painted on every wall. Under the tepee the words "Nikki Club" were imprinted. We could hear the music. It was so loud, and we hadn't even made it to the club.

***

It was late, but Arvette said that she would wait up for me, no matter how late it was. Zay had company with him in a local hotel. He always had women. Every city that we stopped in, there was always a small group of ladies who felt they had what it took to spend the night with the boxing champ of the world. He liked the attention. Sometimes, I felt that he was just a sex addict that couldn't help himself. His infatuation only contributed to my success. As long as Zay was occupied, he didn't have time to ask questions about me and what I did in my spare time.

I didn't like to keep things from Zay; he was more than a best friend, he was the brother that I never had. Our relationship meant more than life itself at times, but I loved his sister. I was in love with her, and I couldn't help myself. I was on my way over to see her.

She had this small condo in South Beach. The back of her crib sat close to the water. She preferred to call it her private beach. I would call her sometimes and she would brag on this private beach of hers. She would tell me that I would have to see it the first chance I could get away.

This was my first time in South Beach visiting her. I was nervous for more reasons than one. In my mind I was going to break up with her. Things could not go on the way that they had. It had been several months since the first time we had given ourselves to each other. It felt so right, but I felt wrong. My subconscious was consumed with feelings of betrayal. I had always called myself a loyal friend, but I was with my friend's sister unbeknownst to him. I knew how he felt. He told me that I was never to cross the line with his sister, but I had, so I asked myself – where was the loyalty in what I was doing?

Arvette saw things completely differently. There was no reason to deny ourselves of what we wanted the most, in order to satisfy someone else's stupid wish. "If two people want to be together, they are going to be together," she would remind me. She had a point, but I still felt that we were both wrong.

I was going to break it off this time. There was absolutely nothing that could change my mind – until she opened the front door. She wore a long, sheer, black dress that stopped about two inches past her ankles. She was barefoot, wearing the diamond ankle-bracelet that I'd bought for her the last time I was Nepal. She had a cute little toe ring with a blue stone in it to match her toenail polish. Back then she had long, black hair. This night, it was pinned up. When I looked into her eyes, I turned into butter. We stood in the doorway a few seconds just staring at each other. "Hey, baby," She spoke.

Don't fall for it. You know what you have to do. You can't give in. Of course you love her. You want to be with her, but this is the right thing for you to do. That is what I told myself before she opened her arms. I pulled her to me and rested my face against hers. "You smell sweaty," Arvette said.

"I won't be here long," I said.

"Where are your clothes? I thought you said that you had clothes to wash?"

"They are in the car," I said.

She kissed me on the lips. "I missed you so much, baby," she told me. I could feel the emotion in her statement. There was so much tenacity in her eyes. There was sincerity in her touch. The mood had already been set. Her place was dark. The only light that we had was the flicker from the television. I liked her place. She had flat screens all throughout the house. She had simple yet eloquent décor throughout. Her furniture was streamlined. The place had a cool feeling that seemed to capture you, but at the same time it wasn't overstuffed. There was balance in the home – not too much, not too little. I walked inside, thinking about what I wanted most out of life at that time. I looked at Vette, and she was it. I was torn between the relationships but at the same time, I knew that Vette was what I needed in my life. She was the one thing that was missing. She was the one thing that completed me. Was I to give that up because of a friend who only seemed to think about himself?

I sat on the couch. Arvette caressed my shoulders. I felt like I was in heaven. She had that touch that could heal almost anything. She felt so good. I could feel myself pulling back from her. She didn't take offense to it. I could feel her back off as well.

I sat there with my eyes closed; I thought about what I was about to do. I didn't want to do what I was about to do, but it had to be done. Arvette was so soothing. I mean, it was everything about her from her voice to her touch. She could have very well been a masseuse in a past lifetime. She had the right type of hands; they could relieve any kind of stress. I loved it when she touched me. I was trying to enjoy the moment, but the whole time I thought of this one song by a dude named Ralph Tresavant. The name of the song was "Do What I Gotta Do". Back in the day, we thought that it was a real playa song. But when I got older, I understood the gist of it – it was really a breakup song. The chorus would go, "I gotta do what I gotta do and break her heart. Though I love the girl I know that the best thing is for us to be apart." That was all that I thought about as I leaned towards the arm of the sofa.

Once I got comfortable, she nestled up close to me. Even though my eyes were closed, I could see her in my mind's eye positioned on her side with her legs folded underneath her bottom. When I opened my eyes, she was positioned just as I had pictured. Feeling her body against mine was the best feeling in the world. She placed her head in the middle of my chest and moved around until her face fit perfectly in the center of my chest. She belonged there. It was as if she was made for me. I didn't take it carelessly, either. When I wrapped my arms around her she would coo like a baby. There was nothing empty or loose about the hold that I had around her when she was in my arms. There was no space in between when I had her in my embrace. She belonged there, she and nobody else. I began to think about all the times that I felt alone. I could have had any woman that I wanted, but there weren't many women that I wanted.

There I was, on the sofa holding the only woman who seemed to complete me, and I was thinking about how to break the whole thing off. Then, I grew angry. For as long as I could remember, I would do the right thing, the responsible thing. I would often sleep on an opportunity because I knew that others wanted it. I didn't want to make them feel like we were competing, so for the sake of argument, I would pass and let others have it. As Arvette moved in my arms, I thought about breaking up, but I saw no real reason to. For the first time, things were clear to me. I needed, loved, and desired Arvette – and I would have her.

I smiled. There was no way I would break up with her that night. I squeezed her tighter when she looked up at me. She smiled. "What, baby?"

"Nothing," I said.

"You sure? Are you okay?"

"Baby, as long as I am with you, everything is okay."

She began to blush. "As long as you are with me, do you mean that?"

"I do."

She adjusted herself. She got up from the sofa and reached for my hand, assisting me as I got up. "I want to show you something." Once I stood to my feet, she leaned over and pulled the throw from the back of the sofa and wrapped it around her shoulders like an expensive stole. She took the lead and reached for my hand once again. I followed her out the sliding glass door. We were in the back of her place, standing on the deck. It looked like something straight out of a movie, the way the moon sparkled off the water. The length of the ocean seemed endless. Her view was so peaceful and relaxing, but I had a feeling that that wasn't what she wished to show me.

We walked across the deck and down the steps. It was cool out that night. I understood why Vette grabbed the throw. We got to the last step, Vette stopped and turned to me. "Wait baby, Take your shoes off." I had on some New Balance running shoes; she was barefoot. We walked as the sand invited my feet, seemed to swallow them. The sand was cool on the top, but once your feet sunk below the surface, the sand was much warmer. I loved that simmering feeling across the pressure points of my feet. She was making it harder for me. When I first got to her place, I could hear the breakup song playing so loud in my head until I almost began singing along, but the way things stood at that point, the song grew faint. I didn't know the words, and I could hardly hear them. All

I could think about was grabbing her ass and throwing her on top of the sand. There was no one around, and it was dark. I could see people ahead, but they couldn't see us. *Fuck everybody that has a problem with me. Fuck Zay and his spoiled ways and egotism.* I lagged behind her a bit and proceeded with my thoughts. I grabbed that soft ass and grabbed her wrist. I didn't have to tell her what I wanted. She just followed suit. I threw my tongue down her throat. She kept up with me and seemed to have a strong appetite for what we were doing. I hiked one of her legs up to my waist and suspended it there. I braced her for stability with one arm and took my other hand and ran it between her legs. She didn't have any panties on. That pussy was dripping for me and me alone. I touched the entrance and my finger was swallowed instantly. She broke contact with my lips. She threw her head back with her eyes closed. I could hear her gritting her teeth. I took my time. She began to gyrate, and I felt that any minute we would lose balance. I didn't want that to happen. I didn't want anything to poison the mood, so I let her leg rest and pulled my finger out of her. She wasn't pleased. When she opened her lust-filled eyes, she stared at me as if she was under due stress and needed relief fast and in a hurry. I thought about helping her out, but the more I thought about it, I figured it would be more fun to leave her like that. I wanted to build up the occasion before I would tear her ass up. She knew that a nigga couldn't do it like me.

"Tracey, let's go," she said, half out of breath.

"Go where?"

She smiled. "I told you that I have something to show you." She gave me that sexy look; the one where she bites her bottom lip and looks me up and down. "Baby, don't look at me like that, Imma fuck you right on this beach."

"And I will fuck you back," she said with a smile. She poked me in the chest and said, "Later, but for now bring your mannish ass and do try to behave yourself."

I took her hand with a smile. I couldn't believe how comfortable I was with her, and it didn't have anything to do with us growing up together. We didn't make sexual comments and remarks when we were little. We didn't make passes or flirt with one another. We didn't feel one another up like consenting adults; we played house and teased each other like rivaling siblings in an extended family. We were like regular kids. We never explored this end of the spectrum. When I thought about Zay, my stomach felt empty. Even though things seemed so right, I felt like I was doing *so* wrong.

I kept my random thoughts to myself and tried to suppress them. I didn't want my separate thoughts to intrude on the time that we were having. I followed her to this spot in the middle of the beach. There was a party going on. I saw signs that read, "Nikki Beach". I had heard so much about Nikki Beach. This place was separate from Club Nikki. Vette told me that Nikki Beach was like a restaurant during the day but converted to a club on the beach at night. At the entrance there were a few couples waiting for the attendant. They were of different nationalities, all dressed in their bed clothes. I looked swiftly over my left shoulder. There was a sign that advertised the pajama party. I looked down at myself. Vette was reading my mind. She nudged me, "Don't worry, handsome, you are fine."

I took her at her word as we stepped down the walk way. Once we got past the main entrance, we hit the mainstream flow of traffic. The dance floors looked like multi-leveled, patio decks made of the most expensive woods. There were thick, wooden beams to reinforce the structure. White curtains encased the tropical environment to give that feeling of a true club. The curtains swayed with the breeze from the ocean. I was impressed. I hadn't experienced anything quite like it.

Zay's sister was all grown up now. She stood there with me in the middle of the dance floor. She didn't wait for an invitation; she just started moving to the groove of the live band. I moved my hips and rocked with her. She rested her head on my shoulder. She felt safe with me, I could tell. She felt so light, like she had not a care in the world when she was with me.

I pulled her in a little and began moving my hips with a little more meaning. I rested my face against her face and smelled her hair. I loved the way her hair smelled. I loved everything about her. I was enjoying her so much and was beginning to relax, when she raised her head. "Tracey, do you know that I have been waiting for you all my life. I don't ever want to let you go."

"I don't want to be let go of," I said. We continued to be sexy as we kept our rhythm. I looked up, enjoying the atmosphere. There was a distinctive breeze and love was in the air. I scanned the area and looked at the couples meandering through the crowd. Some of them looked like they were in aged relationships but still carried on like they were on their first honeymoon. I still couldn't get over the fact that we were at a pajama party and that I was dressed the way that I was dressed. I saw another fellow that made me feel a little better about my attire. He was dressed the same way I was. He had on a button-up and some wrinkle-free slacks. His date was in an unassuming evening dress. I fixed my gaze on the couple, as there was something familiar about the pair, especially the guy. I couldn't figure it out until he turned around. I dropped my head hoping that he wouldn't see me.

There was a stutter in my step. Vette picked up on it right away. "Is everything okay?" She asked.

I guided her slightly to the left. My plan was to turn my girlfriend to the side and eventually move off the dance floor so that we wouldn't be spotted, but my plan didn't work. When I looked, the couple was headed in my direction. Zay was leading his lady friend. I took a deep breath as he approached. By now, I was slowing down. My moves weren't as sharp and crisp as they'd been when we started. I wasn't nervous, nor was I scared. I was caught off guard. Surely my best friend would think that I betrayed his trust.

Arvette raised her head and looked concerned. Her back was still to her brother. She couldn't see him approaching, but she knew something was wrong. I stopped moving completely, but I continued to hold onto Vette. She turned around only to face her younger brother.

"What the fuck is this?" Zay asked.

"What do you mean? What the fuck is this?" I retorted.

He pointed. "You and my sister; what is this?" He asked as he stood there looking like a *straight* victim.

"We are dancing. What the *fuck* does it look like?" His sister answered.

Zay smiled while his escort had this combination of fear and nerves on her face. Zay wiped his face, and before he could form a sentence, I butted in. "Yeah man, what's wrong with you? We are just dancing; some old childhood friends."

Zay smiled again, but this was a different type of smile. He gave the smile that he usually gave when he had been caught doing something stupid. He gave me a pat on the back. "Of course," He said. "Sorry, Trace. I'm just a little buzzed man, that's all." He looked past me and stared at Vette. "My bad big sis, y'all have some fun tonight. Don't let my dumb ass stop you."

Her brother walked off, and we both shared a sigh of relief. At the same time, I could tell that she had grown good and tired of Nyza – and who could blame her? I would sit from time to time and try to figure out why people kissed his ass – why people would go out of their way to accommodate him, and there we were doing the same thing. *Down like pimps without hos*, I thought. That was our saying ever since the second grade. We didn't even know what hos were back then. We sure didn't understand a pimp, but that was what we said. Even though we didn't know exactly what the terms truly meant, we knew that it was something deep. We swore by those words, and again, they echoed in my head. The more I heard the words, the more I knew I would have to cut it all off with Arvette. I was feeling like a punk at the time. My whole intention for the visit was to break things off, but I couldn't do it.

Pentagon City, Virginia

Six months had passed since I had considered breaking up with Arvette. Things had been getting more and more serious. Every time we went some place, Arvette would always hold out her hand for me to grab. I thought it was kind of cute. It was as if she wanted to be led by me. I didn't mind taking the lead. We held hands every place we went. Her little hand seemed to fit perfectly in my hand. More than holding hands, we were sampling each other's dish over the dinner table; we were drinking from the same glass, and we seemed to finish each other's sentences. We understood one another's likes and dislikes. She was more than a confident woman, but she got to the point where she needed my support; she wanted to be reassured by me. I didn't take those things lightly. It showed me how much she had grown in the relationship; it proved to me that she was becoming dependent on me. She needed me to be the cheerleader in the corner. For her, I would wave the pom-poms, it didn't matter the colors.

Along with the overall growth of the relationship, the sex seemed to get better and better. The first time that we did it, it was memorable, but our touches grew more and more intense. I knew her hot spots, and she knew mine. We knew exactly where to touch one another. I knew when she needed to be held. I knew when she needed the pep-talk. I knew when she needed me to be honest with her. She appreciated my honesty. Like I said, from the time we were little I had always looked at her as my dream girl. I knew when I was a kid that Arvette was a bona fide woman. I was totally satisfied with her, and I knew that she was satisfied with me. I liked the way we felt, but there was something else that remained – something that didn't feel so good. I knew that we would have to re-visit the same issue, and I was tired of the lingering situation.

Arvette had come up to visit. I had just picked her up from Dulles International Airport. We were en route to the hotel. She sat in the passenger's seat as I drove. It was in the middle of December. The temperature was fair, but I still ran the heater. I knew how Arvette would get cold quick. She sat upright, twisted the temperature control to the off position, and fell back in the seat. I looked at her. She twisted her bottom before she crossed her legs, poaching her lips like she was pouting.

I smiled. "What's wrong with you, baby."

She looked at me. She pouched her lips out even further before she answered. "Where are we going?"

I glanced over and said, "To the Marriot."

"This is stupid."

"What is so stupid," I asked.

"This whole hotel thing; what the fuck are we going to do at this hotel? I don't even stay in the hotel when I come to visit. I am usually at your place."

"Vette, you know that we have to keep it –"

" – We have to keep it like that for who? For my brother. I don't care about that anymore. Screw my brother." She had tears in her eyes. "I am tired of this, Tracey. I love you, and I don't want to keep it a secret anymore."

I felt the same way that she did. I didn't want to keep the secret either. "Vette, I don't know what to do. You know that we know the same people, and if they knew about us they would –"

" – Let them tell. I don't care any more, baby." Her eyes were watering again and her voice wavered. "It feels good to be in love with you, but it feels bad not to be able to share it with anyone."

I took a deep breath and let it out. We had been down

this familiar road oh, too many times. I didn't know what to do. There were times that Arvette wanted to tell me how much of a coward I was being. She knew that I had never been a punk, but things were different when it came to her brother. She didn't understand that I had a special bond with Zay. Zay was the only person in this world who had never let me down. He had always been there for support and inspiration. Zay had never, ever changed. When one of us had trouble, we both had trouble. Sure, we kicked some ass, and on occasion we got our asses kicked, but through it all, we had fun doing whatever it was that we did, and we always had each other's back regardless. Vette knew that, but she didn't understand the concept in its entirety. She didn't understand that I wanted her brother to trust me like I had always trusted him. To tell him that I had been dating his sister against his will would definitely have been bad.

I continued to grip the wheel with one hand at the twelve o' clock position. I used my right hand to reach for her hand. "Baby, I know how you must feel."

"I'm sorry, Tracey, but baby, I don't want to hear that anymore. I am ready for things to change."

I let go of her hand with a frown on my face. "Come on, Vette. We've been through this already."

Tears rolled down her face by this time. "You are right, Tracey, we have been through this before. We've been through this several times, and I promise you, this is the last time that we will go through this."

I smiled and reached for her hand again. "That's good, baby. We don't need to go through it anymore."

"You are right baby, because tonight we are going to call my brother and we are going to tell him what we have been doing."

I snatched my hand away from hers. "What! You can't be serious. You want us to do what?"

She smiled, but I knew that she was far from joking. "You heard me, Tracey. We tell him tonight. If we can't tell him, then we don't need to be together."

"Vette, you are crazy."

She uncrossed her legs and twisted slightly, as to face me. "Think about it. If you get serious with a woman, you would want people to be happy for you, right?" I nodded. "Especially your best friend; you would want him to be happy for you, if no one else would be happy for you."

"Right baby, but this is a little different."

"No, it's not. It is the same thing. Zay is your best friend."

"But you are his sister, too."

"You are right, but it doesn't matter. You know I don't have a lot of girlfriends, and I have always looked at my brother as more of a friend than a brother. You two are friends and should be able to trust one another."

"Whatever you say, Vette."

"You damned right. That is why we are going to tell Zay tonight."

It was against my will, but I promised my girlfriend that I would call her brother, so I did. I didn't want to tell him over the phone, but Vette was one of those "right now" people. Everything was priority. She lacked patience – among other things. She didn't understand how delivering a message like that via the phone would look. The only thing that she understood was that she wanted her brother to get the news on that same night. If I called him and asked him over, we could have been waiting until the next day.

I took the indirect approach. I made small talk while his sister stood before me with her arms folded, tapping one of her feet at the same time. She had that minding look the look that said, *you better tell him right now.* I knew that was what she wanted, but I couldn't. Zay was in the middle of something, just like I knew he would be. I could tell by the tone he used in the beginning of the conversation. Vette dropped her arms and by that time she was inside of my mouth waiting for what I would say to her brother next. Zay asked if what I had to tell him was

273

an emergency. Of course, I told him it wasn't. "Well uh… How about we meet for lunch tomorrow," He said.

I tried to hide my smile. "I don't know. How about we do the traditional thing."

"Pentagon," he asked.

"Pentagon City it is," I confirmed.

I pressed the off button and looked at Vette, who squinted her eyes at me before walking away. I didn't care if she walked off or not. She would have her way, but not as soon as she wanted. This was best, anyway. Like I said, this wasn't the kind of news that you give to someone over the phone.

It was the second week in January, and we were dressed for the weather. Vette was carefully bundled. Her coat was fastened to the top, where her scarf had been tucked in. I was a vet. I was very much used to the cold. With all the traveling that I did, it was unbelievable how well I could adapt to temperatures all around the world. I looked at Vette and chuckled. She looked down at herself. "What?" she asked.

"You," I said.

She looked down again. "There something wrong with me?"

I had stopped laughing, though I still wore a smile. I shook my head to answer her question. "There is nothing wrong with you."

"Well then, why are you laughing?"

"I'm laughing because you are dressed like its twenty degrees below zero. It's not that cold outside."

"Oh come on, baby, you know how I am." And she was right, I did; I did know her and how she was. That was the crazy part. I think that is what most people look for most of their lives. They look for the one person who truly completes them; they look for that special someone who they care for like no other. The problem is, people take things for granted. They always seem to want what they want when they want it, and when they get it, they seem not to want it any more. As I stood there with my true love, I made it up in my mind that it would not happen within this institution. This institution of ours called "love" was different from what others had. They didn't know, and some of the couples didn't understand how deep our love was. It was deeper than some Bobby and Whitney shit. When I clutched her around the waist, I knew all that I needed to know about myself and all about the fallacies of life. When I held Arvette, I knew that what I felt was real. I knew that it wasn't a dream deferred; it wasn't a falsehood. It was meant to be. Every day that I rose, I felt confident knowing that she had my back. It was a different kind of coolness.

I was cool with our differences. We could agree to disagree, and I liked that. Opposites truly did attract. She stood in front of me, while I reached from behind her to secure her. I held her tight enough just to remind her of my presence. I began to feel nervous. I didn't want to look at my watch, but I knew that Zay would be coming to meet us soon. I hadn't looked at the time but if I had to guess, we had about twenty more minutes before he would show up. Shortly, we would have to move inside the mall to meet him, but in the meantime, my sweetie and I stood outside in front of the ice skating rink. I was never one for ice skating; I'd tried it once and never cared to do it again. I was content watching the other skaters do their thing. This spot seemed to do something for the people. Figure skating was never my thing. I didn't grown up thinking that I would become a skater, but I can say that I did marvel over the figure skaters every time the Olympic Games came on. They came on once every four years, and it was all about competition, but of all the sports, skating was the one event that never felt like a sport to me. It was all about style and grace. Figure skaters seemed too cool to get upset. By watching some of them, you could tell how they channeled their energy. To me, skating was an art – an underappreciated art.

Vette had on gloves, but she still chose to cross her

arms across her chest until her hands were under her arms. I thought it was the cutest thing. I had never seen this side of her before. When we were kids, she came off kind of tomboyish. It was like she wanted to compete with me and Zay, while other times it felt like she was trying to belong. She didn't seem anything like a dude, but when Zay and I hung out, she wanted to hang out too. When Vette did hang out with us, she didn't feel like a dude, but she did fit in like one of the fellas. When confronted with this observation a few weeks back, she confessed that hanging with us made her feel closer to me. "I couldn't let my brother know," she said. We were little, but Vette was all grown up now, and she didn't feel like one of the fellas anymore. She felt like a straight-lady, one who was feminine, confident and sure about me. I kissed her on the back of the neck. She let out a sigh as I did. Then I thought about meeting Zay in the next few minutes and how he might take the news. I didn't want things to get too deep. I didn't want to attract a lot of attention, and I definitely didn't want to embarrass him by getting into a fist fight. Not many people knew, but I was the strongest fighter. I was his trainer. Zay was sharp, but I had always been a sharper boxer than Zay. I just didn't have the passion for it that he did.

Vette called my name. Snapping out of it, I answered, and when she told me that she loved me I knew at that point that it didn't matter what her younger brother thought about us. We were going to do this. We were going to be together. I smiled and focused on the skaters some more. Like I said, there was something about watching ice skaters that relaxed me.

I remember several years ago before this skating rink, before all the outside shops, boutiques and specialty stores, we would frequent this spot. Inside of the large building sat a mall with low to moderate end stores. I liked this mall because of the architecture. There was a carefully constructed glass ceiling. Nineteen-ninety was the first time I had visited the mall. We were in college at the time, all three of us: me, Zay and Vette. Our parents sent us to University of Maryland at College Park. Our parents weren't rolling like that, so we didn't have cars like most of the kids that attended. We didn't stay on the campus; we rode public transportation.

Zay didn't feel like going to school one day and came up with the fancy idea of impressing his new girlfriend by borrowing his momma's new Maxima without her permission. Vette found out about it and threatened to tell if he didn't let her tag along. I was glad he took her for the ride so I could hang too. Me and Vette weren't a pair, but hanging out with her made me feel like we were *more* than just friends. I felt like we were really something. Zay thought he was something too, the way he was mobbing in the Max with the sunroof open, leaned to the side, resting on the driver's side armrest, controlling the wheel with the other hand.

Back then, we didn't play CDs – matter of fact, they were just being introduced. We still played cassette tapes. Zay had just bought that "Momma Said Knock You Out" tape. I liked the tape. One of my favorite songs was Booming Systems. Vette, with her cool ass, liked "The Jingling Baby; Remixed But Still Jingling". We all liked "Around the Way Girl", but Zay seemed to like the song more than all of us. He put the damn song on repeat. The way the system worked, the song would play and when the song reached the end, the play button would click, and the tape would be rewound to the beginning of the song and it would start over. I would say it was a forty minute ride to Pentagon city from the house, and that song played every minute of the ride to the mall. I liked the beat, but after a while I was immune and began listening to the words. Vette was sitting across from me in the backseat. I stared at her and didn't care if she knew it or not. I saw her in a way that I had never seen her before. Arvette was *an around the way girl*. She was plain and sexy, down to earth, nothing to prove and you could tell she was hood a little bit. She sported the bamboo earrings, asymmetric hair style. Some days she wore rings on every finger. She didn't take anything off of them fools around the way. She didn't let anybody call the shots; she was the shot-caller.

She kept it simple. She wasn't into a lot of make-up, she didn't do all the different colors of lipsticks, she was a flavored lip-gloss type of lady. Her lips always glistened when she talked. When it would wear off, she would stop what she was doing to put on a fresh coat. She wasn't high-maintenance, but she always looked good. She could take a long t-shirt, tie the bottom, and mix it with a pair of biking shorts to make it look like an all-original outfit. I liked that. She had lots of style.

I came back to the world. I was no longer living in the nineties. I was back to present day, where Vette clutched the insides of her pockets and I stood thinking about the conversation that would soon take place. I looked down at my watch. I looked at Vette. She knew that it was about that time. We would soon have to move inside if we were going to meet her brother on time. She would be all too happy to be inside, and I would like to believe that was all she thought about for the moment: heat, being warm and in from the winter drift.

We got inside and decided to take the elevator instead of the escalator. I admit, I was a little nervous. I couldn't let her see me sweat. I had to play it off. I looked around, and we were the only ones inside the elevator aside from a young girl. She had her head buried in a book. Seemed she could have cared less about the world around her.

When the elevator stopped, we moved forward while we wondered if the girl would remove herself from the elevator. Ten seconds later, I looked behind me to find the elevator doors had closed and the young girl was nowhere in sight.

We were in the middle of the food court. Straight ahead was the movie theater, with the Sam Goody on the far right. Both Vette and I scanned the immediate sectors looking for Zay, when I heard his familiar voice that seemed to come from above. We looked up to see Zay on his way down the escalator with a light-skinned woman. He smiled big as he waved. I didn't feel good. I didn't feel like smiling. I just wanted to tell him what going on and that was it.

My baby was looking for a suitable table with at least four chairs. Vette stepped off, and we all followed her lead. Zay pulled out the chair for his lady friend. She sat while I stood on the opposite side of the table, pulling the chair for Vette.

Zay sat with a smile still to his face. He looked around. "So, what are we going to eat."

I managed to break a smile. "I'm not hungry." I looked at Arvette and without thinking, she says, "No, baby, we can wait until later." I swallowed really hard because not even I had expected those words to come out of her mouth.

I looked at my friend who had stopped everything to

concentrate on his sister and what had just come out of her mouth. The cat was out the bag. He knew. I didn't want it to come across the way it did, but it was what it was.

Zay took his eyes off his older sister to cut his eyes at me sharply. "Baby," he asked. "She calls you baby?"

I looked at him but I remained silent. I didn't see the point in playing the game. He heard what his sister called me. There was no need to act any other way.

"So," he says. "How long has this been going on?"

We could see the disappointment in his eyes. Vette stood up to him. "It doesn't matter how long it's been. You are not my daddy. If I want to date him, then I will and I have."

Zay looked at me once more. "So that means that you have been *baby* for quite a long time." He scooted away from the table and tapped his lady friend on the shoulder, cueing her to get up from her seat. She didn't know what to think. I could tell that she was a tad uncomfortable, but she scooted from the table nonetheless.

"Zay, wait. Where are you going?"

"Fuck you, Tracey."

"Fuck you back."

He leaned across the table and I was waiting for him. I wasn't about to fight over this, but if he wanted it, I would bring it. "You know what, I trusted you for years, and this is how you repay me. You go behind my back and fuck my sister?"

"You need to get off your fucking soap box, bruh. You know that I would do nothing to hurt your sister. We tried to tell you, but you wouldn't listen."

"Listen, what did you want me to listen to? There was nothing to talk about! I told you that I didn't want you talking to my sister. She was off-limits."

Zay's last statement sent Vette over the edge. She instinctively chimed in. "Off-limits. I'm not a piece of meat – off-limits, like I'm an object!"

I stepped in. I didn't want her to lose her cool. There was too much attention drawn to us. Zay's bodyguards were coming down the escalator. I held my hand up to signal them that things were copacetic. They were coming anyway. Zay was walking away. I walked around the table and grabbed him. He turned around when I told him, "We are in love with each other, bruh. I can't help that. We are happy."

He looked back at his sister, who looked at him with promising eyes. "I am happy, little brother. Tracey makes me happy."

Zay looked at me, disgusted. "I told you to stay away from her." With that, he and his lady friend walked off.

Although we would practice and train – well, I was his trainer – things were not the same. We didn't do the whole get-together at the after-parties. Some of the time, he made the location a secret. If we did do the after-party, he would hang for a few and then mysteriously disappear. I tried to reach out to him, but he was so stubborn. After a while, I gave up.

I continued my relationship with Arvette, and I didn't care if he knew. He didn't ask me about the relationship either. Vette could feel the tension, even though she no longer worked for her brother directly after putting together her real estate business. She would ask me about Zay. She would ask me how we were getting along, even though she knew that we weren't. Some nights she would blame herself for how her brother and I ended up. She would go on and on about how she had come between two friends. There was no way that she could have done that. If anything, I could say that Zay was the one that had come between two friends: her and me. After all, we were *all* friends.

I could tell that she was uneasy about the way everything unraveled, but it wasn't her fault. I tried to explain to her on several instances that we did nothing wrong. "You can't help who you love," I would tell her. She knew that I was right, but I knew that she noticed the change in my relationship with Nyza.

One day I called her from Zimbabwe. I mean, I

was really tripped out; I was having a good time. The culture and history alone was enough to make the average American sit down and think, evaluate his or her own life as they lived it. The same feeling came over me with every visit I would make to a foreign land.

It was natural to want to share everything, with Vette – and why not? That is what people do when they love with each other; they share. All I wanted to do when I made that call to her that night from Zimbabwe was share my sentiments with her, but she seemed uninterested. I was patient. I didn't push. As a matter of fact, I slowed down my conversation, just in case there was something she needed to share with me.

After about fifteen seconds of pure silence, she began to speak. *I will do nothing but listen*, I told myself.

"I don't like how you and my brother have become."

I asked, "What do you mean?"

"You know what I mean, Tracey. You and Zay are not the same."

"Well, people change," I informed.

"Not like that, baby. You and my brother – you couldn't get any closer."

I took a deep breath and let it out. "Vette, I know where this is going, and I will tell you something. I am not going to apologize, and neither should you."

"He feels that we betrayed his trust."

"He betrayed his damned self."

"How do you figure that," she asked.

"He just did. He knows that he can trust me with anything. I told your brother years ago I was in love with you."

"You did?"

"Yes."

"When," she asked.

"A long time ago. His second year in boxing."

I could tell that she was smiling as she talked – maybe blushing, even. "You told him in his second year of his boxing career? We didn't start dating until his third."

I smiled and wondered if *she* could tell. "I know. I had been in love with her long before that. When I told Zay, he was angry. He said "My sister will not date any of my friends, so whatever you think you may feel for my sister, partner, you better let it go."

"Well, he is my brother. Me and him will always be connected. There are no blood ties between you two. It would be easier for Zay to cut you off. I don't want that. You two are good for one another."

She had practically skipped over what I was saying to get back to the same BS. "There is something more on your mind. I can feel it," I said.

"You are right, baby. I do have something to say, but it's nothing you say to someone over the telephone."

"Okay."

"So look, why don't we do it like this; I will be in DC tomorrow and I will be there for three days."

"So you are leaving the day I get back, which is Thursday?"

"Yes, but I talked with my brother and he says that your plane lands in the morning; I don't leave until later that evening."

"Must be important," I said.

"It is."

That was all she wrote. She discontinued our conversation and retired for the evening. Now I would have been lying if I'd said I could wait. I didn't want to wait, but in this instance, I had no choice but to wait. I knew that soon as I got back from Africa, I would find her.

Thursday 1:37 pm

I was on the Metro Blue line, leaving District Heights subway station. District Heights was down the street from my house and right next to the Mazza Gallery Mall. The subway station was right off of Wisconsin Avenue. If you traveled East, you would run into Georgetown.

I thought about only one thing while I was onboard the Metro: seeing Vette. The attendant announced our next stop, Metro Center, which was where I was supposed to meet my lady. When I would see her, I knew what I would tell her. I would tell her how much I loved her, missed and wanted to marry her, but when I got off the train I had an uneasy feeling in my stomach – especially when I saw her. She had on a long, black, wool sweater with a hood. She had on those black, suede boots with the fur on top. Her fitted jeans were tucked into the boots.

She looked so sexy to me. We had no plans. I just wanted to be with her and nothing more.

I wrapped my arms around her. I intended to pour as much love as I could into my embrace. With as much as I poured in, I couldn't feel the return. She was hiding something from me. Sure she said that we needed to talk, but there was something wrong, something she wanted to tell me but didn't know how. I didn't ask. I knew that I would find out if I just held on long enough.

In the busy Metro Station, we stood us two like no one else was watching us. They weren't paying attention to us. They had other things going on in their lives. They had things to do, people to attend to. I had things to attend to also. Arvette had become my whole world. I had to let her know what an inspiration she had become, but when I was ready to divulge, she shut me down.

The platform lights would flash on the platform to signal all passengers that next train was coming soon. The lights were flashing. Most of the patrons stepped back, but I didn't feel like moving. This was it. Vette was about to tell me what she had to tell me. I could feel it. The air was thick. I felt cool around the neck, my hands were in my pocket as I prepared myself for whatever that was about to come.

There was a slight rumble coming from the tunnel, but I couldn't see the light from the train. My hands were still in my pocket. Vette grabbed my wrists as if we were holding hands. I didn't feel like holding her hands right then and there. I looked down at the flashing lights. People were preparing to board the train. I looked at Vette, and she stared deep into my eyes. She stared so deep I could feel it. My heart was beating so fast.

"Tracey."

"Yeah,"

"I just want you to know that I love you."

"Vette, baby, just get to the point."

"I love you, Tracey." The water began to well in her eyes. My heart beat faster. I knew that it could not be good. The rumbling from the tunnel was louder; it seemed that the rumbling was in my stomach. I could see the light, which meant the train was only a few seconds from us. I pulled her back a couple of steps. Separate crowds of people formed around us awaiting the train. I could feel the back draft of wind from the tunnel. The train was here. We didn't move as the train came to a stop. The passengers, with their briefcases and travel bags, crossed the platform onto the train with haste. Still, Vette and I remained in the same position that we had been in.

"What is wrong baby? What do you have to say?"

Arvette let go of my wrists and used her hands to cover her face as she sobbed. I immediately took my hands out of my pockets and wrapped my arms around her. I held her like I didn't want to ever let go. I felt like I would have to let go, whether I wanted to or not.

She wiped her eyes and looked at me. "Tracey, I'm pregnant."

"Okay, that is good, I want kids." I smiled. "I want kids with you."

She wasn't smiling back at me. My joy turned to sadness. "Tracey, you're not the father." She pushed me away. At that same time I heard the warning chimes from the train, which meant that the passenger doors were about to close. Arvette turned around swiftly and stepped onboard the train. I had no time to react. The doors closed before I could take a step. I didn't question her further, nor did I attempt to contact her. I could say that our relationship ended on that note.

Zay

We both stood there looking in the mirror. I didn't want to be up, and she didn't seem to mind. She was the morning type; me I was the kid in school that dreamed about working for myself so I could wake up whenever I felt like it. Even when I went across the country to fight, I would insist on taking the tour van so that I could sleep.

"Maybe we should go and wake my sister."

"Yeah, that girl sleeps like a rock."

Tammy folded her arms across her chest and turned about. I continued to wash my face. I took my time, and before I knew it Vette was in my room looking for a head scarf. It was funny to me. As old as we were, things hadn't changed much. We still carried on like we did when we were little. She would still stick her tongue out at me when she passed me, and she would still make funny faces at me just because. I think I appreciated those moments even moreso because it made me feel like we were still close. I loved my sister.

Tracey pulled up as we were leaving. Vette hopped in his ride and we tailed them to Regan International. Tracey did most of the work. I could see them being together. I could see how happy my sister was with Tracey. I was mad at myself when I thought about how I stood in the way of their progress, how my sister felt she had to lie to the father of her child to protect my feelings. She knew that if she told Tracey about the baby that he would be there. Nothing would stop him. That was such an unselfish act on her part, but I was the one who was so damn selfish. I had a lot of making up to do.

Tammy and Arvette were saying their goodbyes. I was happy that they go along so well. I'd hoped that they would hit it off well. Neither of the two had many friends. They were my two of my favorite people. I used to call my sister my other half, but I knew that it was time for her to pass the title to Tammy. Tracey had a position for her. They would be good to and for each other.

After Tammy walked off teary-eyed, I stepped up to bat. I wanted to get mine in to save Tracey for last. It was only right. I smiled. My sister smiled back. I grabbed her hand. She smiled and said, "Thank you, Zay."

"No need to thank me. I wasn't being a good little brother."

"You know, it's funny, Zay, you are the little brother but I have always felt like you were the oldest."

"I'm not the oldest, though. You were always the one that held me down."

"I didn't intend for it to be that way. I guess it was something that just happened."

"I know I said it before but I am saying it again; I'm sorry, Vette."

"It's okay, Zay."

"No, it's not, sis." I looked over to Tracey. "It's not okay. I know you love him, and if I had looked past myself, I would have known that a long time ago."

She smiled big. "You are right, I do love him. I have loved him for a long time."

"He is my niece's father. You make sure he does right."

"You know he is going to do right. I know what to do if he starts acting brand new." She smiled at me once more. "You remember the reputation that I had."

I nodded. "Yeah, I remember."

"Well you know it was well-earned, right?"

My sister when she was younger had this reputation for beating up boys – especially her boyfriends. Even though she was joking, I knew what she was getting at. She was saying that she would kick Tracey's ass before she would let him disrespect what they had going on. I nodded. There was nothing left to say.

"You be safe, sis. I wish you the best. You keep working on the things that you want in life. It will all come true." I touched her chin and lifted it so that our eyes could meet. "You take good care of Tracey. He is a good man."

Zay

I was restless most of the time. I didn't do planes. Not even a little bit. There were things on the plane to keep us occupied. I could've slept through most of the flight, but I didn't. I found that I would often wake to ear pain. It would feel like pins and needles. I couldn't explain it, but my ears would really hurt after a nap on the plane. For that reason, I would do what I needed to do to stay up. I mean, I watched movies, I worked crossword puzzles, and I read magazines. That twelve hour flight to Korea did something to me. To top it off, we sat in the emergency evacuation section of the plane and there was a man of Arabic decent. There were so many things that went through my mind. I tried to put myself at ease, but at the same time I couldn't allow myself to go to sleep. I watched him every time he made a move, but then that got old, so I pulled out my MP3 player and listened to one of my playlists. Tammy was fast asleep; this was nothing to her. As a matter of fact, that may have been the most rest she got all at once. I didn't mess with her. I noticed how peaceful she looked. I thought about the bitch she could be, and lastly I thought about the brute she was inside the ring.

Nat sat in the row beside us. She was one of those health nuts. She was always trying to introduce some new kind of trail mix or supplement to us. Usually when I'd see her, she'd either have a bottle of water of one of those fruit juices without the sugars or additives. Nat loved to exercise. She was serious about it, too. It was nothing for her to do iron mikes for thirty minutes straight; running ten miles a day, no problem. I remember how Tammy would be so tired after a session with Nat. I thought that she was putting on just a little to get some sympathy until I sat in on one of their sessions.

When I looked at her, she didn't strike me as someone who could really bring it. I mean, she was short in every sense of the word. Her legs were short, and so were her arms. She had this short hair cut, a lot like a dude – I thought she was a little dude at first. Looking into her face, it was hard to tell her gender; her skin was a bronze color, and she had the face structure of an El Salvadorian. She had a hint of an accent. I couldn't tell what type, but she had to be mixed with something. She was a no nonsense type of person. She didn't do a whole lot of

Tammy

Right outside of baggage claims was an aged but distinguished-looking gentleman. He was Asian, and you could tell he had some years on him. He was pretty short and slim. He was holding a sign with my name on it. I saw it before Zay did. I grabbed his arm and pulled him in the man's direction. When I looked at him again there were two ladies with him. When we got close enough, I extended my hand to greet him, "Frank?"

"Ms. Phillips," he returned. He smiled big and took a slight bow. He quickly pivoted to the left. "This is Miss Yim, she will be your tour guide. This is Miss Lee, she will be your translator. Where ever you go, she will go."

The ladies smiled and shook hands elatedly. "Welcome to Korea." Their people took turns shaking hands with my people, and from there the three Nationals led us to our vehicles. The Airport was so clean. They had duty-free stores all throughout. They had my kind of stores too: Blvgari, Fendi, Gucci, and Salvatore Ferragamo. Zay had his eyes on the Cartier shop. We walked a little further behind the fast walking Koreans. Our welcoming party wasn't the only one in a hurry; the whole airport seemed to be rushing. I mean, these people walked really fast, and they seem to have no time to avoid others in their path. They bumped into each other without rendering any type of verbal courtesy.

I looked around some more and saw more boutiques and shops within the airport. They even sold new cars inside the airport. They had Kias, Hyundais, even Peugeots. Zay wasn't surprised; after all, he had been there before. I'm sure things had changed, but maybe not by a lot.

Outside, we were guided to our vehicles. My staff got inside of a black Yukon Denali, while me, my man, the tour guide, and the translator got inside of a black Cadillac Escalade. The seats in the back of the truck were different. There were two rows in the back, but the two rows faced each other. Ms. Yim and Ms Lee sat on one side, and Zay and I sat on the other side.

I'd been tired when I stepped off the plane, but I wasn't tired any more. I was excited. The ladies who sat across from us seemed to smile a lot. They seemed to be nice girls. I'd been told not to try to guess a Korean's age. They often appeared to be younger than what they really are. They were both petite and looked no older than twenty-three years old. I read that Koreans' birthdays are different from Americans'. Americans are born to the parents, and one year later they turn a year old. A Korean is considered one year old the day that he or she is born. One year later marks their second birthday.

The driver turned onto a main street. The lady then turned to Zay. "Welcome to Korea," she greeted. That was one thing I could say about the Koreans; they really wanted you to feel welcomed.

Our greeting party's enunciation was crisp and clear, like English was their first language. With some of the other Nationals, it was hard for me to understand what they were saying. The lady directly across from us smiled. I didn't think she and Zay had been formally introduced.

"My name is Hung Yo Yim." She extended her hand. "What is your name," she asked.

Zay seemed a little nervous. Nonetheless, he extended his hand, gave a clean shake and told her his name. "Nyza Stevenson."

"Your name, it sounds familiar. It is like that of a famous name. Like a movie star."

I chimed in. "Or you mean like a boxer."

"A boxer," she said, puzzled.

"Yes, a boxer – a world champion, even."

Her face lit up. "Oh, Zay Stevenson, the boxer who fought years ago at the sports complex?"

Zay wasn't impressed. He nodded his head. I think I was more excited than he could have ever been upon her discovery.

She looked at me. "So, you are Ms. Phillips?"

I smiled and nodded at the same time. "I am," I confirmed.

"Now, is it Mrs., Ms., or Miss." *What difference does it make?* "Well, I am not married." I looked over at Zay tersely. "So, you can't call me a Mrs."

She looked at Zay just like I did. "Well, what are you waiting for? This is a lovely lady, and she is rich. You don't want a lady like this?" She smiled but I know that Zay wasn't amused. He didn't like pressure, and he didn't like when people tried to make him do things.

"Well, Miss Phillips, I will be your tour guide."

Zay chimed in, "We got that already; you are going to be the tour guide."

I wanted to pinch him for displaying his funky attitude. He was like that sometimes. He was a Cancer, and he was true to his sign. Sometimes it was a turn-on to witness his rough side. Other times it was a turn-off because, in my opinion, some of his comments were unwarranted. His personal attacks were sometimes random. You never knew when it was coming. He was used to being the boss. I wouldn't say that he had a great ego problem, but he was just used to having things his way. They say that money does that do to you, but from what I know about my man, money had little to do with his attitude. They said that Zay was the same person yesterday as he was twenty years ago.

Zay wore his little boy frown for the lady. "So where are we going now?"

"We are taking you to your hotel, sir." The tour guide clarified things for Zay. "Like I said, I am your tour guide. I am from Pusan, Korea, and I am a student at Yonsei University."

"Really," Zay asked, disinterested.

"Yes. During your stay here in Korea, I will be in the same hotel with you, so if you want to do something or go someplace, I will be just rooms away."

"So, you are like our chaperone?"

I leaned back and gave him the dirty face. He smiled.

"No, sir. I just want you and," he hesitated, "Miss Phillips to be comfortable. I want you to know all there is to know about our country. I want you to see all that you can see."

I leaned forward and asked eagerly, "What is the food like?"

Ms. Yim got excited all over again. "Well we will be staying in Seoul, which, as you know, is the capital. There you will find a lot of the food to be like the food in America." She looked to the ceiling of the SUV before naming several well-known American restaurants. "There is an Outback Steakhouse and there is lots of shopping."

The student looked at my bag and then pulled on the straps. "So you like handbags?"

I smiled big. "I do. I love them." I could see Zay rolling his eyes.

"You will find all kinds of handbags in Seoul."

"How about massages? I could really use a good massage."

Right about then, Zay turned to me. I knew that he would be a little touched behind my request. He likes to give me massages – he has good hands but he doesn't always do it quite like I like it.

Ms. Yim nodded. "Yes," she said sharply. "There are several places to get a massage, but you want to go to Total Beauty and Spa. You can lose yourself in there for half of the day."

My eyes got big, I could feel it. "Half of the day," I asked for confirmation.

"Correct. You will be there most of the day. They have lots of activities. They do the facial scrubs, avocado masks, pedicures, manicures, and so much more."

I was excited. Even though I had just come down from the flight, I could go for sitting in the spa for the rest of the day. That would relax me well enough to put me to bed early for the night.

Zay looked out the window. I was sure that he had

tuned us out. Yim continued to talk. "There are so many ways for a woman to get pampered. This is so important to a woman. In Korea, we believe in stimulation and relaxation. For the most part, we benefit from a stress-free life. You won't see many Koreans get upset."

"The streets are very clean," I said.

"We take good care of what we have. You will also notice that the crime rate is considered one of the lowest in the world. Koreans have lots of respect for human life."

The lady went on and was well-informed. She went on to talk about respect and how the people bow to each other. Usually, the more youthful person will initiate the bow. It is also customary for the Koreans to bow to guests in their country.

Hung was a pretty girl. She was twenty years old, and, like she said, she was a college student. Her hair was long, black, and silky. She had a striking personality. She appeared to be reserved but not too withdrawn. I liked her mild Asian features. Looking at her, you might assume that that her parents might not both have been of the same nationality. I wanted to ask, but I wouldn't. I did have manners. That would have been just plain, old rude.

The guide was very enthusiastic. I asked her more about college, and she explained to me and Zay.

"Education is very big in my country. A lot of the monies go towards education, and it's improved over the years."

"Education," Zay asked.

"No, money," She said. The national looked to the top corners of her eye lids before she changed her answer. "Well, actually, both education and money have improved. Seven years ago Korean money wasn't worth much, but now our economy is stronger than ever. Of course, with more money lots of things improve, like education."

"How much is your money worth compared to the American dollar?"

"Well, years ago the American dollar was worth more than the Korean won. But the won is equivalent to the dollar."

"So your money is called the won?" Zay asked. If he had read the welcome packet, he would have known this, or maybe he was just trying to make conversation with her.

She went on to explain her money. "Yes sir, we use won." She leaned forward and tapped Zay on the leg. I looked at her. That was a freebie. I wasn't going to let her tap my man too many times on the leg. "I don't know if you know about our won rate or not, but it fluctuates; like today, the won rate is one thousand won to the dollar, which means the won is worth the same as the dollar." Zay nodded his head. "One thousand won is like… one hundred pennies or one folding dollar bill."

"I understand," Zay said.

"Okay, so five thousand won is like five dollars." Yim

went on to explain the won rate of exchange. She said that we needed to know the won rate because it changes daily.

"Make sure that you check the won rate every day that you are here. Depending on the day, it could be more or less."

"Oh don't worry, we will do that," my man assured her.

I was watching home girl to see if she would hit Zay on the leg again. She didn't though.

"Korea is on a fixed budget, as is the United States. The economy is driven by the education rates. Did you know that twenty-eight point seven percent of Koreans go to college? Those who do not go to college enlist in the Republic of Korea Army. All Korean males have to join the army; they have absolutely no choice, unlike in the U.S. The only other option they may have is to join the United States Army under the KATUSA program."

"What program?" I asked.

"The Korean Augmenter to the United States Army, is what KATUSA stands for. They have to do at least two years in the service. Some do more time in the service."

Zay nodded, and I did too. Her English was very good, which helped a lot, I must say. She told us lots of stories, which made the long ride more enjoyable.

"You mentioned a massage, Ms. Phillips?"

I smiled. "I did. That sounds so good." I needed to

relax. I knew that Nat would break me off the next day. It would be nice to relax, especially after such a long trip.

"Okay, if that is what you still want to do, we can stop right now. We are only minutes away from the spa I told you about previously."

Zay stared out of the dark windows. Yim told us that we were in the heart of Seoul. We were in the middle of a city called Itewon. Like she said, there were lots of American restaurants. We noticed lots of shopping stands and lots of Americans. Some had on plain clothes and others had on Army uniforms. I learned that there was a military base not far from the hotel.

I knew that Zay could see it on my face. I was tired. By my watch, it was 10:30 at night in the States. Usually I would be in the bed by this time, but in Korea it was early afternoon. The Koreans were small people, for the most part. They were so busy, with their cell phones and bags; some of them had one on each shoulder. There were peddlers on the hustle, vendors manning their stands, and lots of traffic between the stop lights. There were just as many people crossing on feet as there were cars making it past intersections. It was amazing how busy the section was. I wasn't used to that, nor did I think I could get used to it. The big signs everywhere made the Itewon strip look tacky. People walked shoulder to shoulder, brushing others while passing. Hung says not to be offended when people bump us in passing without apology. She said that

Koreans are generally in a hurry. She warned us not to show the bottoms of our shoes to the Koreans. She said that it's not good to motion people towards us with our fingers. The American signal for come here is considered rude and offensive. Hung said that we were to hold our hands with our fingers pointed towards the ground while making a sweeping motion; that was the proper way to signal someone for assistance.

Zay didn't say much. He did more looking than anything else. We turned into an alley.

"My goodness, the alleys are narrow." I could believe that the wide SUV actually fit in the alley. I realized how greedy we Americans are. We drive Hummers and large SUVs. Most of the time, we would drive these vehicles on a regular basis. We would drive these trucks to work every day. There would be no one else in the car except for the driver. Here in Asia, the people are so conservative. They did have SUVs, but the largest SUV that I had seen so far was a vehicle called the Rexton. The Rexton was smaller than a mid-sized American SUV. It was smaller than a Chevy Trailblazer, but it was still the largest Korean SUV that I'd seen. They had a lot of small cars and vans here. Most of the vehicles were economical. I could say that I liked the way they rolled. They were a conservative people, for the most part. Again, it made me realize how spoiled we Americans are.

The driver stopped in front of a building with a glass

front. There were ladies in front soaking their hands in Petri dishes. Hung popped her seatbelt. She looked at me and asked, "Are you ready?"

"Sure."

"This is the massage parlor that I was telling you about."

I smiled big. I could certainly use a massage.

"Do you want one too, sir?"

"Yes," I answered for him. He could use a massage. He would like it.

Zay

We had a late lunch at Outback Steak House. Surprisingly, the food tasted the same. Afterwards, the driver took us to a hotel that sat on top of big hill overlooking the entire city. Our bags were put into the room for us. I couldn't wait for them to leave. Hung stayed in the room next to us. She ran down the itinerary for us before she left. I watched her go into the adjacent room to our left. I hated it for her. The way that we get, man, we could make a lot of noise at times.

I was ready, too. We hadn't had sex in about three days, which was unlike us. We were everyday people. If a day went by without sex, something was wrong. Tammy had been stressing over this trip. This upcoming fight was a big one for her. The chick she was about to fight was undefeated. The pressure was there. I'd seen her opponent fight before, she was no punk. I wasn't afraid that my baby couldn't knock her ass out, but it wouldn't be an easy win – she was not to be underestimated.

That massage did it for her. She was really loose. Baby talked and smiled a little more, too. After she laid out her clothes for the next day, the first thing she wanted to do was get in the shower. Usually, I'd get in with her, but when I did, it would be for shower sex. It wasn't for the shower; she liked the water to be scorching. I like to be comfortable with everything I do. She liked the water to be on hell when she took a bath. It would be so hot, I would feel ready to pass out.

I laid in the bed on my back with my arms folded behind my head. She had just turned the shower on. I lay content, didn't quite feel like the shower sex but it was nice to think about – that real good shower sex, the kind where you have to contort your body to hit it right, to ensure satisfaction. I wanted to lay her down and do it to her real good. I just wanted to tear her ass up. I wanted to sex her slow until I worked up a good rhythm, getting progressively faster. I could bang it out until I was hitting bottom, or until she made those hollering noises. Yeah, I would slow it down then, until she calmed down. I would put her in some kind of position so that I could go deep, make it hurt for a little while.

I took a deep breath and let it out. I was making myself horny just thinking about what we do. I let her do her thing. The shower was still running. The bathroom door was open and the steam rolled in. I smiled, yeah, she was getting it. She could have that hot-ass shower by herself. I would take mine later.

Shortly after the water went off, she came in the room wearing a wife beater and her Spongebob boxers. Funny, but I loved to see her walking her sexy ass around in those boxers. She walked barefoot across the wood floor. Her booty shook with every step she took.

"You and those shorts," I said.

She looked down at the shorts and laughed. "I love Spongebob. If I could, I would marry Spongebob," she said.

"You would marry him, huh?"

"Yep," she smiled.

"Well, what about me?"

She touched her index finger to her chin and twisted her mouth, like she was thinking hard about what I just asked her. "Well, I guess if Spongebob fell off the face of the earth, you would do."

She got in the bed and laid her head on my chest. I was on hard instantly. She curled up and got comfortable. "Ooh," she said after reaching down to feel me. "Somebody else is happy to see me." She then put her arms around me like a little girl would do to her daddy. I wrapped one arm around her waist. I could taste the shower gel when I kissed her neck. Her hair was wet and smelled like oranges. Baby was tired; I could see it in her face. I kissed on the face and rubbed her booty. She wiggled just a little more.

"Get some sleep, baby."

"I'm sorry baby, but thank you for understanding. I am so tired. Maybe tomorrow."

"Don't worry about it, baby. That ain't what our relationship is all about."

"I know." She smiled big and looked up at me. "You know I got training tomorrow." I nodded. "You know how horny I get after I train."

She wasn't lying. After she would spar or train, she would want to have sex all night long. She couldn't get enough. Those were the nights we usually explored the different options. I found her more appealing because of her adventurous side. She wasn't afraid to try new things. I think that I was the shy one, though I thought I had done it all until I met her. I liked how she would size me up like she could take me. She knew better, but sometimes I would let her think that she could.

I eased my way out of the bed. I hated to wake her, but I wanted her to be comfortable, so I tapped her so that she could get under the covers. She crawled under the covers and leaned over to give me a quick hug. "Goodnight, baby."

I thought that she would nap and wake in few hours, but she slept the rest of the afternoon. I thought about me and her as we lay. She was so pretty to me; I'm not just talking about the outside, she was people beautiful to me. Before, I would call her crazy and I meant it. I thought she was thrown off some, but after getting to know her I think that I misunderstood her. She wanted what most people wanted: to be understood and loved. Once I looked deep enough, I found the window to her soul. I found the lost episodes of her emotions. I guess when it comes down to it, we all wanted to experience true happiness. What I had to learn is that we have to switch things up sometimes. It's not good to live life the same way that you've been living all your life. I had to learn that. Life is no fun without changes, and you have to know when to make them and make certain that the changes are good and needful ones.

My sister was messing with me. She told me that the Jones would come down hard on me. She told me that when it came down on me, I would change, and that there would be nothing I could do about it. "That love Jones is going catch up with you one day little brother. You can only run for so long." She was right. I ran all of my adult life, and I think I had finally run out of gas.

In that moment, I got scared. I wondered if love meant something bad for me. After all the things I did to all the women who believed that they loved me. The same women I lied to when I told them that I loved them back. I made them believe that I was true when I never had been. Their asses got played like a deck of cards. Thinking about all the lies I'd told, I remembered how I stepped on women's feelings and wondered if love was coming to avenge all the hopeless love-seekers. I never took a woman for serious until a couple of months ago. I was a love-hater, I admit it, but I have changed in ways I never pictured. Sometimes it seemed like I stepped outside of myself. I could see two of myself. I could see the old me and I could see the new me. Was I really that much of an asshole? I said that I love my sister and treated her so bad a couple of weeks ago. I call her my other baby. She had something that most people searched for. She had real love. I knew that Tracey was a good dude. I knew that he wouldn't play with my sister. He wouldn't play with her heart. He loved me as a brother and I trusted him. I trusted him with everything, even my sister. I just didn't want them to be together for my own selfish reasons. She had a baby by him and couldn't tell him to protect him from me. She terminated her relationship with her man because of me. She saw how it affected my relationship with him.

I should be glad that my best friend is my niece's father, and not somebody else. I'd even treated him badly too. They didn't deserve that.

I looked at Tammerine as she opened and closed her cat-like eyes. She'd made me discover so much in such a short time. She wasn't intimidated like most women. She didn't run from me. She put my arrogance and supremacy on display for me to notice. She wanted to make sure that

I understood who I was. *I owe a lot of people. I owe a lot of people big.* I owed myself. I owed it to myself to start being a better person. I had gotten off to a good start. I just hoped that people could forgive me – I needed love to forgive me. I needed love to pardon me, excuse me for reform and good behavior. If love wouldn't pardon me, then maybe it would reduce my sentence.

It was one in the morning, but I felt like I should have been up. I turned on the television. Tammy was still sleeping. I flipped through lots of Korean stations, some Armed Forces Network Channels, and finally I found a football game. I chuckled lightly. *One in the morning and I'm watching a football game.*

I looked over at my baby, who was fast asleep. She was laid in the fetal position, which delineates shyness and sensitivity. The sleep experts say that sleep patterns reveal your personality traits and I believe them. Tammerine was the type of person with a lot of mouth and would be what you consider a stand-up woman, but she was a shy kind of person. That woman was very sensitive when it comes to some things. She played the role because it was easier to do. She played the role because she didn't want me knowing her weaknesses.

Me, I preferred to sleep on my stomach often, and that denotes suspicion; I'm very suspicious. I'm the type who always looks over both shoulders, just because. I had a lot of bad traits that I was trying to make up for, and Tammy loved me anyway. I have been told that being in love and truly loving someone is knowing the worst part of that person.

I watched her as she trained. Nat was on it and didn't take any slack from Tammy. I admired her as she sent flurries at her trainer. Tammerine was on it. For two minutes, Nat challenged her with one-two combos, and from there, she went with the one-two-three-fours. From there, Nat went with one-twos and slipping and coming back with a three four. They went at it with gloves and mitts, and from there Nat put my champion on the speed bag. Hitting the heavy bag was a no-brainer. I even stood by as the toy soldier yelled in her face like a drill sergeant. That was what I called Tammy's trainer: Toy Soldier. Nat looked like a member of the militia. The first impressions are usually lasting ones. The first time I saw the short woman, I checked her out from head to toe. Her eyes were slightly slanted, she had that medium, dark complexion with short hair – her hair was shorter than mine. She was wearing a navy green sports bra with cut-off fatigue pants. She was buff, too. I was amazed a little bit. I couldn't figure her out. I didn't know what she liked, and it was better that I didn't. I didn't like to judge, but at the same time, things were suspect. I didn't know how to take her.

She was a little more aggressive than the most aggressive females I've had the pleasure of meeting.

As short as she was, she could still hang with Tammy, who stood about seven inches taller. Just picture a dark-skinned woman with blonde hair, cut Army style. She could probably pull more women than the average brother who had his act together.

When I got tired of watching the sparring session, I tip-toed out and made my way around. I was told earlier that that there was a fully accessible weight room, a sauna, a pool, and a spa. I decided to check out the weight room. It was a cool, little weight room with all the latest Nautilus Technology – nicer than some of the weight rooms I've trained in. I was taken back to the earlier days when I used to box; I would train before my fights using two hundred eighty-five pounds as a warm up. I would wear my tank tops a size too small – for motivation. I hadn't pushed even two hundred twenty-five pounds in years. I wasn't intimidated by the weight; I just didn't know how much my shoulder could support. Doctor's orders; he said nothing over one hundred fifty pounds.

In the weight room, I looked around until I found a Smith machine. Smith machines were good because they were designed to assist you with some of the weight. The trick was to make you feel like you were the bearer of all the weight. The power bar itself weighed forty-five pounds. After adding fifty-five pounds on each side, I was looking at lifting one hundred fifty-five pounds. I lay on my back, took a few deep breaths, and got my head right. One hundred fifty pounds was not a lot of weight, but, like I said, I hadn't lifted that much weight in a while. I didn't know how much weight my shoulder could support. I couldn't sustain yet another injury. It would not be good for me at all. My shoulder didn't pop, nor did it lock as I lifted the weight. Each repetition was a smooth one. The reps were easy and free-flowing. I was satisfied with myself – even impressed a little. Before I knew anything, I was on my feet adding fifty more pounds to the weight bar. Two hundred five pounds and I didn't feel a thing. There was no resistance on my body's part, but I knew I wouldn't push my luck. Doctors don't know shit. I remember the doc told me that I wouldn't be able to lift more than one hundred fifty pounds without surgery and there I was, lifting two hundred five pounds with no problems. I smiled. I felt so good. Momma said that doctors are liars. Lots of them think that they are gods when they are not. Some of them adopt the God complex, thinking that they predict just how much time you have left on this earth. They would kill me because their word was supposed to be law.

A brother didn't quit; I was too happy to be using free-weights. I felt a sense of accomplishment. Once I got up from the bench, there was a black chick, hair braided backwards, suited and laced up. I heard that a lot of people would go there to train. She would be hard to miss. She would stick out like a sore thumb no matter the environment; besides that, she was the only other sprinkle of color in the whole complex. The Koreans there were a sight to look at. Most of them were on the cardio machines; treadmills and such. They were a thin people.

Tammerine

I'd sparred for about a good eight rounds when Nat called it a wrap. She was taking my gloves off and was about to unwrap my hands when Tischena, my opponent, walked in. We had two more days before the main event. I looked at her and looked away. I didn't have the time for no tiny cat fight. *She is ugly. I don't like to call people ugly, but dammit, she looks bad.* I looked at her again and looked away quickly to avoid confrontation. I didn't have the time for bullshit cat fights.

She was a few years younger than me. I had been holding the Championship belt for a few years, so of course Tischena thought that I was washed up. She thought that she was good enough to take me. Sister had another thing coming to her. She didn't know how good I felt. I'd flown thousands of miles to fight, I was with my man, and I was feeling better than I had ever felt. *I am going to beat this bitch's ass.*

As I walked past, I wondered where Zay was. He started out here watching us, and then he'd wandered off. My opponent giggled after I passed. I didn't turn around, I didn't acknowledge her. I didn't want to give her the satisfaction. Nat could sense my frustration. She had spent enough time with me to know what I would pass and what I would take.

"She is going to try and start some shit with you, Nichelle, but don't give in to her," Nat said. The girl and her crew stopped walking. She was staring at me, I could feel her. She had her gloves resting on the bottom rope.

"You finished training already?" Tischena asked.

Electing to take Nat's advice, I didn't say anything.

"You better do more than that if you plan to beat me."

I couldn't resist. I could feel Nat's hand on my arm but it was too late; I couldn't resist. "You know what, you little scrub? I am the champ. Me, I am the one. There can only be one me. You are trying to get what I got!" Nat looked at me.

"Whatever; you ain't shit, bitch."

I laughed it off. She was a joke to me. We started to walk off when she got started once more. "Go ahead and laugh. You better watch his fine ass; I saw him in the weight room getting busy. I started to give him my number, but I thought I should wait until after I beat yo ass."

I stopped and turned around. Nat didn't stop though. She grabbed me firmly by the arm and pulled me along. Once the Haitian girl got my attention, she was satisfied – that was all she wanted. She just wanted to get my attention. She laughed loudly and walked off. *Ghetto bitch*, I said to myself.

As a part of my boxing contract, I am required to do so much community service and give so much time and or monies to charities. Giving my time for community service was something that I liked to do. No one had to make me do it. Even if it wasn't a part of the contract, I would have done it on my own. You can't the beat the feeling and spirit of giving. On top of all of that, giving looked good on the books, and from a business perspective, I could claim tax deductions for the charities and other odd factions that I gave to on a regular basis. It was funny like that. The way the government is designed, the more money you make, the more you have to give away or be penalized for it, but what the smart people understand is that what you give, you often get back, so really, you suffer no losses.

Charity work was well worth all the effort I would put in. Hung did all the talking for me and Zay at a local Korean orphanage. This orphanage was approximately three miles from the Osan Airbase. In this district, there were lots of Americans, most of them in plain clothes. Most of them had bags in their hands. All the females carried designer handbags; I could tell that lots of the bags were knock-offs at first glance.

We showed up with large, red, felt-like bags packed with gifts. We handled them up the stairs, and at the top of the steps, we sat the bags down so that we could take of our shoes. Even though I had taken a shower and was wearing a clean pair of sweats, I still felt like the same, tired, old lady. Hung finished talking to the lady who had originally pointed to the floor when we'd reached the top of the stairs.

"You have to take your shoes off, Ms Phillips; Mr. Phillips." I smiled as Zay grimaced. "You will have to walk in your socks, or you can you put on a pair of house slippers." She pointed to the box next to the doorjamb.

There were at least six pairs of house shoes, but I wasn't jiving with that. I decided to walk around in my socks. Hung didn't put on the shoes either. Zay and my bodyguards followed my lead. As we walked, Hung went on to tell me about the floors.

"I love the floors. The floors are heated by what are called flues. They are pipes built underneath the floor. In some domiciles, you will find that the flues are heated by water. These heated pipes, heat the floor, which heats the room. Americans say that heat rises."

I liked the concept, and it seemed cost-efficient. I liked how they did some of the things in Korea, but I still wasn't too comfortable walking around in my socks.

Hung looked back to us as we walked up yet another set of steps.

"Also, you will find that Korean customs promote togetherness. You will not find many kitchen tables larger than twenty-four inches by thirty six." The tables were very low to the floor. The Koreans sat on the floor Indian style when they ate their meals; it was much different from the American standard of life.

I found it very awkward to walk the floor in a strange place with my shoes off. I could hear the children before I saw them. They were running wild, but they were the cutest kids. I got all mushy on the inside, just thinking about the day when I would have a little one to call my own. The kids came closer, and the first commonality that I noticed was that they all had big heads. Now, generally, kids have larger heads compared to the rest of their bodies, but the Koreans just have large heads, period.

It didn't matter how large their heads were, I just wanted to hug and kiss all of them. I wanted them to feel some love. Those children had an optimistic glow. I could tell that they were cared for. They didn't know why they were there – some of them. Some of them thought that they belonged there; that was where they were supposed to be. The older ones seemed a little bitter. They knew why they were there. They knew what they wanted. They wanted and needed to be a part of a family. Some of them were as old as thirteen. They had been told that the older they got, the less of a chance they would stand of getting adopted by a family.

Zay stood beside me and clutched my hand. I clutched his back. Hung told us that it was time to pass out the gifts. Zay let my hand go so that he could secure the red bag. I had only two colors of wrapping; red and blue. All the gifts wrapped in blue paper were for the boys, and the gifts wrapped with red paper were for the girls. Hung passed me a list with all the students' names on it. She stood alongside me to help me with the pronunciation of the names when I needed it. She also was there to let me know if the names were male or female. Some of them I could figure out. As I called a girl's name, Zay picked a red box.

It was such a great feeling on the inside to be doing what I was doing. I watched the kids' faces light up as I called their names one by one. It didn't matter what was in the boxes, though me and Zay had bought some pretty expensive gifts. Price didn't matter; we just wanted to do our part to touch someone in a special way.

Each child bowed when they came forward to receive their gifts. I would return the bow, though Hung told me that it wasn't necessary. Zay, too would bend at the waist with a smile. We were enjoying this and felt blessed to have been a part of this.

Once the red bag had been emptied, one of the ladies from the orphanage stood before the kids and started saying things to them. Of course I couldn't make out what was being said, but the kids were intrigued. Their little faces lit up at once. The kids started speaking amongst each other while others started swinging their arms like they were boxing. Zay looked at me and started smiling. "I guess she told the kids that you are nice with them hands."

I leaned over to Hung, who was smiling, herself.

"What did she say to the children?"

"She told them that you are the strongest woman in the world and that you will be fighting in our country."

I smiled. That was cute. I looked at the children once more. Zay went to help the little boys open their boxes. One of them had a remote control car nearly as big as he was. He couldn't figure out how to make it work.

"You will need batteries," Zay said.

"What size will you need, Mr. Stevenson? There are plenty here."

I caught myself stuck in time. I wasn't caught up in a day dream; I had zoned out for a brief period. I thought about how much we took for granted. We were spoiled as Americans. The Koreans were simple. These people were well-to-do and didn't seem to make a big deal out of the things that we as Americans would fight over. The children in the orphanage didn't require much. They wanted what all of us would require as people: love, kindness, and affection. Some of the children referred to the others as brother or sister. For some of them, they knew that they were not like the others; they knew they were not kin, but to them, they were all family. There were at least two hundred of them.

I snapped out of it. I was back in present day. The children had only one present apiece, but they were happy. The average American is used to abundance. Even the less fortunate families have facilities that they can turn to for assistance. There are so many charitable organizations that donate their time, money, and service to ensure that hard-stricken families enjoy the same privileges as the affluent families.

I didn't know these kids that stood before me and Zay, but I felt that they deserved much more. I looked at my security that stood in the hallway, and I pulled Hung to the side. I walked over to Nyza, feeling so maternal. Felt like I had fallen in love with him all over again. I wanted everything to be with him; I wanted him to be a part of everything that I did. I even wanted to have my children with him. I was more than confident that I had the right man. A child would only complete us. I looked at my man some more and I all at once I felt the urge to work on having a child with him. I had more than enough money. After I whip ole girl's ass, I could take a break. I wouldn't have to stop boxing. I could do like the other athletes – retire and come back when the time was right.

Zay stood, waiting for me to say something.

"You know what, baby?"

"What's that?" Zay asked.

I grabbed his hand. "I think we should make a contribution to these kids for Christmas."

He smiled. "I'm with you. I was thinking the same thing. Why don't we go out and get a bunch of gifts?"

"We could do that, or we could just make out a check to them."

Zay quickly protested. "I don't like checks. Checks could go to repairs, light bills, or other stuff." He rubbed my hand. "Why don't we get someone to go out and get started on that? We can have them to go out and get some gifts – matter of fact," he pointed at Hung, "maybe we could give that job to her."

"Okay, Santa Claus," I said with a quaint smile.

"Okay, Mrs. Claus."

I liked it when he referred to me as Mrs. I wrapped my hands around one of his muscular arms. "So does this mean you're going to wear the suit?" I looked him straight in the eyes, trying to contain myself. I was turned on by him. I was turned on at the possibility of him putting on the Santa suit for me. We could role play. He knew that

I loved that kind of shit. I wanted his sexy ass right then and there, but I couldn't. There were too many people around.

I asked him again if he would wear the Santa suit.

"I'll wear the suit," he said.

"You promise?" He nodded. I leaned over and said in a low tone, "I want some of that long dick right now." He smiled. By then, Hung was walking up. I was sure that she heard me but I didn't care.

Hung smiled. "Are you ready to eat?"

***

I wore make up two shades darker than my skin tone. My hands were covered by Isotoners. It was about fifteen degrees out, so I was bundled up pretty tight. Even though it was cold out, the sun still shone, so I had on my stunner shades, giving dirty looks at the things I didn't like without being noticed. The shades were also a part of my disguise.

We went this quaint Filipino restaurant. It was very small upstairs, but the downstairs was much larger. I didn't want to sit downstairs; there were diners singing karaoke. My people went down there. I asked them to leave me and Zay alone for a while. I knew they wouldn't leave us alone completely, but we settled for a compromise.

One guard stayed upstairs with us while the others went downstairs.

The people of the establishment seemed to speak good English, so we didn't need the college student at the time. I ordered a chicken dish that was rather tasty. Zay, on the other hand, wasn't too happy. He took a few seconds to stare at his food when the waiter sat the plate before him. I wanted to laugh at him but I didn't so I hid my smile from him. *Poor baby, I know he's hungry, too.* On the same token, Zay got exactly what he asked for. He ordered fish, but I don't think that it came the way he expected it to.

"I ask for Tilapia, and this is what they give me?"

I started laughing. I couldn't hold back any longer. Zay asked for broiled fish and they did just that. They brought him the whole fish, including the head and scales.

"It's looking at me," he said.

I laughed hysterically. I could tell that he didn't find it funny. "Oh, baby, I'm sorry." I leaned forward to rub his cheeks. "Why don't you just send it back?"

He didn't respond; he just poked at his food while he made faces at it.

"You shouldn't play with your food," I said, still smiling.

He looked up. "You know what; this is the ugliest fish I have ever seen in my life. This makes me never want fish again." I laughed some more. "I mean, really, who in the hell cooks a fish with the head still on it?" He asked.

The server looked at us and came over and asked if we were okay. "Is everything alright?" she asked.

"Sorry, he asked for Tilapia, but we are not quite used to the fish being prepared this way."

She laughed. "That is how the fish comes. I can take it away for you if that is what you would like."

I smiled. "Please, take it away."

"I will," the waitress said. "May I recommend the Chicken Adobo?"

"Chicken Adobo?"

"Yes, sir. The Chicken Adobo is a boiled chicken, seasoned well and served with vegetables. It also comes with steamed, white rice.

I looked at the fish as the lady lifted the plate. I started to tease him some more but I felt that I had already messed with him enough.

Zay seemed satisfied with the chicken dish. I knew that wasn't his cup of tea. He often complained that chicken didn't fill him up. He ate it just the same.

Nyza

The food was different. I liked the American food the best. I told myself that I would try something different whenever I would get to Asia. That is why I agreed to try the Asian restaurant in the first place. They did me wrong on the fish. I have never seen anybody cook the whole damned fish. The chicken stuff wasn't bad, but it wasn't enough. We got back to the hotel with lots of bags. Tammy wanted to go shopping off the economy. The first thing I did was call up room service. I couldn't take it. I needed some real food. I could understand why Asians were so small. Their diet consisted of many vegetables and lots of rice.

Tammy was quite happy with herself. She was able to spend lots of money. That was one of the things that she did best. She bought all kinds of jeans, dresses, nightgowns, sweat suits, and such.

"The shopping is great here," she said.

"I told you that you would love it."

"Yeah, it is nice."

She stuck her face in one the brown bags. "You know what these bags remind me of?"

Tammy laughed. "These are like those bags they give you in the hood when you go to the corner store."

I nodded. "Yep, it reminds me of going to the swap meet. They always give you these cheap plastic bags, no matter what you buy from them."

Tammy leaned over and searched her bags until she found what she was looking for. With a big smile on her face she stood up. She handed me a big bag.

"What's this?" I asked.

"It's for you."

I had a grin on my face. "For me?" She nodded. I held the bag with each hand by the handles as I looked inside. Whatever, was in the bag was big, red, and fluffy. My smile faded. "What you want me to do with this?"

"Take it out of the bag, silly."

I set the bag down and began pulling the outfit from the bag. It was nothing more than a Santa Claus suit. Tammy stood there grinning and clapping her hands like a four year-old on Christmas morning. "You promised me, Mr. Claus."

I thought about the conversation we'd had earlier at the orphanage. I did promise her I'd wear the suit. I ran my mouth too much. I didn't expect her to find a Santa suit, and I damned sure wasn't going out to look for one. I looked at the suit, shaking my head. "It's a little big. You want me to put this on?"

She didn't say anything; she just hit me with that seductive look that she normally gives when she feels like being bad. "Tammy, I thought you were talking about putting on the suit for the kids."

"I am a kid, a big kid. Besides, none of that matters. I asked you if you would wear the suit and you said that you would." She had me. I was locked in. I had to put on the suit.

"Baby, this is really different."

She folded her arms and pouched her lips as if she were pouting. "We don't even have a chimney, girl."

"You are Santa from the hood. They don't have chimneys in the hood. You got to be gangsta."

"Alright," I agreed.

So I was in a Santa get-up. I tucked the red and white hat in my pocket to where the ball stuck out, and I put a red baseball cap on my head instead. I turned the cap to the side, took off my glasses, and replaced with them a pair of shades I had bought earlier in the day.

I knocked on her door, laughing at the same time at how ridiculous I must have looked. When I thought about it, I guess it was kind of a cool thing to do. I didn't know what my acting skills would be like, but I would soon see. I guess I could only do as well as she could. I had a bag in one hand and a small box in the other.

She came to the door in one of those short, sheer nightgowns. She had on a thong that made it hard for me to concentrate on what I was supposed to be doing. Her ass was hiked up on her back, and I could already smell sex in the air. I didn't want to role play; I wanted to play with her. I was ready to grab her and take her on the floor. A brother was ready to tear that ass up, but I decided to play the game anyway.

She smiled. "Santa, please do come in," she sang. I came in and she closed the door behind me. "You're too small to be Santa Claus. Santa is usually bigger."

I just looked down to my stomach and said, "My fifteen-day program works wonders."

"Oh, okay, but where is your beard, and what is up with that baseball cap you got on?"

"It's a New Millennium, baby."

"Okay."

She walked around, teasing me in that sexy outfit. She walked away from me as I followed her. She looked back at me and shot me one of those flirtatious smiles. "Are you ready for your milk and cookies, Mr. Santa Claus?"

"Hell nah, I don't want no milk and cookies. I want to get high with you, I want some Hennessey."

"You want some Hennessey?"

"Yep a couple of shots too; it's cold out there. I need something to warm my chest."

"You want ice, or no ice?"

"Drop a couple of them thangs in there."

She brought back two glasses. She handed me one, and she held on to the other glass. "Do you have something for me, Santa?"

"It depends; have you been naughty or nice?"

"What if I have been both naughty and nice?"

I looked her up and down and winked at her. "In that case, I got something for you." I took a couple of sips of the Cognac and then reached for her bag. "Here you go. This is for the part of you that has been nice."

"For me," she asked. I nodded. She looked in the bag. "Can I try them on?"

"Certainly."

She took the bag to the back room. She came out before long wearing the purple nightie. She modeled it for me. I took a couple more sips of the drink. She left and returned wearing a green, two-piece set. The top was cut low in the chest, and the bottom of it stopped mid-thigh. It came with a pair of matching shorts with lace around the thighs. I ran my eyes across her thighs down to her knees and then down to her calves, to her ankles, to her pretty feet.

I looked back up. She could tell I was feeling her. She began turning for me so that I could get a good look at her from all angles. She then turned her back to me. She spread her legs and bent over at the waist. I could see the print of her cat, it looked like two knuckles. As a matter of fact, that is what I called it: knuckle. Some men prefer to call it a camel toe. I hardly considered that sexy. If I was thinking about sex, I didn't want to relate anything with a camel. I was different like that, I guess. When it came to the pussy, I would call it my candy. I liked to touch it, smell it, eat it, and taste it.

Tammy stood up and asked me if I liked the outfit. I was feeling nice. The next thing I knew, she was asking me about my Santa hat.

"What's that?"

"The hat, the Santa hat, where is it?"

I was feeling silly. "The reindeer stole it," I said.

She grimaced slightly, "Oh, well. It's too bad you don't have the hat, it really turns me on," she said in a soothing, yet sexy tenor. Right after, she licked her lips, she winked at me, and then began to grope her breasts.

I got up from my chair without reservation as I was eager to touch her. "Come here and let Santa help you with that."

"I don't want any help. Besides, you are a guest, you shouldn't be working. I should be asking if there is anything I can do for you."

"Something for me?"

"Can I get you anything?" She looked my glass. "Like, can I get you another drink?"

"Well, I'm good for right now. I would like some candy. Do you have some?"

"Do you like candy?"

"I do. I love candy."

"In that case, I think I have some candy for you."

I sat there and waited for her to come to me. She walked up slowly, hiked her right leg up and placed her foot on my thigh as if she were about to take a step up. With her legs gaped open, she placed her hands on the sides of my face and pulled me closer until my head was between her legs. I smelled her; I took a few deep breathes and exhaled deeply. That candy smelled so good. Her panties were soaked. I pulled my head back so that I could reach for some of that candy. I wanted to touch it. I rubbed it with the tips of my fingers. I slid the panties to the side and stuck a finger in the candy dish. After feeling around for a few seconds, I pulled my finger out and licked it to taste the flavor.

"Okay," she said, "That's enough candy for you."

"That is some good candy."

"So let me ask you; has Santa been a good boy or a bad boy?"

"Oh, Santa has been a good boy."

"Really?"

"Yeah, and if you sit on my lap, I'll tell you all about it and how good I have been."

She straddled me as I continued to sit in the chair. She moved her hips, causing friction. My manhood was rising. She continued to move her hips as if she were in the saddle for real, like she was really riding. She didn't make noise at first, but I could tell that she was into what she was doing. The chair rocked meaningfully. I began to get bigger for her, and she could feel it.

"What is that in your pocket, Santa?"

"It's a roll of quarters."

She smiled. "No, it's not."

"Do you want to find out what it really is?"

"See, Santa, I knew it. You are bad."

"A little bit," I confessed.

"But how bad can you really be?"

"Real bad – so bad that right now, I just want to do something bad to you."

"Like what?" She asked.

"I want to lay your ass down so I can sip some of this Hennessey from between your titties, rub your nipples with the ball of this Santa Hat. When I finish there, I'm going to tickle your clit with the whiskers of my top lip, and then I want to eat some of your candy."

Tammerine

Goddamn, he was making me so hot and wet. I knew I was the one who wanted to role play and it was fun, but I wasn't too sure how much more I could take before I was ready to fuck him. He was smooth and seemed to fit right in with the role that he was playing. A sister was tempted to say fuck the role playing game, but I started it, so that meant that I would have to finish it.

Even if I was dead serious about stopping, he had his ace in the hole. He started whispering all this kinky shit in my ear until he knew that I was hot. He could tell because I started to squirm around, though I was trying to keep it together. I tried to concentrate on other things, but his request to taste some of my candy started to affect me; I tried to block it out. Thinking about what he had just said would only draw me in to him. *Fuck it. He says that he wants to taste my candy; how bad does he want to taste it?*

When he did, I moaned for him. I had to brace myself, gripping the arms of the chair so tight. I threw my head back as he felt my hard, throbbing breasts. I thought I would love on myself when did this. "Santa," I called to him.

"Yeah," he called back to me.

"Santa, it's been a while since I had my titties sucked." I breathed harder. Between breaths, I ordered him to suck my titties. He had me in the air before I knew it. He placed me on my bottom in a sitting position before he pulled off my nightgown. I raised my arms for him, offering no resistance so he could pull the garment over my head, and I shimmied out of my green shorts. I couldn't wait for him to get me naked. My pussy was throbbing already. Once he pulled off my stuff, he got on the floor with me and nudged me in the direction in which he wanted me to fall. I leaned backwards with his nudge until my back met with the wooden floor. It was warm and felt good against my back. That jolly old man sucked on my titties like popsicles. I didn't mind one bit. I forgot about where I was, I blocked out everything that could have been going on around me and allowed myself to get lost in the moments. Nothing else mattered more than what was going on at that very minute. He sucked and he slurped. The more he did those things, the more I squirmed. I was so wet; he didn't understand. He would have to do something to me quick or I would have to take the dick from him. Still with my eyes closed, I was feeling it... when... he... stopped. *Is he fucking serious? I can't believe that he is leaving my body like this – on fire for him.*

He hung his mouth over my ear, when he said something. "I want a taste."

I was a little irritated. Santa was fucking with me. "You want a taste of what?" I asked.

"I want to taste your candy."

I knew exactly what he wanted and what he meant when he said that he wanted to taste my candy. I didn't give him the satisfaction of tasting it before I reached down between my legs and stuck my own finger inside of me. I didn't move it around, but I left it inside long enough to get a sample for my own benefit. I pulled out, put that same finger to my mouth, and licked it. I smiled. Even though I couldn't feel it, I knew that his dick was getting harder. He was more aroused. He got up and announced that he would be right back.

He returned wearing the Santa hat half-cocked to the side. He had the bottle of liquor in one hand and a bottle of coke in the other. The man did exactly what he said he would do in the beginning – poured the blended liquor down my cleavage. He lapped it up quick like a thirsty dog. Right after, he chased the liquor with Coke soda. Santa then kissed my nipple and repeated the process. Before long, he was pulling down his pants.

"Hold up, what do you think you are doing? Do you think you are getting some of my goodies?"

"Only if you are willing to give me some," he said.

"Willing to give you some? Just what exactly are you going to do for me if I give you some of my stuff?"

He smiled and said, "I got a candy cane. Do you like candy canes, little girl?"

"I love them, so long as you have the great big ones for me to suck on."

"Damn, baby, you are in luck. I got a real big one that you can suck on. I don't much believe you've had one this big before."

I smiled back at him and said, "Never know what I've had. For all you know, I could have had bigger."

"I doubt it." He leaned over and sucked my neck as I grabbed his long candy cane and kept pulling on it. He didn't lie. He candy cane was long, and it was big. He reached down and then cupped my wet pussy. It was tingling slightly. I didn't know what was going on with my body. I couldn't control it, and he hadn't even penetrated me yet. I guess it was the anticipation that was getting to me.

I closed my eyes once again, and the next thing I knew, he was separating my lips with his tongue; they made that smacking sound when he did. I was expecting him to stick his tongue inside, but he threw me for a loop by dropping his tongue between the crack of my ass to absorb my running water. Santa was good – so good. This is what all women wanted. They wanted to be wide open for a man, they wanted to lay ass-naked, free to be a freak without being called one. This was one of those freaky nights where I would allow him to do whatever he wanted to do to me. If he wanted to fuck me sideways, I would let him. If he wanted to fuck me hard in the ass, I would bend over and take it like a straight trooper and cuss his ass out in the morning.

I hadn't drunk in a long time, and I was buzzed off my ass. I didn't know if I drank enough to qualify as being drunk, but I was sure tipsy if nothing else. I was feeling nice and my head was rushed.

I felt a mild vibration as Santa licked my clit. He played with it like a cat plays with a ball of yarn. Oh, that shit felt so good. He used the tip of his tongue to press down on the center of my clit. He would lick and then just hold pressure there. He knew exactly what to do to me to give me the level of pleasure that I desired. I could smell myself and became more excited. That sex smell was in the air. The only problem was, I hadn't been penetrated, and at first the whole teasing thing was okay, but I was good and bothered.

I breathed hard and heavy – not because of what he was dong to me; I breathed that way because of what I was thinking as he ate me out. I wanted him to dig this pussy out. I wanted him to dig me out so good the neighbors would want to call the cops to report domestic violence because they were sure that I was being violated because of my screams. I wanted him to take it like it truly belonged to him. I wanted him to make me remember this night for always. I wanted him to leave his mark on me. He kept me on the edge, squirming and moaning. He was licking me so good, I was reaching for things that weren't there. I began slapping him on the back, warning him that I was about to come, but I was mad because I didn't want to come like that. I wanted to come on that hard, long dick of his. I was right there, I was about to bust when he stopped. I let out a shriek. "Baby, what are you doing? Why did you stop?"

"Not yet."

I was glad that he stopped, but at the time it was feeling oh so good. His mouth was wet and sticky. He gathered himself and quickly got up to get a towel to wipe off my fluids. He was taking too long. I heard no water running, nor did I hear a toilet flush. When he did return, I was on my feet waiting for him. He had lost the top of his Santa suit and he had some articles in his left hand. It wasn't my concern what he had in his hand. My only concern was what he had in his pants. I reached in the lower half of his suit. My mind was made up; if he didn't give it to me, I was going to take it.

I looked him in the eyes when I demanded that he take off the rest of the suit.

"What's that," he asked me.

"You heard me, Santa, I said take this shit off now."

He smiled. "So, you are ready for your candy cane."

I felt him, and smiled back. "I've been ready for this dick," I confessed.

His pants fell to his ankles. He took one foot out at a time and then kicked the pants to side. I was already on my knees, ready to be his slut-puppy.

He looked down and said, "I see you are bad when your momma ain't home."

I put my mouth on his dick, licking it as if it were really a candy cane, prepared to lick the stripes off of that thing, fondling his balls at the same time. I knew he liked it when I did that. He told me that I was the only woman in life that knew how to make him feel good in that respect. He said that the other girls would be too rough and that they often hurt him when they grabbed his testicles for pleasure – not me. I guess I just had that right touch.

I stopped licking and just let it sit in my hand. I looked up at him, and when he opened his eyes I inserted his pole that I called a candy cane into my mouth. I went deep the first couple of times, but then I stopped. I was going to spoil him like that at first, but I had to see him make the *face*. He made some of the ugliest faces when he was feeling it. I loved to see him make those faces. Yeah, he could make the noises, he could talk trash and blurt out obscenities at the same time but when a man makes those faces, it tells the true E! Hollywood story.

My pussy was pulsating as I continue to suck my man off. He just didn't know how bad I was hurting for him. I wanted to have been on my back with my legs in the air, but first, I wanted to return the favor; I wanted to do something special for him. Zay was breaking down. He could hardly stand, so I slowed up enough to allow him time to reposition himself. He flexed his knees slowly until he was on his knees. I stopped long enough for him to have a seat on the warm floor. I pushed him on his back so that I could finish the job. I grabbed his hand and pulled it between my legs. He started playing with my pussy as I was on all fours sucking him. He had two fingers inside me, then a third, but it wasn't enough. I needed more. A sister felt cheated. His fingers were making me mad, though I put them there.

As I took my mouth off of him, he moved his fingers inside of me faster. I opened my mouth and squeezed my eyes shut, while my arms were shaking. "Santa," I called

He answered, "Yes."

"I can't take it anymore. I want you to fuck me. Take me in the room. This floor is uncomfortable."

He grabbed the articles he brought with him, and then he picked my ass up and carried me to the room. After he laid me on the hard bed, he grabbed a tie from his collection of articles. He asked me to close my eyes before he tied it around my head. Not being able to see, I would have to rely on my other senses just a little bit more. Next, I could feel him on top of me. He told me to relax before stretching my arms out. I could feel something around my wrists. *This kinky motherfucker is tying me up. Do you believe this shit?* I smiled, anxious about what he would do next. He spread my legs, and the next thing I know he was in me so deep I could feel it in my chest. I took it, feeling pain and pleasure at the same time. I asked for more abuse – which is what it felt like with each hard, concentrated thrust. I begged for it, even though it hurt. I wanted him to do me harder. I wanted to feel like I was getting disrespected.

"Is that all you got, you black motherfucker?"

"How do you want it?" He asked.

"Just keep doing what you are doing. Don't stop fucking me."

"Do you like it?"

"Shut up and fuck me. Just fuck me," I breathed. I raised my legs and bent them, squeezing my thighs against him. I was rocking with it as he continued to penetrate me the way I liked it. I was trying to hold on, but that shit felt so good. This was one of those nights where I knew I would have multiple orgasms. Sometimes he would make me come for him back to back. There were some nights where I couldn't stop coming. It could be hours later and I would still feel it.

There it was. I was at my climax, yelling, screaming obscenities, pissed because my wrists were bound. "That's right, Santa, fuck me, I've been such a bad girl this year."

"Really," he said as he handled business.

"Yes, I have been such a bad bitch."

"You *are* a bad bitch. Goddamn, you are such a bad bitch, but you are my bad bitch."

"Don't talk to me like that," I said to him but I really liked it when he talked to me like that. It did something to me. He kept talking. I had just come for him, and there it was; I was coming right on top of the first one. My legs were shaking uncontrollably, and the rest of my body was tingling. My sensation of touch was intensified. I hadn't felt quite like that in a long time. I didn't know how to describe it, but if he would have stopped our session right there, it would have been alright with me. I didn't need no more, momma was more than satisfied.

He slowed down and pressed his body against mine – but he still hadn't come for me yet. Wiggling my arms, I had forgotten that I was still tied up. I moved my hips slowly as he moved with me. It was a slow, consistent groove. He made love to me like he meant it, and I knew that he did. I couldn't see, but I could feel every touch and every stroke. It was like magic as we both hit our orgasmic peaks at the same time. I felt for him because it was his first one, I'd had many.

His body slowed down before I could feel his muscles relax. I could tell that he was getting good and relaxed; he was getting heavier. I always knew how to signal him when he was getting too heavy for me. When I signaled him, he knew exactly how to shift his weight so that the both of us could be comfortable. He removed the neckties from around my head and wrists, and then he shifted until we both felt comfortable.

I rubbed his back and smiled. "You always know just what to do. God, I was so tense, but you know how to loosen me up."

"I just want to spoil you. Nothing is too good for you."

"The little things are what count the most to me."

"And that is what I am talking about, the little things."

He was tired, I could tell. He had this dance that he would do on the way to bathroom after a good love-making session. When he knew he did a good number on my body, he would do what he called "The Beat it Up" dance. Doing this dance signified a victory for him. He won, he had conquered me to a point where I was incapable of moving or doing anything, I was so drained of energy.

"I guess I should be the one doing the beat it up dance tonight, huh?"

"Please, girl, I did all the work."

"I didn't help?"

"Of course you did."

"But you are so tired that you can't even do the dance, so that means that I must have really worked you out too."

"I guess you are right," he admitted.

I looked at him. "I didn't know how much of a freak you are."

"What – what are you talking about girl?"

I laughed. "You know what I'm talking about. This was a great night and I had never seen this side of you."

"So you saying that I don't take care of you; I don't handle mine?"

I tapped his butt. "Oh hell no, you know better than that. You never heard those words fall out of my mouth."

"I'm glad you enjoyed tonight."

"You know what," I discovered.

"What's that?"

"You know how they say people do things behind closed doors that others would never know about?" He nodded. "And you know how they say things about keeping things in the closet?"

"Uh huh," He acknowledged.

"Well it seems that you keep all of this; you keep all your freak shit in the closet."

"Sometimes we need to keep some things in the closet."

Tammy

"You ever think about quitting?" Zay asked me.

Not sure where this was coming from or where it was leading, I took my time before I delivered an answer.

"Quitting? I'm not so sure I know what you mean."

"What does quitting mean to you?"

"Zay, don't talk to me like I'm stupid. Quit what?" I began to get a little irritated.

He took his glasses off and came a little close to me. I became nervous and I didn't know why. Staring into his green eyes, I had a feeling that I wouldn't like what he was about to say.

"Have you ever thought about quitting boxing?"

"For what – why would I want to do something like that? I love boxing. You know that."

"I'm just saying that we have a future ahead of us," he reminded.

"I believe we have one together, but what does my career choice have to do with it?" I made an expression of deep concern. This was my way of reasoning with him. "I want you in my future."

"So what about family, don't you want that?"

I smiled nervously. I was unsure where this was coming from. I touched him on the arm. "Baby, yes, I want a family… eventually." I smiled some more.

"Eventually?" The man asked.

I held my hands out. "Yes, baby, eventually. You can't expect me to rearrange my life right now. Things take time."

"Well, I am just saying that I am damned near forty."

Is he serious? Is this the best he can come up with, 'almost forty'? Give me a break. "Here we go with that forty stuff."

"No, listen to me, I don't have any kids, and I've never been married. I want to start making this family." He dug into his pocket and pulled out this little white box. I couldn't believe it. Zay opened the top to reveal the prettiest set of diamonds. He got on his knees, pulled the ring out of the box, and smiled at me. His proposal sucked, but it was a beautiful ring. I covered my mouth with both hands.

"I'm not asking you to quit. I'm just saying that carrying kids and boxing don't always mix."

I was still stunned, waiting for the shock of surprise to wear off. I took my hands away from my face. "I guess I could take a break," I said in a child-like voice.

He smiled and held the ring up to my finger so that I could take a better look. I stuck my ring finger out to better assist him.

He began to slide the ring onto my finger, when I pulled back. I paused to get his attention. He looked up at me. "Is this what you want Zay – do you really want to take things to this level?"

He frowned as he quickly placed the ring back in its respective box. "You know what, Tammy? You could fuck up a wet dream."

He got up, and I was waiting for him to walk off, turn his back on me like he normally did – but he didn't. I was glad. "Baby," I called. "Understand me; I want this," I started, "I mean, I really, really want this." I paused and looked up to the ceiling. "I guess I just want to make sure that you really want this too, just as much as I do."

"I got you," he said.

"The situation just caught me off guard; you know, the proposal and all. We never discussed this before."

Something was wrong with him; I could tell. I think he wanted a different answer when he asked me about boxing. I could only tell him how I felt. That was all I could give.

After a long recess on his end, he finally responded. "I'm sure about you, Tammy. You are all that I want."

I threw my arms around him and wrapped him up with them, squeezing as tightly as I could. As we released each other, something was still bothering me. I looked up at him and asked, "So what was the real reason you asked me about quitting boxing?"

"I told you already."

"No, baby, sorry I don't believe that. There is something else."

He was getting frustrated, but we needed to get to the bottom of things. I grabbed his hand. "Baby, I know that you don't always like to see me out there in the ring. I know it is dangerous. I see your face every time I am out there. Every night I fight, there is different look of concern for me."

"I don't know, but it's like you are some kind of ravenous beast when you are in the ring."

"I don't like how you put that, but I will take it as a compliment. It is what makes the difference between defeated and undefeated; I prefer the latter."

"Nah, what I'm saying is just – you are like a different person when you fight."

"Is that too much for your ego?"

"What is that supposed to mean, my ego?"

"I am not two different people, and you know this, Zay. I am one person; there is only one me. Who you see ringside is who I am when I am around you – in and out of the ring."

"Well, you sure as hell don't act like it."

I put my hand on my hips and got in my stance. "Well, what is that supposed to mean?"

"You don't act like it. You don't, and you get in this joint and put on this front like you have to constantly impress me – impress your femininity upon me like you have to remind me that you are a lady."

I disrespectfully rolled my eyes. "That is not true."

"Yes, it is. I know who you are, but you try your damnedest to be extra girlish to cover your boxing image."

I chuckled. "That makes absolutely no sense."

"It's like you even have a problem figuring it out. Sometimes you climb in the bed and forget. You want to take charge; you want to act like you are the man."

I rubbed him lightly and pursed my lips as if I were really sympathizing with him. "*What-da-matta*? Does the baby feel intimidated? You scared to let some one else take control," I mimicked, laughing right in his face. I didn't care if he got mad. This had turned into something ridiculous in no time flat.

"So you think this is funny." He was ready to walk off, I knew it.

"So you think something is wrong with me; you think

I'm a dyke or I'm butch cause I box and do it well; it makes me less of a girl because I like to box?"

"There's a difference," he defended.

"So I'm different in the ring, but you want to fuck me every night."

"See, that's what I am talking about. Everything is about sex with you."

"Are you telling me that I am not sexy to you unless my hair is straight and hanging down my back, or am I just too ugly for you to stand when I come home with a swollen face and black eyes?"

"You know what I am saying."

"No," I shook my head. "I don't. I really don't know what you are saying. I am confused. Then you are saying that everything with me is about sex. Well, you are wrong; everything with us is about sex."

He breathed heavily. He, too, shook his head.

"So tell me, Zay – tell me that I'm not sexy. Don't you want to make love to me right now? Don't you want to fuck me from the back?" He was fighting it. I could see the bulge in his pants getting bigger. I knew I had that type of control over it. He didn't have to admit it, I already knew.

"Come on, Tammy." What did I just say? He was fighting it. "You know that I love you. I always want to make love to you, but we don't need to use sex to mask our problems – or use it to smooth things over, for that matter."

"I don't do that. I just believe in the old saying, 'make love, not war'. Some things just aren't worth the time and attention we give to them."

"You know what, Tammy, you can apply all the theories that you want. I told you what it is."

"Zay, we are sexual people, and I guess I am the only one who sees it that way."

"You'd rather chase an argument with a good sex session instead of dealing with the problem."

"And you'd rather run away like a little girl, instead of dealing with the problem – and if that is solely the case, that I chase an argument with sex; I don't ever recall a time where you stopped me. You went right ahead and took this pussy, didn't you?"

He shook his head and dropped his hands to his side. "Unbelievable. You are right; this got ridiculous fast."

I looked at the box that he still carried with him. *Am I ready for this?* Zay was usually the one to walk off, but this time I thought I would be the one leaving. I was a firm believer in resolution, but I didn't feel like getting into another emotional battle, not with him. I loved him, and one of us needed to be the bigger person, or the level-headed one, and maybe that is why Zay seemed to be the one to walk off most times.

I guess if we were going to be together, there were

some things that we would have to work out. I looked at the box again and thought about the responsibilities that came along with being a wife. I had never been one of those before, but I was sure that I could be one for Nyza. This was the first major conflict we'd had thus far, but I knew it wouldn't be the last.

As I stood there, breathing not a word to him nor he one word to me, standing on separate sides of the room, I continued to reflect. Things had been different ever since he had taken me on as a trainee. I felt that he really wanted the job, but I don't think that he could take all that came with it. Maybe I'd made a mistake when I asked him to take the position.

There was something, somewhere in him that couldn't be touched. It was as if he was battling with something; he had an issue or two of his own. It was like his heart were in two different places, or maybe he just needed some healing. Maybe he just needed some time. I was ready to give it to him. I walked off. He called for me, but I didn't stop. I needed to get away for a while.

My man had just proposed to me – told me that he wants to give me everything and that he wants to be everything to me. He told me that he wants me to bear his children without circumstance. I should have been happy, but there I was, crying like a baby. I was angry. I didn't want to be happy. *Who proposes in a fucking living room?*

I was taken back to the end of our argument. I actually asked him the question.

"I'm not decent enough, that's all I get, a living room proposal?"

"What difference does it make where you hear the words or where you receive the seal of our solidarity? Would it have been better if it were more traditional, like, let's say in a dining room setting?"

"It would have been better than a living room." I was being catty. My feelings were bruised, and I needed a way to get back at him. Granted, he could have done it somewhere else, but honestly, the time and place shouldn't matter. As I was being mean, he shot one back at me to my surprise.

"Guess you are right, baby, I should have got down on one knee inside of McDonalds."

I smiled a cocked smile and squinted my eyes in response to his stupid comment. "That's cool, at least I would have expected something like that from you, you fake Donnie Simpson look-a-like."

"Shut your perpetrating ass up."

"Perpetrating? You are the one that's all fucked up; judging me like you are perfect; telling me that I'm not a lady, and that I don't know anything but sex."

"You damned right. That is all it is with you is sex. We never solve anything because whenever I have an issue, you try to shut me up with sex – like that's supposed to make everything all better. That is some bullshit."

"Is that all I feel like to you, sex?"

"That is all you fell like to me, sex!" He roared.

His words were like a strong blow to the chest, and for a couple of seconds, it felt like I lost my breath.

I had to play it off. I couldn't let him see me sweat. I managed to laugh at him. "Funny, that is exactly what you are to me is sex. The dick is good – real good – but the conversation sucks. I get more out of a conversation with a dead person than I do with you." I was raw I know it, but I had to hurt him like he'd hurt me, and it seemed to work, judging by the expression on his face.

"So that's all that I am to you; Sex?"

I hit him with the iced grill. "What else do we have? You don't even know me. How many times have you tried to get to know me? Tell me, what exactly do you know about my life – and you are talking about marrying me."

I stood there all alone remembering how we stood in front of each and after all those awful words, neither of us had anything else to say to one another. That was when I decided to walk out.

Zay

Some people were diehard college football fans. Some needed to watch Monday night football just to get their heads right for the rest of the week. You got your NBA fans posted up in their living rooms yelling at the players as if the athletes could really hear them. Some of them boys couldn't get enough of the Redskins, despite their horrible losing streak, but everybody has their own. Boxing was what always did it for me.

I lived for Fight Night. It was the most exciting thing in life to me. I had friends that liked to watch the World Wrestling Federation, but at that time, me and Tracey were outside with gloves on reinventing the Ali/Spinx fight. We would fight over who got to be Muhammad Ali. I never liked to be anybody else but Ali because at that time, he was the greatest that had ever lived. I never wanted to be anything less than the best. Man, we practiced at it.

When the VCR came out, the best gift that my momma could have ever given me was the video of some of Ali's best fights. Man, I must've watched that thing over a hundred times. I would take turns sitting and standing as I studied his moves and combinations. Tracey watched it just as much as I had, and he knew the moves better than I did. He knew the moves and combinations so well that he would watch me and tell me what I was doing wrong. I would box out some of the cats in the neighborhood just for fun and Tracey called himself my manager and trainer. He was good at what he did. He made sure that I was my best.

Now, I wasn't a violent child. I just liked boxing as a sport. I learned all that sportsmanship stuff by watching the pros, which helped shape my character early in life. It was hard for me to understand how two big, grown men could beat the hell out of one another for ten rounds and then turn around, shake hands, and hug one another. I admired that. It took me a while to get to that point. It wasn't until I fully understood what sportsmanship was really about that I started practicing the same.

Momma didn't understand how serious I really was. I wasn't one of those kids just taking the talk, I had always dreamed of walking the walk. I knew at an early age that I wanted to be a boxer – I knew I would be a boxer and I would be good at it. My mother thought it was a passing phase, but she supported me any way. She went out and got me jump-ropes to improve my stamina. When her co-worker learned that I frequented the boys and girls club, momma went out and bought me wraps for my wrist and new pair of gloves. Momma was there, and I will always love her for it. Little things like that showed me how deep a mother's love could go. I will forever be grateful for that.

Momma's love and my own determination took me all the way to the Olympics. Momma got sick when I was competing. I wanted to break down and cry; I wanted to give up. I took my time in my dressing room reflecting, feeling sorry for myself, when it occurred to me; the best thing I could do at that point – the thing that would make momma happy – would be winning. By winning, I could show her that her love and continued support was appreciated. I could show her that it wasn't in vain. That was what would make momma feel better. That was my way of giving back. I had to win. There was no other way to look at it. My sister, Vette, was there, and so was Tracey. They were there to cheer me on every step of the way.

I took the gold that year in 1985 and never looked back. I was approached to do commercials and offered several endorsements. Momma got better and she was so proud; she never stopped talking about the Gold medal. As soon I touched down, I made sure I went to see her so that I could place that medal around her neck. My mother asked, "What is this?"

"It's my medal, momma. I want you to have it."

"Is this your medal from the Olympics?"

"Yes, ma'am."

Momma breathed a little heavier. She looked worried as she looked down and touched the ribbon, rubbing with both hands. When I bent over, I could see a small puddle in each of her eyes. "Ma, you okay?"

"I'm okay, baby."

"You sure?" I asked.

"I can't take this from you, baby. I can't accept this."

"Momma, this is yours; you earned it. I didn't. I won this medal because of you. You supported me all these years and I don't know how to pay you back."

My momma squeezed my hand, biting her bottom lip at the same time. She was trying to hold back her emotions, but it was okay. I knew that she was happy, and it's okay to cry if you are happy.

It was the main event. I was in the corner instead of sitting ringside or actually being in the ring. I was there as a part of Team Phillips. There were flashing lights and thousands of cheering fans. The mic dropped from the ceiling as the ring announcer waited. It was the best high to me. It was better than sex. I don't know how Tammy felt, but I still felt that high, even though I was only there for support.

The ring announcer grabbed the mic as the crowd settled some. The bell rang, and people perked up a little more. The fight was about to start. The announcer presented the fighters one at a time, starting with the challenger. He used his powerful voice in the most distinctive way.

"Introducing the challenger from Queens, New York, wearing green trunks, official weight at 154 pounds, with an impressive record of 20 wins, 12 by way of knock out, and zero losses, she will be fighting for the Championship tonight; ladies and gentleman, Shelita Henson." Shelita came to the middle of the ring.

Typically, some cheered, while others booed. When they'd settled some, the announcer continued with his introduction. "Now ladies and gentlemen, tonight, our fight is scheduled for twelve rounds where we have the reigning, undefeated champion defending her title. She is coming to you by way of Inglewood, sunny California, she wears red trunks and weighed in at 150 pounds even. She has a blemish-free record folks; 33 wins, 27 by way of knock outs and zero losses. Ladies and gentlemen, I present the Champion, Ne – She-e-e-e-e-e-l Lo-o-o-o-o-o-c Phil-i-lips. The crowd went wild. There was a tingling in my stomach as well. I could tell that my baby was a bit nervous, but it was quite alright to be a little nervous; as a matter of fact, it was only natural. The night before last, I'd told Tammy the story about the Olympics. I told her that every fight, she should remember that story and when she would think of that story, she should think about someone who has supported her or encouraged her in some shape or fashion. I was hoping that the story would drive her to greatness with each bout, especially those times when she felt she didn't have it in her.

The boxers met in the ring, Shelita, looking everything like a tall man with braids, and Tammerine, soft, yet powerful. They sized each other up before touching gloves. I could see the intimidation in the competition's eyes. She was trying hard to use the fear factor on Tammy, but I knew it wouldn't work. She was the Champ, and it would stay that way. Parting ways, Tammy came back to her corner. At times it was hard to keep things professional in the ring. I couldn't pet her up, and I couldn't be too rough, I had to somehow maintain a medium. I think that was the hardest part of the job. I just looked at her and told her to keep what is hers. We had a couple of seconds left before the fight would start, and when she looked at me I knew what she wanted from me; she wanted to hear some words from me. It was like she had grown to depend on it. "Go out there, and take it easy at first. You know what I mean, right?" She nodded. "Go out there and get a feel for her punches and throwing patterns. I will be watching too. Then, after a couple of rounds, you go back out there and beat her ass." Tammy smiled, and then the bell rang.

What I told my little boxer sounded good and briefed well, but she could not hold up to my advice. She couldn't stay away from the opponent. Tammy tried, but Shelita kept coming after her. In the blink of an eye, Tammy threw a fast combination. She hadn't even tested her reach, she just drew in for the kill. Shelita took a couple of steps back and winked her eye at Tammy. Tammy stepped back as well but kept her guard up. I would remind her on several occasions to stay covered. Tammy landed a few solid head shots while Shelita stayed to the body. This went on for about three rounds.

The fourth round would be the tell-all. I just knew it. Shelita didn't have the wind. Most of her fights only lasted about five rounds. If she hadn't seriously damaged her comp by the end of the fourth round, it was pretty much a done deal. I remember watching a special once, and her trainer said that her problem was stamina. She would train hard, but for whatever reason, she just couldn't go the distance. She was not known for her distance. She was known for her ability to quickly finish her opponent.

The scorecards were two to one, Tammerine "Loc" Phillips. In round four, I could tell that the champ was tired of playing. She could sense the challenger's fatigue and used it well to her advantage by throwing power shots. She got in the groove and, like always, she dropped her guard, and when she did, Shelita caught her on the side of the ear. Tammy stumbled backwards. The crowd jumped out of their seats, some cheering, some booing. The ref stepped in, giving the champ a few seconds to recover, issuing a warning to the contender at the same time.

"Keep your guard up," I yelled as the fight continued. Tammy found her groove once more and delivered a flurry of punches. Shelita could do nothing. Her frustration shone; she covered up and attempted to block the shots. They were coming so fast, she was in the corner helpless. "Get out of the corner," her team yelled. Making a desperate effort to get out of the corner, Shelita used her weight by charging at Tammy, head-butting on the way out. Dirty fighter. Tammy jumped up and down and held the top of her head with her glove. The ref responded by standing the middle of the two fighters. He issued another warning to Shelita and resumed the fight.

The ten-second warning chime sounded, and the two fighters were brawling. Shelita was beyond tired, while I was wondering if the champ could do it. Could she knock out her opponent? This fight was different. It seemed more like a personal thing. The two had fought two years ago, and the world anticipated the rematch. Nichelle had the title and Shelita wanted it, but my baby would not lose her title – not on this night. Every athlete knows the day that it is over. They know when they are going to lose. It has something to do with how you wake up in the morning.

Not sure how Shelita woke up that morning, but I do know that she had lost her second chance at becoming the Female Boxing Champion of the World. Tammy knocked her slam on her back in round five. There was no standing eight count, and you couldn't be saved by the bell. Tammy landed a hard right that folded Shelita up and sent her to the canvas. When she couldn't get up in time, the bell rang and the ring filled with people from both teams.

They came just when I knew they would. The commentators had their mics in hand, walking up. One of them put their arm around Tammy.

"You know something, you are remarkable. That is all I can say. You are still the undisputed champion of the world." He looked back to me and smiled. "Then again, with a man like Nyza Stevenson on your side, how can you lose?"

They then turned to me. I didn't want to talk. It wasn't my interview. I had a big problem with that. Tammy was the professional athlete, not me. People said that I had what it took to be a great. I was mad at the sport for a little while. They offered me a job – seat for commentator on the Home Box Office Network. I didn't want it at the time. I couldn't handle being the one talking about it and not being able to be about it. I hated when they talked to me like I was a used-to-be or an athlete that was all washed up. I was neither. I did have a short-lived career, and that was about it. More and more I would think about going back to the doctor to get another professional opinion regarding my shoulder.

Tammy was basking in her moment of glory while Shelita was on her knees crying. For some odd reason, her tears didn't seem like tears of defeat, her tears were for some other thing.

There was an after-party following the fight. The next night we would be leaving for Washington.

That same night of the fight, we went to the after-party and got tore down drunk. Fans were there throwing beer and alcohol across the club. The security and our bodyguards had to step in a few times to keep order. People were having a good time, there was no doubt about it. In the front, there were topless Korean dancers on stage. They were nothing like American women. The women there were very small, they had hardly no figure at all. There were men that were turned on by it, but I didn't see why. I watched them shake their little asses at us when Shelita walked in. She looked like a little boy with a fur coat and two diamond earrings. She looked around until she spotted Tammy. I didn't know what she wanted with her, but whatever she said to her was serious. Tammy looked nervous once Shelita walked away. We were on opposite sides of the room, so I didn't know what was said.

Nyza

"So, what's been up?" I asked my sister.

"Not much. How was your trip?" My sister returned.

"It was a trip."

"Really?"

"So what are you doing?" I decided to change the subject. I didn't want to talk about Korea.

"What am I doing – sitting online looking for a new job."

"New job," I asked in surprise.

"Yeah, a new job. Tracey wants me and the baby out there with him."

"But you sell real estate. Why do you need to find new work?"

"Well, I don't know the market out there, and besides, I don't have the time to test the waters."

"Come on, Vette, you know that Tracey has money. I don't know why you are worried about money."

"I'm not, Zay." I could hear her punching the keys on her laptop as she conversed with me. "I'm not worried about money, but I definitely don't want it to look like I am just moving in with him and living for free."

"What the hell, are you two roommates or lovers?"

She laughed. "You are right bro. You know me, I like working. Tracey already told me that I don't have to work. He told me all that, but you know me, Zay, I will go crazy sitting home all day long. I can't do that."

I smiled. "Yeah, I guess you do have a point." I looked at my watch. "Wow, you two really move fast."

"Well, I guess we do, but we love each other, and he is really serious about us being together."

"Is that right," I said dryly.

Vette took a deep breath and quickly let it out forcefully. "Don't tell me, Zay, you are still hung up on that, because I mean –"

" – Nah, baby," I chuckled, "Believe me, I'm cool with it. I just got some things over here that I'm dealing with."

"Well, maybe big sis can help."

"Nah sis, I need to work this out on my own. I'm good."

"Come on, baby. What's wrong?"

I didn't want to tell her what was really up, but I had to give her something or else she would take it personally.

"Tammy's manager walked out on her, and she asked me to be her manager."

"I bet that is a lot of stress."

"Well, it was sudden. I didn't have time to react. I didn't want to do it. I couldn't just leaver her hanging like that though."

"Wow."

"I guess I liked things the way they were."

"I guess," she said.

I could tell she was concerned, but she was preoccupied with something else. I could picture her getting distracted from her computer work, standing in the mirror with the phone pinched between her cheek and her shoulder. She'd be holding a piece of clothing trying to imagine what it would look like on her. On the side, she'd be wondering what Tracey would think. Honestly, I was glad that they hooked up. They were two of my favorite people. I felt bad for being the barrier in their way for so long. I was an inconsiderate fool. I admit.

"Business and personal stuff don't gel, you know what I mean."

"What is that, you always say; business is never personal?"

"I know, but it complicates things."

"You say it complicates things, but work never seemed

to affect the relationship that you and Tracey had together. You were the boxer and he was your trainer."

"Me and Tracey are men; it was different. We are not as sensitive as women can be."

"I guess so," My sister said.

"Look sis, it's obvious that you are doing something else. I can call you back another time."

"Yeah, Zay, it's just a lot for me now. I'm trying to get all my business in order. I got a lot to do."

"I know," I said.

"And you are sure that you are okay?"

"I'm chillin."

"As long as you're okay, little brother."

I got off the phone and cracked half of smile. She could've cared less. She just wanted to be nosy. That was the only reason she wanted to know what was wrong. She didn't lend a possible solution or any advice, but at the same time, I guess I didn't present her with a real problem, either. I didn't want to tell her what was really wrong with me. I didn't want to tell her that me and Tammy were on the outs. That was too much information, and frankly I didn't think she was capable of yielding an unbiased opinion when it came to the subject of me and Tammy.

A brother had a killer headache. Usually I would lie down, but I didn't really feel like it. I felt like thinking. I had to arrange some things in my head in order for things to make sense. It seemed, since I got back from Asia, my personal life was in complete disarray.

Tammy had been working and I'd been working right along with her. She had more than enough on her plate, but she had no choice but to deal with it. I mean, that management shit was crazy. I didn't want the job, but how I could I have refused. She was my partner. I had to back her up, whether I wanted to or not. It is just the type of man that I am. Besides all that, she would have taken it personally, had I said no. I wanted to work on the personal side of us. They say business and pleasure don't mix. That is not true; you have to find the right ways to make them work.

I had to admit, I was changing in a major way. There were times when I didn't know who I was sometimes. Me and Tracey were cooler than we ever had been before. I was thankful for that. He was more than a friend; he was family. He got me over a lot of humps in my life. If Tracey'd been a woman I would have asked him to marry me – well, not really, but I loved that dude.

I looked for the Tylenol, but there wasn't any. Tammerine eats them shits like candy before and after her cycle. I'd had some ibuprofen, but she put those in her purse last night. After grabbing my keys, I headed for the front door. My original destination was the drugstore, but I went to the coffee shop instead. Tracey's house was on the way. To my surprise, there was a fresh For Sale sign in the front yard. How was his wife taking it? It serves the bitch right; all she tried to do was use my boy. She didn't deserve him. I don't even think she had changed her last name legally. All she wanted was the money. Regret ran so deep for me at that moment when I thought about the short time I had been sexual with her – sexual with her and neglected to tell my friend what had gone down. I shook my head at the thought and continued towards the coffee shop.

Tracey was sitting on one of the sofas with the lounging chaise. He was leaned back relaxed-like but his feet remained on the floor. He hadn't kicked them up on the chaise as of yet. He had an easy smile on his face. He held his hands up as if he had been expecting me to show when I did. "It's been a minute, hasn't it?"

I looked at my watch before I took my seat. "Yeah, it has been a whole minute." I slapped him a five. "We have been busy on the road."

"I understand, but do you like the new gig?"

I smiled. "It's okay. You know me."

Tracey smiled, but he still wasn't convinced. "So are you ready to sell or what?"

"Sell what," I asked.

"I got a couple of potential buyers looking at the club."

I scratched my head. "Wow, you don't waste much time."

"Well, that is what we both decided to do right?"

"Well, I guess it was, originally. You just got to excuse me, it is all happening just a tad too fast for me – a lot for me to digest in such a short time."

"Well, I got their info. They want to stop by when we are both present." Tracey dug into his pocket and pulled out a folded three-by-five card that he glanced over before passing it my way. We can get out of this thing and split everything down the middle."

I choked on my words. "You were serious, you really want out?"

"You were right I am – we are getting older; too old to be running some night club. Let the youngins tend to it," Tracey mused.

My headache just increased. I covered the sides of my head with the palms of my hands. Tracey was growing up. "Are you serious about this, Tracey?"

"Well, yeah, I am serious. Are you changing your mind?"

"Like I said things are just moving pretty fast around here. I didn't know that you had your house on the market already?"

My friend smiled smartly. "Got my mind made up. I know what I want to do. I know where I want to be. Shit, all this time I had been spinning my wheels when I knew what I wanted all the while." He looked me in the eyes long enough for me to fill in the blanks. "I love her man, and I am going to be with her."

"Have you got it all worked out?"

"Man, when something is right, you don't have to work hard at it, you just do it." He leaned forward and extended his right hand to me. "Thanks for your blessings, brother."

I gave him my right hand and we gripped. I didn't say anything. I was still bothered a little bit, but I was sure that he knew it.

At once, concern was painted on his face, causing it to wrinkle some. "Zay, you good?"

I hid my emotions with a smile. "I'm good. Actually, I am happy for you and my sister. I really am, just got my own stuff that I am working out."

"Stuff you are trying to work out? Does it have anything to do with me and Vette?"

I laughed. "Nah man, me and Tammy," I answered.

"You know, I'm still ya boy, Pimps without hos since the second grade. You know you can holla at me whenever you need to."

Sitting there, he didn't push. I didn't talk, and neither did he. I sat in the tripod position, with the palms of my hands resting on my knees. I took a deep breath.

Tracey got up and tapped me on the back. I couldn't pull one over on him. He knew me all too well. "Take your time, bro. Whenever you are ready to talk, I am here."

Tammy

Me and my man hadn't been right since the trip overseas. Every now and then, I caught him wandering off. This had become the norm. Me and my man hadn't been making love for a while. That was routine for us – it was what we did best. Maybe he was right, I do love sex. Most of all, I enjoyed sex with him like I had never enjoyed with any other man. Zay made me feel that I had it all in a man to the point where I didn't have to look no further. I felt complete. He had no idea how that made me feel. I felt that there was nothing else to it, that it got no better than the blissful feel of our rock-solid institution of a relationship.

I had been a fiend for the dick lately, but he continually refused me. He always managed to come up with some kind of quick excuse. I would let it ride when he would tell me he was tired or that he had things to do. I knew the brush-off when I got it. That was what he was doing to me – giving me the brush-off. I was tired, too, but I still found the time for my man. Between training days, interviews and such, I was worn out, but there was that time that I held in reserve for a man who didn't want it. I didn't know what to do. I mean, I had never felt a man the way I was feeling him. He just didn't know what he did to me. He literally awakened all of my senses and reminded me of the ones that I forgot about; he was the one that did it for me.

Zay had become so distant and cold. He didn't seem to care about much in the last days. Once again, I decided to reach out by stopping at his place. That night he came to door wearing his glasses and holding a book. He stood there, and I wondered if he was even going to invite me in. I looked around. "I mean, can I come in, or are you just going to stand there and let all the cold air in?"

He stepped to the side and stood in the hallway, looking around like I had never been there before. What was his problem? I had my arms folded. Though it seemed longer, it had only been two weeks since I had been there to visit.

As the evening progressed he looked less and less interested in what I thought or had to say. He sat on one couch and I sat across from him on the other while he read this fucking book. Bullshit.

"How come you've been avoiding me?"

He dropped the book in his lap, like he was disgusted, like it was such a problem that I was there. I was ready to cry. I loved him, and I thought that he loved me – but there we were acting like we were in a dead-end relationship. Finally, he was ready to say something. I was all ears. "You got something you want to tell me?"

Instantly I frowned. *Where in the fuck is this going?* "Something I want to tell you about what?" *What could this fool be talking about?* There is nothing to tell.

"You know what, Zay, I don't' think I like the way this is beginning. Why don't we try this again tomorrow? This is going to be some silly shit." I stood up and started towards the front door before he finished his thoughts.

"Are you going someplace?"

"What are you talking about, Zay?"

"Okay, I am talking about Asia."

I felt cross-eyed as I looked up to the ceiling. "What are you talking about, what did I do in Asia? Nothing happened." My demeanor went from confused to concerned in two seconds flat. *Asia – I thought we had a good time in Asia.*

"I'm talking about the night of the after-party. I am talking about when I went to the bathroom – what I saw when I came out."

I felt as pale as a ghost. *Did he know? Is he talking about what I think he is talking about?*

"So you two got some history?" He asked.

Devon Callahan

"Zay, baby," I pleaded, "that was all before you."

"I believe it was before me, but who in the fuck are you? What are you?"

"I didn't think it mattered, Zay. Me and Shelita had a thing years ago, back when I was curious."

I didn't want to have this conversation, but I was already having it – avoiding it would only make things worse. "So you think something is wrong with me based on a decision I made almost ten years ago – a mistake I made almost ten years ago?"

"So that is what you are going to go with, curious?"

"That is what it was, Zay. I was experimenting. I was having issues. People talked about me, and it wasn't easy. People didn't appreciate the idea of woman being able to do what a man could do. They didn't appreciate a woman that had a passion for the sport of boxing. They thought that I was weird – they thought I was a dyke. They wondered if I liked women."

Discounting my explanation, he said, "That woman felt something for you."

I touched his chest. "And maybe she did, but that is not me. That was one time, baby. I was young back then. I love men – I love you and no one else." It may have been wrong, but at that point I didn't feel like convincing him. I didn't want to be judged, and it used to happen all the time. It wasn't until I started making myself look like a baby-doll, overexaggerating the make-up before press conferences, that people started to consider a softer side of me.

Zay had his hands on his hips like Tom Hanks did when he played in Forrest Gump. He was waiting for something. "It has been over between us. That is something I never want to go through again, Zay."

"So it's been over," Zay tried to confirm with a non-convinced look on his face. I nodded. "So if it's been over then how come she kissed you that night? I saw you two."

He was mad and he was hurt. "A kiss, Zay? She walked up and kissed me on the neck. It was totally unexpected. If you were looking so hard, you would've seen that I frowned when she did it."

Zay kept at it. "How deep was your relationship with her?"

"Goddammit, Zay. If I told you it was over before it started, then how deep do you think."

"How deep?" He insisted.

If he wanted to play a game, then I could play right along with him. "I didn't ask you how long your relationship was with that bitch that you took me to go see."

"I expected you to say something like that."

My eyes watered, and I felt weak. I could hear my voice waver. "And I expected something better from you." *Don't make me do this, Zay. Don't make me go back to that*

time. I don't want to go there. It is all about forward progress.
"Look, Zay I am sorry."

"How would you feel if some woman walked up to me and kissed me?"

"You are right, I wouldn't like it."

"So how long did you and her see each other?"

I didn't want this. The questions were coming like I knew they would; what made us want to experiment like that; am I bi-sexual; have I had a threesome; am I fronting with him – do I really prefer women over men. I didn't feel like I had to go through it. I thought about walking off, but I wanted him, and I didn't want to let him go. I wanted him to understand that I loved him and him alone.

"So you still like women." He smiled and shrugged his shoulders. "I mean, I just have to know so I can stop wasting my time."

Walking up and getting right in his face, I yelled, "Listen to me. What difference does any of this make? None of this mattered, and you were sure about me until now. What you're unsure of is some pretense bullshit of something that I put behind me several years ago. She was a woman I used to see. It was wrong; it didn't feel good, so I quit – and if you want me to be honest…"

I was about to show him the worst side of me. This was the side I kept in the closet. I hid this side because I didn't like hurting people with sudden reactions and comments. I went to anger management for two years, and I'd promised myself that I would lock my other side away.

"I didn't know what I wanted at that time, Zay, I was still young. I didn't know who I wanted to be. I didn't know if I liked girls or boys." I pointed at his dome, close enough to poke him. "Is that what you wanted to hear?" Zay shook his head. "I just wanted to be loved. You don't know how it was for me growing up." I could feel my face wrinkle, but I didn't want to cry. "That short time of my life was hell and nobody knew what that was like for me."

"Is that why you stopped?"

I slapped him right in the face. I was frustrated. "No stupid. I stopped because I was convicted, Zay. Convicted, I do believe in religion. I knew that it was wrong, I felt nasty and dirty, and I never want to do that again!"

His expression changed. His look softened, turning apologetic.

"Fuck you Zay," I said and headed for the front door."

"Look baby, I'm sorry, but I have one more question for you." I kept walking. "What if you found out that I slept with a man – let's just say it was a very short-lived relationship, but it was with a man; would it matter?"

I stopped and turned around. "I don't care, Zay; this relationship can be over for all I care. You can't be serious about me. You don't take the time to try and understand me – the little things about me. Think about it; what do you really know about me, Zay?"

"What?" He asked.

"What you do know about me?"

"I only know what you tell me."

I shook my head, and in a calm tone I said, "Such a cop out."

"It's true."

"Okay, playa, when is my birthday?"

"It's in October."

"October, what?" He didn't know. "See that is what I'm talking about." He picked up his book, when I knocked it out of his hand. He then, pulled my purse straps off my shoulders. I pushed him, he pushed me back. I punched him in the chest, he tagged me with a swift one. It wasn't hard, but he used enough force for me to feel it. He grabbed me at the shoulders like he wanted to shake me, but he didn't.

"What is wrong with you?"

"What is wrong with me – what is wrong with you?"

"Why does our relationship feel like a boxing match – a competition scheduled for twelve rounds, but we always seem to go an extra one?" I asked.

"The thirteenth round is what it feels like to me too," he retorted.

Tracey

I came to the door in a grey tee and the hospital scrubs I wear for pajamas. *At this time of morning, whoever is at my door had better have a good reason. That is all I can say.* I wiped the sleep from the corners of my eyes as I walked across the bare floor of the living area. There were more hard knocks at the door. There were only three people who knew where I stayed. I looked through the peephole, and I couldn't believe who was on the other side of the door. Taking a deep breath, I undid the dead bolts and took a step back so I could open the front door.

Zay stood with his hands buried deep in his pockets. He was smiling, but I wasn't. A brother looked at his watch, and then I looked at him. "Zay, it better be important."

He breezed right past me. Once inside, he started pacing. *Not the pacing. This is not good.* I was patient. He would talk soon. "We had a fight," Zay informed.

"What kind of fight?"

He looked at me with a stern expression. I shrugged my shoulders. "Well, one may never know. I know the first time you and her ever got into it, ya'll ended up fighting in your basement. So that is why I ask what kind of fight you got into."

My friend put his hands on top of his head. "Argument," he confessed.

"Okay… and people do that… especially men and their women. Welcome to the club. It just means that you are normal."

"Look, don't be condescending. I don't need condescending right now." Still pacing, he looked at me and said, "I asked her to marry me, Trace."

I woke up quick. "Whoa – what the fuck; you did what?"

"Yeah, I asked her, and she said no."

"Well… that's what you get."

"That is dirty. I wouldn't say that you."

"You are right; you would say worse."

"Well, she didn't exactly say no, she just didn't tell me yes either."

Still stuck on myself, I asked, "How are you going to propose and not tell me?" He didn't much pay me any attention. It was alright, I understood. "That's cruddy, Zay."

He still didn't say anything, but he continued to look

around, back and forth as if someone were following him.

I yawned. I couldn't help it, a brother was tired, but I couldn't turn my back on my friend.

"I need a drink," he said.

"You don't need a drink, Zay." If I gave Zay a drink, he would ramble on and I would never get any sleep. I wasn't in the mood for that.

"Yeah I do. I need a drink."

I laughed at him.

"Why are you laughing at me?"

"Nothing, bro." I attempted to wipe my smile clean, but it was hard. It was amazing. To me, looking at Zay was like looking at my own child that had just done something great – accomplished something, even. "Zay… you're in love."

He threw his hands up, frustrated, and said, "I know it. I am in love and that is what's fucking me up."

He sounded like a young woman feeling sorry for herself after learning that she was pregnant. I couldn't resist. I had to laugh. "First, it was your mid-life crisis; now this." I shook my head and walked off for the kitchen to make him a drink.

"You know, it's not funny, Tracey. I didn't ask for this. I didn't ask to feel this way." He paused. "Listen at me, I sound like I have some type of disease or something."

"That is what it feels like sometimes, my man – a disease that you can't get rid of or one that drains everything from you until you feel you have nothing left. Other times, love makes you feel like you're on drugs. Believe me, I know."

"Tracey, I just want this to be so right, but I'm fucking up. I know I'm selfish at times."

I threw my hands up and yelled, "Hallelujah." *He is finally admitting it – selfish. But he is doing better.* "Damn."

"Damn, what? What are you dammin about?"

I smiled. "She is good. I mean real good."

"See, what I'm talking about, why you keep saying stupid shit to me? I only came over here cause we are boys and this is what we do."

"Listen up, bruh, you've always been the same old selfish Zay. You want what you want when you want it, and it has to be how you want it."

"Selfish?"

"I tell you because I am your friend, and I'd like to see you make some changes."

"I asker her to quit… I asked her to quit doing what she loves most."

"Zay, you asked her to quit boxing?"

"I know I was wrong, but I don't like to see her get hurt." He shook his head like he was confused. "Man, I just want to be her bodyguard, her protector, brother, father, mother – you know, her everything. She could do something else besides boxing."

"That sounds good but you have to tell her these things." I paused, "Did you tell her this?"

He shook his head once more. In a low tone he confessed, "I can't find the words, Trace."

"Wrong answer; you have got to find the words."

"I know."

"Well you need to find the words quick because she needs to hear the words right now."

Right then there was another set of knocks on the door. These had less power than Zay's. These were more like taps instead of knocks. I breathed heavily and got up from the sofa to answer the door. I looked back at my friend who looked like he was really going through it. "See what you've done." Zay looked at me puzzled-like. "I got this crazy-assed old man next door. He swears that he can hear me open my cereal boxes in the mornings."

I didn't have time for this. It was late. I didn't want to be bothered. I only put up with Zay because he is my brother. The old man was liable to get told off, if it were it up to me. When I looked through the peephole, I started laughing. I looked at my watch. *Will I ever get some sleep?* Before opening the door, I looked back at Zay and whispered, "It's Tammy."

I read his lips that said, *tell her I'm not here. Tell her you haven't seen me.*

I opened the door. Tammy stood there with her hands

folded at her waist. "Tammy, baby, do you know it's one forty-two in the morning."

"I'm sorry, Tracey."

"Do you know what normal people do at one forty-two in the morning – especially at my age?"

"Tracey, I'm just looking for my man."

"Oh, you are talking about," I pointed over my shoulder, "Nyza, he told me to tell you that he's not here."

She didn't wait outside in the hallway any longer. She marched right on in, brushing me with her thick coat as she passed. I gladly closed the door behind her with a smile.

Zay was sitting down with a frown on his face. "That is fucked up, Trace. I told you to tell her that I wasn't here," my friend griped.

"Forget about all that; talk to your woman." She stood with her arms folded. He sat with his back to her like he didn't know what to say to her. I couldn't take it no more. I didn't mind helping my boy by covering for him, but this was stupid. They needed to talk to one another. Their solution was simple.

I wanted some sleep. I turned to Tammy, who was ready to put her man in the hot seat. "Zay was just talking to me, and I think he has something to say to you."

He shot me dirty looks, but I didn't care. It was time that he grew up. "Come on, Zay, why don't you tell her how you feel. Tell her what you told me. Tell her that you love her and how you've never felt this way before.

Go ahead," I prompted. Tammy's shoulders drooped a little, and she allowed the rest of her body to relax. She was already letting her guard down. I looked at Zay, who appeared to have stage fright. It was cool. This only meant that I would have to do all the talking for him.

"He said all those things, and he called himself a fuck-up. He admitted to being selfish for asking you to give up what you like to do." I winked at Zay. "See, there it is."

"You said that?" Tammy asked. My stubborn friend nodded. "Tell me yourself, what you told him."

"I've said enough."

"See, that's what I'm talking about. Why do you say stuff like that?"

Throwing a counter-punch, Zay asked, "Why do you say anything at all?"

Tammy threw her hands up in the air. "See, I don't even know why I came over here for his stupid ass." She turned, looked him in the face and said, "That's fucked up."

"And so are you, Tammy. You are fucked up, too. I just told you that I want you and I want you for life and you have to think about it? You act like I asked you for a piece of a sandwich instead of your hand in marriage."

She laughed. "I did not, baby." She chuckled some more. "No I didn't, baby."

"Then you ask all these damn questions."

"If a person asks all the kinds of questions I asked, you

think maybe that person just wanted to make sure that the other person meant what he asked?"

It confused me at first, but when I thought about it, I knew that she asked the questions that she asked of Zay because she wanted to make sure that Zay was serious about asking for her hand in matrimony.

"You should know that a person wouldn't ask you a question like I asked you unless he was serious – unless I really meant it."

"But, Zay," she pleaded, "What do we really know?"

"About what?"

"About us, Zay?"

"I know enough to know how I feel about you."

"But we argue and fight a lot."

"We are going to argue and fight, and I am sure that we will argue and fight some more, but that is the only time when we really hear each other baby." He took her by the hand. "Look it up in the dictionary; arguing is healthy. That is how we work out the kinks. It is how we get better." She smiled.

I smiled too. I didn't mind them sharing my space any more. They were making progress, and that was about the best you could ask for in an instance like this. He had always been my boy, but that day, he became a man. I was thankful for Tammy; she was the voice of reason. She was the long arm of the law and the only one that could get close enough to Nyza Stevens to influence change. Me and Vette talked about it and wondered if Zay would ever grow up and what it would be like if he did. We didn't have to wonder any longer. The time had come.

"It's how we get better," Zay repeated.

"You want me? You want a family?" His soul-mate asked.

"I want you. You know I do. I want a family."

With the eyes of a small doe, she said, "If you want me to quit boxing, Zay, I will do it for you." My face lost its luster.

Zay quickly put his fingers over lips. "Shh, don't say stuff like that; boxing is your life." He meant that, and I could tell.

"Maybe so, but I could get a new life." She looked off shyly. "Maybe I *should* be off making babies somewhere."

"Okay, this is good. Looks like y'all done made up, want to make babies and all that other shit, but you can't make the babies over here. Y'all have got to let me get some sleep," I said.

They smiled at each other; then they embraced. I felt good on the inside. I was happy that I was used as a vessel that night. Despite their flaws, they were good people. And besides that, we all have our flaws.

They let each other go, when Zay grabbed Tammy's hand, Zay winked at me. "We can take a hint. You're kicking us out." Tammy thanked me on the way out the door and with that they left.

Tammy

I stood at Zay's side as he waited on the doctor to give the results. He was hopeful, and for that same reason I was disappointed for him. I knew what the doctor would say to Nyza; he told me a week ago that Zay would be unable to go back into the ring, professionally. I advised Zay, but still he wanted to go in and see the doctor anyway. Me, being the supportive mate, who was I to tell him that he couldn't go and see the doctor? I told Zay not to get his hopes up. Boxing was his life, and I knew that he wanted to get back in the ring more than anything in the world, but everything has an expiration date. His time in the ring had long passed.

So Zay smiled at the doctor as the doctor looked at the x-rays. The doctor had finally put the films down long enough to look Zay in his face.

"So tell me Doc, what can be done?"

Doc pushed his glasses up on his nose before picking up the x-rays for a second time. This time the doctor pulled a pen from his breast pocket. "Better yet," Doc turned to the side with the film in his hand, "let me put these on the viewer so that you can see them better." The retired boxer's smile faded.

"Well, Mr. Stevenson, the tear is here and the break is still here. The break in your bone will not heal itself – even with the pins –"

" – Well, I was told that there was a possibility that broken ends could fuse, and if that happened, they could take out the screws."

"Well, Mr. Stevenson, it happens, but not always – not in your case."

My heart dropped when Zay hung his head. I usually had something to say to him to make him feel better, but not on this day. There was nothing I could think of that could make him feel better. Then I felt guilty for not telling him sooner what the doc had said; then again, it was better that he saw things for himself so that there would be no doubt.

The doc tapped on the viewer with his ink pen. "Well, you see, Mr. Stevenson, the break is here, so we would have to go through your shoulder here." He tapped on the screen to make sure Zay understood what he was looking at. "Open you up right here."

Zay smiled hopefully. "Okay. What's the problem then? I can go back to boxing after the surgery right?"

The doctor shook his head.

The whole way home, he was silent. I knew what he was thinking about. He was thinking about what was said at the doctor's office. He didn't need to fight any more. It was a dream that was well-lived at the time, but the fact of the matter was, it was over now. He was not hurting for anything, he still had his pride and his respect – which is lot more than others could say.

I watched him for the past few weeks. He moped around, feeling sorry for himself. A couple of times I stood over him, waiting for him to open up. The last time I did this, I put a hand on his shoulder, and in a soft voice I said, "I know you love boxing. You can still love to box, but maybe you love it more because you can't do it anymore."

He looked up at me almost cross-eyed. "That don't make no damn sense."

"Sure it does, baby. When you were little you hadn't been outside in two weeks. That was the longest two weeks because in *those* two weeks, it seemed like you missed out on everything. You wanted to go outside even more than ever because you were restricted by your momma – she punished you for that period and told you that you couldn't go outside; she took a privilege from you." He looked up as I continued. Maybe I was getting the point across to him. "When someone takes something from you, all you can think about is how you can get it back. What is the fastest way to get back what belonged to you?"

He was tired of my talking but I kept going. "I like boxing, Zay. You know this. You know that I absolutely love boxing, and I will continue to love boxing as a sport, but boxing is not for me anymore."

He turned around slightly. "Look Tammy, I told you that I used a poor choice of words that night when talked about your career. I had no business asking you to quit."

I reached for his hand. I squeezed it to let him know that I was serious. My smile was most sincere. "No, Zay I don't want to do this anymore. I really don't. I have been thinking about a family and normal life. Besides, if I leave the sport right now, I can leave undefeated."

"Really," he cracked a half-cocked smile.

I looked at him and squeezed his hand a little harder this time. We were looking each other in the eyes. "Baby, if you ask me again… to marry you, I promise I won't say anything stupid." I slipped the ring from my finger and dropped it in the palm of his opened hand.

"Right now?"

"Right now," I confirmed.

He stood up. He was a bit hesitant. "But, Tammy, what will we do if you quit boxing?"

"Be together, that is what we will do Zay."

Two Years later

"So how is the girl?" I asked.

"The girl is fine," Arvette said. "Tracey was just playing with her. She is good –

She is a happy baby."

"That is good to hear."

"Yeah, she is knocked out asleep."

"Okay girl, I just wanted to check on our girl," I said.

"Come on now, you know she's in good hands. You and Zay don't have to worry."

I smiled. "I know she is in good hands. You tell Tracey that I said hello."

"You know I will. Good luck with the fight, sis."

"I will see y'all tomorrow if the Lord is willing." I pressed the red phone key on my cell phone to end the call. I knew that any minute they would be calling for me. I left the room and made my way down the aisle. When it was time, lots of people were looking at me. My husband negotiated a huge purse for one of our trained professionals. We had really been working with this girl. We'd come too far to mess this one up. The manager took his spot and I took my spot along with him as the boxer's trainer. At the end of round one, we got up and did our thing. The cut man was in front of her with a cold compress to keep any swelling down as I stood on one side of her while Zay stood on the other. We were both giving *our* boxer tips and strategies to control the scorecards to ensure a win in her favor. She was off to an excellent start.

The bell rang as I tapped the boxer on the shoulder. The chair was pulled from the corner as the boxers both met in the middle of the ring for round two.

Zay looked at me. "How is the baby?"

"Your sister said that she is knocked out, sleeping like a champ." He smiled. I smiled back.

The media had their cameras rolling as they talked about us. The sports commentators talked about us as well. It was a good feeling, being able to do what you love to do most but from a distance. They talked about us, the dynamic husband and wife franchise. My husband, Zay, and I had three boxers signed with us under contract. We managed, trained, and supported them to fullest. We went by the name Team Stevenson. We had even started a small team of our own. Our first player was our baby daughter, Armenta Tracy Stevenson.

Zay promised his best friend that he would never have kids, but if he did, he would name the first after him. Though it's not her first name, we slid it in there, giving it a different spelling.

I smiled. I felt really good on the inside. I hadn't given up boxing and neither had Zay. We found a better way to capitalize on the sport. Though we weren't boxing under the spotlight, there were those times where Zay and I would go home, glove up, and go at it. Our bouts were scheduled for twelve, but some nights we would go into the thirteenth round. We wouldn't stop until we reached mutual ground. Sometimes our relationship sent us into overtime. It was just our way.

End

ABOUT THE AUTHOR

I am a Washington DC native with 10 years experience as a writer, whereas 5 of those years have been spent professionally. I have been writing for the Rock E-News magazine (<http://the-rock-newsmagazine.com>) Some of those published works include articles about Entrepreneurship like; Don't Quit Your Day Job; Taking a Risk; and Dime Piece. Within the same five years I have had two books published; Fire and Rain and Nappy is Good under my name. Nappy is Good, published in May 2005 kicked off my professional start as an author. The latest published work; Fire and Rain was published Oct. 2006. With an experienced publicist with creative ideas I was able to make many aware of my work. I took some time off from writing so that I could market my work the way it should have been. When I wasn't marketing I spent time in churches talking to the young people in the community. When I wasn't in the church I was in the schools talking to some more of our young people, exposing them to some new stuff. Not enough of our young people realize the career opportunities in writing. I made as many aware as I could. I love what I do. I love what I do more than my usual occupation. Being a 12 year U.S. Army Veteran, I was afforded the opportunity to make a difference - the kind of difference that would continue to multiply. It is all about giving, FAM. You never go wrong by giving and you will always get what you give.

I took a little bit of a break but since then I have written about five almost six novels neatly fitting the genres of romance, suspense, street crime and erotica. I mean, I have been real busy. I met Michael Baisden a few years ago in Dallas and he told me to find my passion if I hadn't already. He then told me to make sure that I purchased a digital recorder and be sure to capture everything. I do that.

I haven't lived in the City of Washington for a long time but I have roots there and there are so many stories to tell and I am the right person to tell them. All of my stories talk about the life, struggles and times of the District. I use my experiences from my travels to enhance the plot points and story lines but you can be sure that Washington D.C. is tied in there somewhere. That is my trade mark, baby. I use that recorder that Baisden spoke of to record the highlights and memories of the city and I bring them to life.

I got some romance for yo ass, and I got some gangster shit among the suspenseful "Who done its." So check me out. I am currently seeking traditional publishing. My work is not by any means average and I don't plan to stop with writing books, my work has that screen play appeal. Whoever you may be, feel free to inquire. I am free for signings, public talks, interviews and appearances. Let's do some business together. To my fans, thank you for the continued support, but like I promised you before, I will not stop and I have a lot in store. Help me to keep it going.